Dimensions of Fear

DIMENSIONS OF FEAR

Sandra Maxwell

MERANO WRITERS PRESS
LOS ANGELES

Front Cover Art by Lucinda Seaman
Book & Cover Design by Christopher Askew

ISBN #10 0692445811
ISBN #EAN 13 9780692445815

Printed in the United States of America

Acknowledgements

Books are not written alone in a dark room; just you and your computer, ideas pouring from your imagination onto the blank screen with such ease you need no one else.

I wish to thank:
My husband, Robert, for all his support and patience.
The Merano Writers Workshop, the best workshop I've ever attended.
B.K. DePaolis and Jane Hallenger for taking me by the hand and showing me the way.
The Iseum of Isis Shanti Bhavan for all the magic.
Pedro, who kept my computer going through thick and thin.
Chris Askew for all the work preparing this book for print.
Lucy Seaman for her brilliant artwork, although gone, she will always be at my side.

And a very special thanks to Harlan Ellison for always being there for me since the first Clarion Writers Workshop in 1968.

ONE

NOTHING broke the flawless silvered surface.   Carol's heart pounded. Nowhere to hide. The smooth horizon stretched forever. Power charged through the air. She knew it would destroy her. She could not stop it.

Shreds of thin, lifeless clouds marred the clear sky turning it a sickly gray as the pale weak sun began to set. The clouds rotted to a deathly purple when the sun sank even lower. Wind whipped across the surface growing stronger and colder with each blast. She hunkered down, her face sheltered by her knees.

An unseen force pulled against her mind; unwelcomed, strange and alien. Her terror intensified. All light vanished. Her scream echoed to nowhere.

The ever-increasing wind threatened madness. Nausea roiled in her stomach as she struggled blindly to maintain her balance. Carol clung to what sanity remained, but the force gained entry into her mind, invading her thoughts, controlling her emotions. She shrank from its advance. Agonizing pain seared her mind and spirit. She fell into the void, blind and terrified.

Carol's eyes flew open. Brilliance blazed and she threw her arm over her eyes, her breathing hard. Lowering her arm, she slowly focused on her surroundings. Sitting up, her senses returned. Her breathing slowed. An early morning breeze wafted through an open window, bringing in fresh spring air. She was home. In bed.

1

God! What a nightmare! No, terror. She actually felt as though she'd been there. That she'd just returned from Hell. Her throat was raw and sore.

Still groggy, she swung her legs over the side of the bed and lingered a moment. Her forehead throbbed. Standing, she felt dizzy and sat back down. Maybe she had the flu? She took a breath and fumbled for the robe at the foot of the bed. She tried standing again. Blood dripped onto the back of her hand. Nosebleed. She grabbed tissues from the side table to stop the bleeding. It ended quickly.

She had never had a dream like this. It had terrified her beyond anything she had ever experienced awake or asleep. She shuddered as she remembered every detail. A cup of coffee might be her salvation. Surely waking up completely would make it all fade away.

Curling up on the couch, wrapped tight in her robe, she gripped a mug of black coffee n both hands and tried to shake the remaining night terrors. She decided she did not have the flu, yet she shivered. The nightmare still haunted her no matter how many cups of coffee she had. It dominated her spirit, as though her very soul held a chill that would never be warm again. Fear returned to her as she remembered the presence of someone she couldn't see in the dream, trying to take over her mind.

She began to worry that the nightmare held something more foreboding. No! It was just a bad dream. It was over. Taking her half empty coffee cup, she marched to the shower, convinced that starting her routine would brighten the day.

The shower helped wash away some of the chill. Drying herself off, she began to feel the comfort the atmosphere her home always provided. Built in 1913, it was part of a bungalow complex that sat right in the middle of old Hollywood beneath the famous Hollywood sign. She loved history and having it related to her love of film was a bonus.

Fluffing her long dark brown hair, Carol frowned at the natural curl that always went its own way. Her thoughts drifted back to the nightmare. She shivered again as a sudden feeling of suffocation made her take a deep breath and turn away from the pale face in her mirror.

She lived alone. She dated but quickly got bored. No Prince Charming had come to her rescue as yet. At twenty six, perhaps she should give up looking. She kept herself busy with the film club and her job as a production accountant in the movie industry paid well. It allowed her to furnish her home in early twentieth-century antiques and collect her favorite films. She slipped on jeans and an old I Heart L.A. t-shirt and returned to the kitchen for a fresh cup of coffee.

Emptying and rinsing her mug, she turned. Carol jumped, startled by the dark human-shaped shadow that sat at her kitchen table. "Mornin', George," she mumbled, addressing the ghost who shared her bungalow. "Sorry. Not awake yet."

George disappeared.

"I said I was sorry," she called after him.

She felt bad about startling him like that. She knew he hated it. It was the nightmare that made her jumpy, not George. She had gotten used to his silent comings and goings the past five years. She had tried to find out who he had been and why he was attached to her place, but without success. Even her landlady, who had been there for thirty years, could not remember anyone who died in her bungalow. Finally, she just accepted his presence. In fact she relished having a ghost in her home, although some of her friends did not share her enthusiasm. She named him George after a character in one of her favorite movies, Topper, with Cary Grant as the ghostly George.

She refilled her cup and stepped outside her front door to sip her coffee, taking in the pleasant courtyard she shared with six other bungalows in this section of the complex. It always calmed her. The very air brought comfort. The golden hue of the light filtering through the trees brought tranquility.

Her eyes followed the familiar red brick pathways that led to the front door of each ivy-covered bungalow from a central circle and the final path that led to other sections of the complex. In the circle a large urn-shaped fountain bubbled into a basin of water lilies and koi. Around the basin various plants grew in abundance, as if worshiping the fountain for the life-giving water it provided.

Carol heard a meow and turned to see a chubby gray cat trotting towards her.

"Good morning, Dinah." Carol bent to stroke the cat's long soft fur. "On duty as always, I see." She stood and looked around. "Where's Marguerite? She never lets you out alone."

A short stout older woman with dyed black hair rounded a corner and toddled down a path towards the fountain. Marguerite held the title of on-site manager, but everyone referred to her as mother-in-residence.

Carol waved. "Mornin'."

The manager laughed, a bit out of breath. Her eyes twinkled. "What are you doing out so early?"

Carol grinned. "Now do I have to tell you everything I do?"

"I may be nosey, but it keeps the peace around here. I'm getting too old for most other hobbies." She chuckled and shuffled on towards Dan's apartment farther down the path. Dinah trotted after her mistress.

Carol, headed back inside. The effects of the nightmare still lurked, ready to ruin her mood. She grabbed her cell phone, dialed.

"Sarah, want to join me for breakfast at the Canteen?"

"Sure. You okay? You usually don't call on a work day for breakfast."

"Yeah, I know. Please. Just come."

Near Franklin and Gower, The Hollywood Canteen served the best brew in town only ten minutes' walk from Carol's place. Like the bungalow complex, it too possessed red brick pathways, this time leading to sequestered courtyards filled with delightful flowers. Small round tables held people sharing the sun with their favorite beverage.

Carol, with Sarah following, chose one of the crowded courtyards. They finally found a table near the Fountain of Wishes. Carol put down her coffee and food, plopped into the chair with a sigh of pleasure, and tossed a penny into the fountain for luck.

"Now this is what I needed," she said to Sarah, watching her juggle eggs and coffee before sitting down. Sarah's short bouncy blond hair

4

framed a heart shaped face making her blue eyes appear even bigger than they already were.

Sarah also tossed a penny into the fountain. "What's got you so willing to have a casual breakfast on a Monday morning, Ms. Workaholic? Don't get me wrong, I think I like this new Carol. All work and no play..."

"Had a horrible nightmare last night. Worse than anything Freddie Kruger ever created." Carol took a sip of her cappuccino.

"Can't think of a better therapy for a bad dream than coffee." Sarah's blue eyes twinkled with mischief. "Except good sex!"

"Just needed to get out and be with a good friend. I—"

"Whoa." Sarah whispered, leaning forward. "Check out the hottie coming our way." She gave a slight nod to her right.

Carol turned slightly so she could casually take in this vision. She almost lost the casual part as she glanced at the drop-dead gorgeous dark-haired man searching for a table. Slender but powerful looking in his black pullover and slightly worn jeans, he looked for a place to sit with a slight frown that only added more charm to his chiseled features. His black eyes glanced in their direction.

"You can join us," Sarah called brightly to the stranger.

He smiled and wound his way towards them. Carol had wanted to talk to Sarah about her nightmare. She shrugged. Maybe after breakfast she could get her friend's opinion. Sarah would probably steal all the attention, assuming he wasn't gay. Carol could relax and enjoy the view.

"I don't know whether to thank you or strangle you," she whispered to Sarah as the man approached.

Putting down his mug of coffee, he pulled out the chair at the end of the small table between Carol and Sarah. As he sat his long black hair fell over his forehead. Carol liked long hair on guys. Today's adventure might be taking a turn she might actually enjoy. Maybe it had been that penny she just threw into the fountain.

"Thanks." He raked his hair back into place. "Even on weekdays this place is crowded." He gave them a charming smile. "Name's Darren."

"Hello, Darren, I'm Sarah and this is Carol."

Carol only smiled. When she didn't speak, Sarah continued. "Perfect day, don't you think?"

Darren looked up at the blue cloudless sky and sang,

"Everybody's happy,
'cause the sun is shining all the time,
looks like another perfect day."

Sarah finished the verse with a flourish,

"I Love L.A!"

She laughed. "You have a nice voice."

"Thanks." Then he noticed Carol's t-shirt. "No offense."

Carol just smiled. Sarah could have all the fun. She'd rather relax.

Sarah liked to flirt. "So what brings you to our coffee shop this morning?"

"Your coffee shop? Really?"

"No silly. But it seems like it. We're here so much."

Darren turned to Carol. "You're quiet."

Sarah interrupted. "Carol is an accountant to the stars."

Blushing, Carol felt obligated to explain. "Actually, I'm a production accountant. I work for the studios, not the stars. Nothing glamorous."

Carol realized Sarah wanted her to join the fun. Yes, he's very good looking, but she hadn't come to the Canteen to meet guys. But as she looked into Darren's dark eyes a shiver crossed her shoulders. The air seemed still. She felt somewhere else, distant from everything around her.

Sarah's voice brought her back. "Maybe not glamorous, but certainly interesting. Once she had to determine the value of a camel to finish the cost expenses of a reality show because some local got paid a camel for his work."

Darren's smile dazzled. "I'm not surprised. I work in the Industry myself."

Carol spoke before Sarah could say anything else. "What do you do?"

"I'm a location scout. I find locations for filming." He took a sip of coffee. "When that well runs dry, I try acting. It's mostly commercials these days."

Carol watched his face in fascination. Common sense spoke from somewhere far back in her mind. What's wrong with you today? He's just another man. And an actor! He'll only be interested in himself. "I find other work when my regular show is on hiatus. Being an accountant has its advantages."

Sarah announced with pride, "I don't work."

Darren looked at her, his brows raised in question.

"Well, they say if you love what you do, you'll never work a day in your life. I create apps for phones and tablets. Have some pretty interesting clients." Sarah flashed a brilliant smile at Darren. "I'm busy, but I like to get out and have fun too."

Carol expected Darren to become very interested in Sarah. Most guys hoped they could cash in on how much money Sarah probably made in the often lucrative aps business. If Sarah wanted to attract Darren that way, so be it. Carol had tried to dissuade her from doing this, citing how dangerous it could be, but Sarah didn't agree. Taking another sip of coffee, she leaned back in her chair, thinking that the pressure to be a part of the conversation was over and she could finally relax. It surprised her when Darren turned back to her.

"Are you working on a show now?" he asked, his dark gaze melting into her brown eyes.

"Ah. No." She began to wish this would end. "I'm only doing my regular accounting for a private client. Pays the rent until my show 's next season starts."

Darren leaned forward and reached into his back pocket, pulled a card out of his wallet and handed it to Carol. "Let me give you my card. Maybe we can help each other stay employed."

"Thanks." She smiled politely. "Networking's the best tool in this town." She slipped his card into her purse, pulled out one of her own and handed it to him.

Sarah leaned forward, catching Carol's eye. "I need to get back home." Then she turned to Darren. "Sorry to hurry off, but I have clients coming."

He turned back to Sarah. "No, please. It was a pleasure meeting you both."

Carol laughed. "At least you get a private table out of the deal." She rose to leave too.

Darren stood politely. Carol noted his manners. These days, you rarely met a gentleman. She liked it; very Cary Grant or Gary Cooper. As she turned to grab her purse, she felt Darren's hand on her forearm. Startled, she yanked her arm back and turned to face him, frowning. It had been as though an electric shock had spread through her arm. She could still feel its warmth.

"Sorry." He had a sheepish grin. "I just wanted to tell you that my offer to network is genuine and not just a come-on."

Carol, not sure how to respond, merely gave a quick smile and nodded. She moved past her chair and into the aisle, walking away as fast as she could without losing grace. What was the matter with her? Did she exaggerate that shock? He was wearing a sweater. Must be the damn nightmare. She turned around when she reached the brick pathway back to the front of the restaurant.

Sarah followed her with a look of confusion. She put her hand on Carol's arm to keep her from walking on. "Are you okay?"

"I'm fine," Carol answered too quickly. She felt out of control. She preferred her life to be as predictable as her spreadsheets.

Sarah changed tack. "He's a hottie and très charming. He's really interested in you. Why not see what happens?"

Carol snapped, "I don't need your advice."

Sarah took a step back and frowned.

Carol tried to smile. "Sorry, I'm really jumpy today."

Sarah became serious. "You wanted to talk, didn't you? I shouldn't have called him over."

"It's okay. Really, I'm feeling better. You're right about Darren being a hottie. Can't blame you for asking him over. I didn't tell you I wanted to talk."

8

Sarah smiled. "Hope he calls you. Have fun! You don't have to marry him."

"Look, I have to get some work done too. Thanks for the coffee. I really needed your company."

Sarah looked at her with a knowing eye. "Okay, we don't have to discuss Darren. Sure you're gonna be okay?"

"Sure."

Back home, Carol gratefully worked on Brown & Associates' monthly expenses. Seeing all the figures match up and come to a satisfactory and correct result felt normal. The horrible dream had receded to a mere shadow. At six o'clock, she decided to order delivery from her favorite Thai restaurant. Once her dinner arrived, she poured herself a small glass of plum wine, popped *The Uninvited* into the DVD player and settled onto her couch to watch one of her top ten favorite old movies starring Ray Milland. She had a soft spot for this particular ghost story. On the scary side, true, but it portrayed how love could conquer all fear and horror. It had actually become a "comfort" film for her over the years. That should put her nightmare back into its proper perspective once and for all. George's shadow joined her, gathering his darkness into the leather chair by the fireplace. He always came when she watched a ghost movie. She assumed he couldn't resist. Smiling, she pushed the play button.

After the guilty pleasure of good food, wine and a great movie, Carol felt the warm security she always got from watching the film. Yawning, she said goodnight to George and headed to bed. The sheets were cool and smooth on her nude body as she settled in for the night. She rolled over and snuggled into her pillow.

The air chilled her. She crossed her arms hoping to warm herself. The hill she stood upon overlooked someone's garden. No moon shone but small lights hanging in the garden's trees showed her glimpses of pathways and a couple of benches. It had to be late. The dark sky only held distant stars. Their coldness made her feel the chill even deeper. If she left the hill and entered the garden it might be warmer. As she descended, a dog

9

howled in the distance. It didn't sound like a coyote. She picked her way a little farther in the darkness. Another howl answered the first although much closer. Then a third joined in. Panic overwhelmed her. She flew down the hill, her terror rising with each step. The howling became constant as others joined the hunt. Carol fell and slid a few feet before she could regain her footing. Rising, she saw something dart into the bushes farther down. The dogs were surrounding her. She must reach the garden. A low menacing growl made her whirl around. The dog seemed deformed. The size of a lion, long matted black fur covered its humped shoulders. Its short snout snarled again, long fangs dominating its maw. Not a dog, a demon! Carol heard more rustling and turned to see four more advancing, their eyes glowing blue in the darkness. She screamed for help. Her only answer came in the form of a cold controlling presence. The same that had tried to take over her mind the night before. She fought its advances. The demons moved closer. Her mind began to surrender to the invader as terror filled her. No, she would not allow it! She clutched her head as pain seared her entire being.

TWO

SHE WOKE UP screaming. Leaping from bed, Carol realized the demons were gone and she stood in her own bedroom. Her nose started to bleed. Still dazed, she headed to the bathroom and stuffed some toilet paper into her nose. Turning on the shower, she leaned against the tile wall, praying the cold water would clear her mind. Her head ached like it had yesterday. As the water began to heat, she felt more attached to her surroundings and less apart of the dream. Why, all of a sudden, was she having horrific nightmares? Two! One right after the other!

She pulled on her robe, headed to the living room, found her insurance card, and picked up her cell phone. She was told to go to the Urgent Care section of the clinic to get quick service.

After three hours of waiting, the doctor told her she had nothing to worry about. He assured her the nightmares were temporary and gave her a prescription for the headache and sleeping pills to keep the dreams away. He assured her the nosebleeds came from tension and would go away when she could get some sleep. Sounded good to her. Stress did odd things to people. She hadn't realized she had so much tension.

Returning home, Carol tried to prepare her spreadsheets for the next month's receipts from her client, but she was so tired after two nights of horrific dreams, she gave up. After a light supper she popped in the Lord of the Rings, The Fellowship of the Ring. She only watched one disk before her eyes became too heavy to stay open. Turning off the player, she decided to take the sleeping pills the doctor gave her in spite of already being tired, and went to bed.

She was lost. She had no idea how she had gotten here. The forest reeked of rotten leaves and fungus. The air, heavy and stagnant, provided

11

no breeze to rid the lifeless trees of the stench. The sky draped the dismal landscape with a monotone gray that leeched out any cheerfulness that might have been there. A branch creaked overhead, and a raven flew away, cawing at some annoyance. She glanced down the trail she stood upon. It got even darker ahead. Other than the raven, no sound came to her deathly surroundings. Damp crept into her bones and she decided to walk on hoping movement would warm her. Most of the trees were bare and although the forest floor was deep in damp dead leaves, the trail was clear. The sky remained gray. The rain had stopped but would soon start again.

Unsure what direction to take, she headed down the path. It had to lead somewhere. Shortly the path took a steep downward turn becoming muddy and slippery. Something large and black swooped at her, pulling her hair as it passed overhead. The raven settled in a nearby tree staring at her, its head moving from side to side as it watched her, first from one eye then the other. A few stands of her hair were in its claws. She hurried past the bird. Its bold attack made it sinister and all she wanted was to get away from its stare.

A voice whispered from nowhere, "Run. Get away. You can't stay. Run."

The raven cawed and leaned forward ready to take to flight. A hand pushed her but when she turned, no one was there. The raven launched himself into the air and started towards her with deathly purpose. She ran. Slipping in the mud she fell, sliding out of control down the sloping trail at an amazing speed. The raven flew after her.

She landed at the muddy bottom, splashing into viscous cloying mud too deep to find her footing. The raven grazed her head as it flew over and landed on a nearby stump to caw at her as though laughing. The mud sucked at her body and she slowed her struggles to stop her descent.

The raven spoke. "You wish to be free?"

She knew the voice. She had heard it in her nightmares. Her panic grew.

The raven tilted his head. "I cannot allow you to be free."

She grasped at twigs lying on the surface of the sucking mud. She had to escape!

THREE

SHE AWOKE trying to claw her way out of her bed. There was blood from her nose everywhere. The nightmares were so real, so terrifying. The sleeping pills hadn't worked. She didn't feel comfortable about seeing a psychiatrist, but what should she do? She didn't want to have another nightmare tonight. She would rather stay awake the rest of her life! She reached for her cell.

"Sarah? Have some time to talk today?"

"Sure. What's up?"

"Another nightmare. This one would've scared Clive Barker. Gotta get out of here for a while."

"You starting out now? You okay to drive?"

"Yeah. Getting dressed. Should be there in about an hour."

"I'll put on a pot of coffee."

Carol quickly dressed in jeans and t-shirt, locked up, and crossed the street to the parking area, feeling better now she was going to Sarah's. After a couple of false starts, she fired up her classic cream '62 Volkswagen Beetle and maneuvered it out of the tight lot onto the street.

She knew Sarah had seen a healer of some sort recently. She raved about how he had helped her deal with some personal issues at the end of last year. Carol hadn't been interested at the time. He was some kind of guru or something. Maybe she could get that his phone number and get her reality straightened out too. She felt anxious. But could anyone really help her? She worried that her problem sounded too insane or too complex for an easy solution. She calmed herself. At least she could ask Sarah for his number.

Carol relaxed the moment she entered her friend's home. She was always fascinated by Sarah's jumbled décor which unapologetically ran the gamut from Victorian jumble sale to *2001: A Space Odyssey*. Her eyes fell upon the picture on the ornately-carved mantlepiece of her and Sarah in Spain taken two years ago. Maybe they should consider another trip? Get away from it all?

Sarah closed her front door. "You look like hell."

"Is that coffee you promised ready?" Carol asked, ignoring her friend's remark.

"Of course."

They each poured a cup. Sarah's was more cream and sugar than coffee, Carol's black. They took their cups into the sunlit dining room next to the kitchen. Original movie posters for the George Pal 1960s' versions of *The Time Machine* and *War of the Worlds* adorned the walls. Carol had given them to Sarah for her birthday a couple of years ago.

"So, you've had another nightmare? I thought you were done with all that."

Carol blurted in frustration, "They're making me crazy."

Sarah motioned with her spoon. "People usually have horrible nightmares because they're crazy in the first place, don't they? If you want my opinion, I always thought you a bit too sane and needed some insanity in your life."

"I am very aware of your opinion, thank you," Carol said in mock indignation. She looked down at her cup and added quietly, "This is different."

Sarah became serious. "Why is that?"

"I went to the clinic yesterday and all they did was pat me on the head, tell me the dreams would pass, and gave me some pills." Carol slowly began telling her friend about the nightmares, but it brought back the terror and tears started flowing. She didn't get emotional like this. Her tears embarrassed her. "The pills do nothing to keep the nightmares away!"

Sarah hastened to grab a box of tissues from the bathroom. "When you said nightmare, I thought you were talking about the kind everyone gets from time to time. This is weird!"

14

Carol blew her nose. "It just doesn't make any sense and I don't know what to do!" She looked directly at her friend for the first time since beginning her story.

Sarah looked pale. "I don't believe nightmares make you crazy. But these dreams don't make any sense at all. And the nose bleeds aren't good."

"No they aren't and the headaches are awful." Carol pushed her cup away too upset to finish her coffee. "And there's something else that doesn't make sense." She swallowed hard to stop further tears. "There's always someone I can't see trying to hurt me."

Sarah leaned back in her dining chair. "We've got to get to the bottom of this. None of it is even remotely normal. You remember Dr. Cameron? I told you about him."

"Yeah, I was hoping I could get his information." Carol still struggled with her opinion of psychiatric help.

"I'm not sure what's happening to you, but I am sure Dr. Cameron will help. Or if he can't maybe he knows someone who can. Dr. Cameron's different. He's easier to talk to. It's a good place to start."

Carol frowned. "What do you mean different?"

"Dr. Cameron practices a holistic approach. He incorporates ideas from history and science and all religions."

"Is he actually a real doctor?"

"Yes, just not a traditional one. He has PhDs in Psychology and Physics and I remember seeing Master degrees in Chemistry and History on the wall. Oh, also a yoga master and I know he meditates."

"What does he do? Read your fortune in a crystal ball?"

"Yes! If he thinks it would do you any good!"

Carol knew she'd stepped over the line. "Sorry. I'm just not sure anyone can help."

Sarah took a deep breath. "I understand. Dr. Cameron gets results because he is willing and capable of looking into many ways to help people. He knows what he's doing."

Carol trusted her friend. That was the only thing she knew for sure. Sarah's experience with Dr. Cameron had helped her. Carol had to admit she liked the idea of holistic approach. Surely, it would be easier to

15

work with him than with someone who would just prescribe some pills and ask her to call them back later. Or worse, have her committed.

"Here, judge for yourself." Sarah handed Carol the doctor's card. "Call him now. I'm worried about you. Your nightmares could be a symptom of something worse."

Carol looked into Sarah's eyes and saw genuine concern. She nodded, found her cell and dialed the doctor's number, making an appointment for the next day. She hugged her friend. "Thanks."

Sarah smiled. "Say, do you want to stay the night here? Maybe it would keep the nightmares away?"

Carol laughed. "Now that's brilliant. Yes. Just need to get some work done and throw some stuff in a bag. I'll see you later tonight. Thanks!"

As Carol turned her car onto Briar Cliff Canyon, her cell rang. She hit the button on her ear piece.

"Hi, it's Darren, the guy you met at the coffee shop yesterday?"

"Oh, right." Carol was surprised he'd called. "What can I do for you?"

"I have a short-term production accountant position you might be interested in."

"I'm listening. Who's it for?" Maybe this would turn into a good thing.

"I've worked for these people before. The name is Spartan & Associates. Their production accountant broke her leg yesterday. Guess it's bad enough to put her in the hospital for a couple a days. They need someone to cover for her."

Carol had heard of the company. "Sounds good. Who do I contact?"

"Listen, I'm on my way to location for this commercial I'm doing. Can you meet me at the Hollywood Canteen in fifteen minutes? That way I can give you the entire package of information before you call them."

"Sure. I'll meet you out front."

16

Turning her car around, she headed to the Canteen. She remembered how Darren had upset her yesterday when he touched her arm. She must have imagined that. Maybe he accidently touched a raw nerve. A vision of his alluring dark eyes made her thoughts wandered in a different direction. He had been a perfect gentleman. He had not been the typical bore of an actor. He'd assured her his motives were to network and, here he is, keeping that promise. Well, she could take care of herself. If this was the least bit suspicious she was under no obligation to accept the offer.

Ten minutes later Carol waited in front of the Canteen. The usual crowd of people made it difficult to keep an eye out for Darren. Then she saw him hurrying down the street. Carol waved her hand, and seeing her, Darren jogged up, an envelope under one arm. She was impressed. He was not even breathing hard.

"Here are the W-4's and other forms they want you to fill out if you decide to take the job. Oh, and a job description."

Carol took the package. "Thanks for the opportunity."

"My pleasure." Darren turned to go but paused. "Say, I know I told you exchanging business cards would be strictly for business, but could I take you out for a drink sometime?"

Carol hesitated. Here it comes. Nothing is ever free or easy. But she didn't feel angry. As she looked at his smiling face and into his dark eyes full of hope, she caved. "Sure." What harm could a drink in a public place do?

"How 'bout tonight after I finish work? I'll pick you up at the office you'll be working at."

"Why so sure I'll take the job?"

"Life can't be that cruel." He smiled. "See ya tonight." He hurried away down the sidewalk.

Carol watched him go. Damn, he was growing on her. She shrugged. Maybe it's what she needed to take her mind off the nightmares.

She took the job. It came with a bonus for coming to the rescue. She started that very afternoon. Her assignment was a commercial. It was only a five-day shoot, but there were a pile of bills and receipts already waiting for her when she got to her desk. Her boss, Mr. Daily, was patient. It made things much easier for Carol that her predecessor had used her own account codes and not those she was familiar with.

"Hey, Carol," cried the young man who delivered mail. "Got some more work for ya." He looked like many young men these days, drooping trousers, shaved head and tattooed arms.

Carol liked him. "Hey yourself, Adrian. You can stop bringing more work, ya know," she kidded.

Adrian leaned over the side of her cubical. "Hey, I heard Darren got you this job."

"You heard right."

"Great guy, Darren. He got me this job. Say, you goin' out with him?"

Carol smiled calmly. "That's none of your business."

"Yeah, right, but you should if you're not already. I'm truth'n here." He winked and pushed his mail cart onto the next cubicle.

Carol's cell rang. It was Sarah.

"Hey, thought I'd call and see if you'll be here for dinner or after," she said brightly.

"Sarah, I was going to call as soon as I could grab a moment. You'll never believe what happened. On the way home from your place I got a call from Darren. You know. The guy we met at the Canteen?"

"Really? Askin' for a date, I suppose."

"No, he set me up with a short term job. I'm sitting at a desk sorting receipts as we speak."

"Wow, he really meant it when he said he would network? That's a first."

"He wants to go for drinks after work, though."

"You goin'?"

"Probably. You'd think Darren was a saint the way they talk about him here. First the man I report to thanked me for coming in. Said he knew I must be good if Darren referred me. Just had the mail clerk tell me what a great guy Darren was and that I should date him."

Sarah laughed. "How much did he pay them to say all that? Well, with those references, why not? Just be careful. You've got my key."

The bar was a local hangout for industry people not far from the Art Directors Guild in Studio City. Carol had been here before. She sat at a small table, watching Darren order drinks from the bar.

"A martini for my fair lady." He smiled as he handed her the four-olive drink she'd asked for. "How was your first day?"

"Good. More bills than I thought there would be, but then I've never worked on a commercial before. How was your day?"

"Interesting. It's a high end commercial so we can afford several takes for each shot and even some green screen work next week."

"When do you think it'll wrap?"

Darren took a sip of his Guinness. "Schedule says next Wednesday, but the way we're going, I'll believe that when I see it. Company's pretty good at staying on time and budget, though."

"Mary called today and she'll be back to work Thursday, so day after tomorrow's my last day. I want to thank you for this opportunity."

"My pleasure. When they said they needed a production account-ant fast, I knew who to call." He laughed. "You're the only production accountant I know."

Carol liked his laugh. He seemed genuine, not the usual actor who only liked to hear himself talk. She felt comfortable with Darren.

He leaned forward. "I'm sorry your last day is so soon, though. I was hoping to get to know you better." He reached for her hand.

Carol let him touch her. His hand felt warm. "How about coming to my Film Club with me Friday night? They're showing a rare Georges Méliès hand-tinted silent film. All proceeds go to film preservation."

"What time should I pick you up?"

She smiled. "Seven."

Carol got to Sarah's house around nine o'clock. Her friend sat on her couch watching a science fiction show; something about time trav-elling in a blue police box. Carol put her bag down.

During a commercial Sarah asked, "How'd your day go?"

"Great. Darren's growing on me. I really had a good time after work."

19

"I set up the guest room for you. Let me know if you need anything."

Carol nodded. The show had started again. She found herself getting hooked into the plot and sat riveted until the end.

"That was actually a great show," Carol acknowledged.

"One of my favorites." Sarah beamed.

"I don't know about you, but I'm ready for bed. Thanks for letting me stay."

"May your dreams be sweet." Sarah crossed her fingers.

Carol picked up her bag and headed to the guest room. On the small side, it was comfortable nonetheless. She set the alarm on her cell phone and gratefully slipped out of her clothes, threw on a long t-shirt and fell into bed.

Huge dark clouds threatened rain. She could hear the low rumble of thunder in the distance. A fitful breeze caught her hair and she brushed it out of her face. Glancing to her left she saw only dirt and rock with a narrow road that wound off into the rolling hills. The dirt held a red hue that cast an eerie bloodiness into the dim light. To her right, the road was visible for miles over flat land and it was paved. The air seemed thin and her breathing deepened to get enough oxygen. Where was she? Taking the easier route to her right, she reasoned that she could find help of some sort, perhaps someone driving a car or a town. The breeze strengthened into gusts and the sky darkened from gray to a deep purple. Carol worried she was in for a soaking. No rain fell yet, but the gusts were getting stronger and colder. Lightning webbed the sky. She ran down the road seeking any shelter she could find. Thunder cracked making her wince then duck at the power of its rumble. Wind shrieked past her. She had to stop unable to see the road through the whirling red dust. Lightning lit the scene before her. The thunder clap so loud and immediate, Carol knew it had struck the ground. She huddled down, trying to keep away from the wind and the thick dust to think. The hills were directly behind her. There could be shelter in the rocks. She stood just as another bolt of lightning hit the ground. The smell of ozone urged her to hurry. A hand on her arm startled her and she backed away in terror. A shadow in the swirling redness rushed towards her. Carol ran but tripped, falling hard on her side. Before she could regain her footing, the shadow's hand grasped her hair and roughly pulled her head back allowing the dusty wind to scour her face. Carol couldn't breathe! She fought her attacker as hard as she could. The sense that her mind was being taken over engulfed her and she stopped struggling. "No!" I won't let you..." The shadow backhanded her across the mouth. She screamed.

FOUR

CAROL SAT bolt upright, the scream still echoing in her head, consciousness returning bit by bit. She heard knocking at the door. Someone called her name.

Before Carol could understand, Sarah rushed into the room. "Are you all right?" She was frantic.

Carol just stared at her, still trying to regain her senses.

"Carol, talk to me," Sarah cried, sitting on the side of the bed. She handed tissues to her.

Tears ran down Carol's cheeks merging with the blood from her nose. "Nightmare," she mumbled.

Carol's head throbbed. The pain coming in waves. Her nose would not stop bleeding. Her alarm went off. She just stared at it. Sarah reached for the cell and gave it to her to shut off the alarm.

Sarah touched Carol's hand. "I'll get you some water."

Carol felt sick. This was the third night in a row!

Sarah rushed back into the room and handed Carol a glass of water. "Will you be all right?"

Carol only nodded as she pushed a tissue against her nose.

"You can't go to work today."

Carol turned to her in alarm. "Have to. Want to. Gotta get away from the nightmare."

"I don't think that's a good idea," Sarah pleaded.

"Please. It's okay, my nose has stopped. Go make some coffee. I'll shower and dress."

"I'll make some coffee, but I think we should discuss this some more."

After showering, Carol walked into the kitchen. Sarah filled two cups with coffee and motioned for her to sit at the breakfast bar.

"Feeling better?" Sarah asked.

"Yeah, I'm beginning to function. The coffee will get me back." She reached for her cup.

Sarah stirred sugar and cream into hers and pushed a bowl of fruit and yogurt toward Carol. "I think I understand why you want to go to work. I would want to be busy so I wouldn't think about a nightmare, but don't you think you should call Dr. Cameron and see if you can see him earlier today?"

"You're probably right. But I would feel better doing a good job. I like this company and I hope they hire me back sometime. And there's Darren. He got me the job."

Sarah looked at her coffee. "I don't agree but I understand. Call if you need me. I'm here all day."

Carol's work day was thankfully busy. She did find it hard to concentrate at times, but she managed to get a lot done. As he gathered her purse and keys to leave for her doctor's appointment, Darren came into the office. She smiled as he walked up to her desk.

"I volunteered to bring you these." He grinned.

"Thank you." She took the envelope of receipts. "I call this job security."

He laughed. "Let me escort you to your car."

"I would consider it an honor."

Darren walked her to the security parking lot next to the office building and waited while she unlocked her car door. "Remember our date for drinks tomorrow," he said and turned to leave.

"I'll wait for you in the office," Carol said, as she got into her car and closed the door. When she turned her key nothing happened. "Damn!" She turned the key again. Nothing. She heard knocking on her window.

It was Darren. "What's wrong?"

She lowered her window. "Won't start."

"Got roadside assistance?"

"Sure." She dug in her purse for her card then dialed her service. They would be to her rescue in thirty minutes. She looked at Darren. "Well there goes my doctor's appointment." She dialed the doctor's office and changed her appointment to tomorrow evening. "And there goes our date for drinks."

Darren leaned against her door. "I would feel better if you allow me to stay until the service arrives."

"Thanks. Never had car trouble. I keep my car serviced. What do you think it is?"

"I'm afraid you're asking the wrong guy."

"Sorry, just thinking out loud. It's very nice of you to stay." She glanced at the time on her cell phone. "How'd your day go?"

"Interesting. First time working with a green screen." He laughed. "Director said I got the concept fast. He was happy with what I did."

"I've heard it can seem weird acting to something that's not there," Carol said.

"That's for sure. Just a few props and a stunt man in a black diver suit with green balls stuck on his arms and legs. He also had a stick coming out of his head with one of those balls on top of it. Caused a few laughs at the beginning."

"What's he supposed to be?" Carol asked.

"The giant of high prices. I'm the knight who rescues customers from said terrible high prices."

Carol had to know. "Were you in shining armor?"

"No. I'm afraid I had to wear tights and a tunic." He hastened to add. "At least the tunic was long enough to save any embarrassment on my part."

"I bet you looked charming," Carol purred.

Darren, his face red, laughed. "That's me, Prince Charming."

Carol changed the subject. "I'm sorry I have to cancel our date tomorrow night, but I have to make this doctor's appointment."

"We have our date Friday at your film club." Darren offered.

"Thanks for understanding."

"How old is your car?"

"1962. A classic," Carol said proudly.

"Maybe you should consider a new car."

Carol looked at Darren, a frown on her face at his comment, but when she saw he was smiling she knew he was joking. They both laughed. At that moment a tow truck honked to be let into the security parking lot. It turned out to be nothing more than a loose battery cable. She was greatly relieved.

Darren laughed. "Good, everything's back to normal."

Carol smiled at him. "Thanks for waiting. Now you qualify as both Prince Charming and my Knight-in-Shinning-Armor."

Darren reached for her hand and touched it to his lips as a proper Prince Charming would, laughter in his eyes.

Arriving home, Carol bounced down the sidewalk to her front door. She felt so alive and happy. She giggled to herself as thoughts of Darren's long dark hair and those wonderful slim hips danced through her head. She had suggested the Film Club for Friday, but she couldn't help wanting to see him sooner.

Going into the kitchen to fix a bite for supper, she saw George standing at the window next to her table and chairs.

"Hi, George. Have I had a great day!" She grabbed some left over chicken from her fridge. "I've met a wonderful man."

George's shadowy shape turned to listen.

"His name's Darren." She put the chicken on the table and sat down. "If things go well, you'll be meeting him soon."

George faded away.

After dinner, Carol called Sarah. "You'll never guess what happened."

"Dr. Cameron stopped your nightmares?" Sarah's voice held hope.

"'Fraid not. Car wouldn't start and had to change my appointment to tomorrow night. But there is a bright spot. Darren's going with me to the next Film Club Festival."

"Isn't that kind've nerdy for a date? Just my opinion." Sarah laughed. "I told you he was interested in you. Is he nice?"

"Seems so. He's not like other actors I've met."

There was a hesitation. "You sure you want to date right now?" Sarah asked.

"I can't help myself. He's too damn charming." Carol hesitated. "But you're right. I don't know if I'll have more nightmares."

"Want to stay over again?"

"Might as well stay home. Doesn't seem to matter where I sleep."

"You sure?"

"I hope to fall asleep so deep with happy thoughts dancing through my head that a nightmare can't find me."

"Hope your right. You're welcome anytime, you know that."

"Thanks."

Carol decided the distraction of a favorite movie might help. She cuddled into her couch pillows and tried to watch *Robin Hood*, but every time Errol Flynn appeared on screen she thought of Darren. She loved Darren's old-fashioned ways. He was a gentleman. She wondered why he was like that. What was his background? Maybe he'd been raised in another country.

As Errol Flynn flirted with Olivia DeHavilland in Sherwood Forrest, Carol remembered he was supposedly having an affair with his leading lady during filming. He also insisted that his tunic be shorter than the rest of the Merry Men. He was very proud of his manliness. Unlike Darren's tunic and it's more appropriate length. She laughed to herself. Perhaps she would find out about Darren's manliness soon.

Carol had a glass of sherry before going to bed, hoping it would make her sleep deeper. Still aglow with her thoughts of Darren, she snuggled into her covers, not without a private thought about what he might be like in bed.

Carol grabbed the sides of the small boat and shifted her weight, hoping to keep the tiny craft from capsizing. The air was charged with energy she had felt before, an energy that brought destruction and fear. Looking up, the sky glared a deep magenta, no color a sky on earth had ever been. Glancing around, she could barely make out the barren shoreline of what seemed to be a gigantic lake. But the clear water was far too still for such a huge body of water, yet the little boat floated on towards the middle. A deep dread descended upon her spirit. Where was the boat taking her? Looking around for paddles, she saw there were none. Slowly the little boat crept on. Looking into the clear water she was amazed that she could see all the way to the bottom. It felt like sitting on the edge of a cliff staring down into the depths of a deep canyon. A dark shadow slithered through the water in the rocks below her. What was that! She couldn't see it now! There it was again!

Frantically she used her hands to paddle the little boat to shore but she almost swamped the craft and had to stop. She glanced below to see if the creature in the water still lurked. Horror closed her throat. A dark snakelike prehistoric monster swam up towards her. Lightning flashed in the heavens and with the thunderclap that followed, a torrent of rain began to fall, rapidly filling the little boat. The surface of the lake now seemed to writhe as the drops of rain plunged into its glassy surface. She could not see the monster any longer! The boat would soon sink. She could not swim fast enough to escape the creature coming from below.

Laughter! She heard laughter from somewhere, everywhere. Mocking, derisive laughter getting louder as her terror rose. Her mind felt the unwanted touch of someone wanting control over her. Carol panicked and stood. The boat flipped her into the water just as the monster broke the surface, rising high, towering over her tiny form. It began its downward plunge.

FIVE

PAIN EXPLODED in her head as she awoke clutching the side of her bed, her breath coming in short gasps. Blood soaked the sheets.

"God!" Carol moaned. Tears flowed. It took several minutes for her to even sit up. When she could, she took a shower, but it did little to reduce her pain, let alone her unnamable terror. But she couldn't let it beat her. She had to pull it together. She had to go into work today no matter how she felt. She couldn't leave her work in a mess and she had her appointment with Dr. Cameron. She took one of the pain pills they'd given her at Urgent Care and got out some yogurt and fruit to go with her coffee. .

She sat down to her breakfast, unable to take a bite. George joined her. He remained silent as ever, but Carol felt better having someone to talk to.

"I can't stand it anymore." She took a sip of coffee. At least that felt good going down her throat.

"Is there something stressing me out I'm not even aware of?"

George's shadow floated closer as though to comfort her. Whether or not this was his intent, it made Carol feel better.

"I see a new doctor today. I've got to find out what's wrong. It's messing everything up."

Carol got to work earlier than usual; hoping she could ease into her day and feel better by the time everyone else came in. Her headache was now bearable. But a dark mood hung over her. When anyone noticed she simply said she was sad to leave and how wonderful it had been to work at such a great place.

Around noon, Darren called. "Hey pretty lady, I thought I'd check in and make sure you and your car were still okay."

"Yeah, we're all right." Darren's voice cheered her.

"Glad to hear it. See you Friday night."

"Thanks again for staying around until help came."

She felt much better after Darren's call. She had something pleasant to look forward to.

Although her day had been crazy busy, she cleared her desk. Everyone told her how wonderful she had been to step in at the last minute. She at least had the satisfaction that her dark mood had not affected her work.

Driving to Dr. Cameron's office, she wondered how to tell the doctor about her problem. She was nervous yet hopeful. She comforted herself by remembering how successful Sarah's treatment had been. By the time she parked her car, most of her courage had returned.

Doctor Michael Cameron saw his clients on the top floor of an old hotel on the Santa Monica beachfront that had been converted into offices. She walked into the soft green waiting room. Sitar music played low and the light scent of incense wafted through the room. Beautiful pictures of forests or sea shores graced the walls. Carol tried hard not to let the décor influence her opinion, but it did seem a cliché. Hopefully Dr. Cameron was not a charlatan.

She had already filled out the necessary forms over the internet. The receptionist, Laurie, greeted her with warm brown eyes and a smile that would make any one smile back.

"Please have a seat." Laurie went through the door behind her. She came back before Carol could find a magazine. They all seemed to be about meditation or yoga. "You can go right in, Ms. Knight."

As she entered, she was immediately struck by the incredible view of the ocean through the wall of windows behind Dr. Cameron's desk. His office felt serene. Any apprehension she still had eased as she surveyed the comfortable furniture, the Oriental carpets draped the floor all giving the dimly lit room a sense of warmth and calm. She noticed his collection of exquisite crystals on a bookshelf to her left. Her previous remark to Sarah about using crystal balls surfaced and she smiled. She looked up at the sound of the doctor's voice.

"Ms. Knight, glad you're here," he said as he stood.

Tall and slight, Dr. Cameron walked around his desk with a graceful stride, his shoulder length blond hair tied back at the nape of his neck. He wore white cotton deck pants and a white Indian tunic style shirt. As he smiled, his tanned face lined with character. Carol relaxed, comforted by his warm and gentle manner.

"Please have a seat." He motioned to the chair before his desk. "I understand you are a friend of Sarah's?" He returned to his desk.

"Yes." She sat down, anxious to get started or get this over with, she wasn't sure which. "First, I should tell you I've never tried alternative medicine before. I'm not sure you can help me."

"I'm here to guide you towards solutions. We'll work together to balance your mind, body, and spirit. I have discovered that involving my clients in their own solutions brings faster and more lasting results. I have no hidden agendas, nor do I keep information from my clients. Is there anything you'd like to know? I want you to be comfortable." His blue eyes held his concern.

"What kind of techniques do you use?"

The doctor leaned back in his chair. "It depends upon the problem. We use yoga, tai chi, massage, acupuncture and hypnosis basically. All our vitamins and health aides are natural and herb-based."

Carol wondered if he had dealt with her type of problem before. Was he just going to give her some vitamins and hope for the best? That would be no better than the Urgent Care.

Dr. Cameron smiled. "I'm here to listen and. As I said, guide you toward solutions., not hand them to you. I can help you, but you will need to trust me with the details of me why you are here – what experiences and feelings are causing you problems."

His eyes seemed to see right through her, yet it did not make her uncomfortable. She wanted to be normal again. She tightened her jaw, hoping to get through without breaking down.

"I've been having nightmares."

"Nightmares can be the symptom of many things." His voice remained calm, reassuring. "Can you tell me what happens in your dreams?"

Carol looked down at her hands, they shook. "They're not like any nightmares I've ever had." She paused. "They're horrible. I dream of places I can't even imagine exist. There's always someone there I can't see. I'm afraid of him."

Dr. Cameron nodded for her to continue. As she gave him more details of each nightmare, she found it easier to talk than she had expected. For the most part he just sat and listened, gently interrupting only when he needed clarification.

"Doctor, I should tell you that my nightmares cause horrible headaches and nose bleeds, and it takes hours for the fear to go away."

"Have you seen a doctor about the headaches?"

"Yes. It was a 'here's some pills, call me if you get worse' scene."

"I want to pursue your case. Do you have time tomorrow for at least a half hour session?"

Carol felt rushed. "Is there something really wrong with me?"

"Your nightmares need to go away quickly. They are interfering with your life, your health." His voice was caring. "We'll work together and get to the bottom of it all; the sooner the better. You want the nightmares to stop and so do I."

"What are you going to do?"

"Would you allow me to put you under hypnosis?"

"Will it help?" Carol felt uncomfortable. She had expected to talk about her nightmares in a more conscious way.

"I want to see if anything in your past could be causing your nightmares now."

"I don't know of anything. How can hypnosis help?"

"If something traumatic happened to you, you could have blocked it. You wouldn't remember. Using hypnosis can break the block. Perhaps we will discover what's causing your nightmares or rule it out and go on to other possible causes."

"Have you been successful? Will this hypnosis cure me?"

31

"Hypnosis can only provide an indication of what is wrong, not a cure. And, yes, I have used it successfully on many occasions."

Carol just looked at him, not knowing what to ask next. Her mind whirled, not wanting to stay on any particular subject.

The doctor added, "I've studied the techniques of hypnosis for over a decade and have used it as a diagnosis tool almost that long. I have developed hypnosis therapies for people suffering from extreme phobias and fears. I had better success curing patients that way than all the drug therapy that is used. Drugs don't cure; they just treat symptoms."

"I'm afraid," she confessed.

"If you start to have any problems while you are under, I will immediately bring you back."

"Dr. Cameron, I will be honest with you." Her brows knitted. "No matter how hard I try, this is difficult for me. Don't get me wrong, I want to stop the nightmares, but…" She bit her lip. What choice did she have at this point? She pondered her fears, her alternatives. Then, to her own surprise, she found herself saying, "All right. I'll try your treatment. I want to see if you can help me."

He had a kind smile. "Laurie will make an appointment for you."

As though in a trance, Carol left the doctor's office, made her appointment and headed slowly to her car. Could he help her? She shivered and realized how tense she had gotten during her visit as she turned her VW towards home. Then she was struck by a new worry. Would she be able to hold her side of a relationship with Darren? She didn't feel she could confide in him and tell him all her troubles. They'd just met.

Her mind took a different turn. Perhaps she had been premature in taking steps in seeing a doctor, particularly an alternative one. Surely it would all turn out to be something logical and easy to fix. She realized, as she turned left to head into Briar Cliff Canyon, she did not remember how she had gotten to this point, her mind had been so preoccupied by her visit with Dr. Cameron.

After a small supper, Carol sat up watching movie after movie. If she exhausted herself, she hoped to go straight into a deep sleep and skip nightmare land altogether.

Carol heard laughter, cynical and unpleasant. She turned only to see a dense fog bank floating towards her. It breathed dank rotten air into her lungs. Carol put her hand over her nose and mouth, but it was a useless gesture. Again laughter crept from the fog. She took a step back from the crawling mist. Tendrils of vapor seemed to reach for her. Turning, Carol started to run but the fog was faster. It enveloped her; it held her in its fetid embrace and made her retch. She could not move. Carol sensed a presence behind her but the mist would not allow her to turn around. Struggling only made it tighten its grip. The laughter roared right behind her. Carol jumped. Hands grabbed her shoulders. She struggled but still could not turn around to see her tormentor. Hands groped her body, caressing her breasts and hips. Pushing her to all fours, he tore off her shirt. "You are mine to do with as I choose." He roughly pulled her pants to her knees and forced himself into her.

Pain seared her body and she awoke on the couch, TV still on. Grabbing tissues for her bloody nose, she moaned her agony into the empty room.

SIX

CAROL SAT before the doctor's desk. It had been a struggle, but she had made it to her appointment on time this morning. She felt Dr. Cameron's warm energy flow through the room as he pulled a chair closer then reach for the digital recorder.

Pushing the record button, he asked, "Can you tell me about your nightmare last night?"

Her hands shaking, she filled in the details of the dream, the sense of entrapment and gross violation. "I'll be crazy soon, if not already." Carol looked at Dr. Cameron hoping he would stop her nightmares here and now.

"The dreams are all about someone having control over you. Let's try the hypnosis we discussed. Perhaps we will find information that will confirm or deny a couple of theories I have. Please lie down on the couch. It will make it safer when I put you under." He picked up the digital recorder and followed her to the couch.

Carol took a deep breath as she lay back, still apprehensive but determined to see if this would work. Dr. Cameron pulled a chair next to the couch and pushed record on a digital recorder.

"Close your eyes and take a slow deep breath. Feel your body relax with each breath you take."

Amazingly, her muscles obeyed and began freeing themselves of tension. A sense of deep contentment filled her. The room seemed to darken as she took another slow breath.

"Visualize a white light at the top of your head. Watch how it slowly descends through your body relaxing every muscle, every nerve."

She felt even more peaceful and calm. As he started to slowly count backward, she concentrated on his voice and it alone.

"You will awaken at the count of three. One, two, three."

She opened her eyes and took a long deep breath before turning her head to look at the doctor. Her question about not being hypnotized froze in her throat when she saw his face. He looked pale and shaken.

"What's the matter? Why didn't you hypnotize me?"

"I did hypnotize you," Dr. Cameron said slowly.

"Now you're scaring me. What happened? You look like I confessed to being a serial killer or something."

"Sorry, just thinking. Don't mean to frighten you. I tried a regression to your childhood to see if your life held any clues to your nightmares."

"Did they?"

"You went back beyond your childhood, beyond your birth."

"How could I do that?" Carol scoffed. Maybe she had misheard.

"It's called past life regression. You had another life before this one, perhaps many other lives."

Carol fell silent, unable to think of what to say or ask.

"Want to hear what you said? It will help you understand."

She frowned. "Ah, sure."

He set a number and started the recorder.

"Where are you now?" Dr. Cameron's voice asked.

She heard her own voice answer. "I'm waiting."

"Waiting for what?"

"To be born."

"Can you see anything?"

"I see a bright light. It's wonderful, you get energy from it," her voice a whisper of awe.

A few moments passed and suddenly Carol's voice came again but this time in a lower tone. She spoke with authority, "Their reason for being is to learn. By knowledge they become complete. They rest awhile then return to teach and by teaching learn more."

Dr. Cameron's voice asked, "Who is there? Who tells you these things?"

"The Masters," Carol's voice whispered. "The Master Spirits tell me I will live again many times."

Carol shouted, "Please stop!"

He stopped the recorder. "Are you okay?"

"I'm not sure. What was that all about?"

Dr. Cameron sat back in his chair. His face calm and reassuring, "I would like to pursue more sessions before I come to any conclusions. I think we might be able to get to the bottom of many things as we learn more. Indications are favorable. I didn't see anything traumatic in your childhood; at least not yet. Perhaps being able to explore former lives will reveal what is happening to you."

Stunned, Carol said, "I don't understand how any of this can help."

He leaned forward and held her hand, comforting her. "Please understand that it may take time to uncover the reason behind your nightmares. I want to be able to stop them as soon as I can. I'm positive I can help. Will you trust me?"

Carol could only stare at his hand on hers. She felt calm with it there. She felt she could overcome whatever may happen if it would only stay where it was.

"I want to schedule another session for Monday. I need a little time to analyze this recording. We need to aggressively find a solution. Your nightmares have to stop. Will you help me help you?" He removed his hand.

"Sure, I'll be here." It seemed practical to try again.

"If you have another nightmare tonight, will you call me and let me know immediately? It's important that you do." His deep blue eyes were serious. "In fact you can call me anytime. I will be here for you. I'll answer any questions that may come from this session. It's important that we remain in touch." He handed her his personal card and phone information.

"Of course." Her words came slowly as her mind whirled around what had happened during the session. She looked down at his card not really seeing it.

Dr. Cameron looked relieved. "Here are some melatonin pills to help you sleep. Only take one, a half hour before bedtime. They are natural and safe."

Carol paced her living room. The session had brought even more confusion and concerns. Why did she agree to another session? Common sense did not seem to factor in anywhere. She was afraid. But what had President Roosevelt said? "The only thing to fear is fear itself"? If she wanted to be rid of nightmares she had to trust that Dr. Cameron could do it. He had listened to her. He had believed her. He wanted to help her. She remembered his hand on hers and it brought back the feeling of calm and trust again.

Trying to make sense of her unbelievable situation made her think of her ghostly roommate. Most people would point to that as a symptom of mental problems. She lived with and talked to George. That didn't seem real to most people. But she knew he was real.

But ghosts were one thing, her nightmares seemed totally different, important and complex. She had heard her own voice talk of a bright place where Master Spirits spoke to her. But how did that prove anything? Perhaps it was just a figment of her imagination. She plopped down on her couch and put her head in her hands. God, it was her own voice! How could she doubt her own voice?

"But the mind is easy to deceive," she said aloud.

It was getting late. She looked at the bottle of sleeping pills the doctor gave her. She took them into the bathroom and poured herself a glass of water. She swallowed two instead of one, deciding it might ensure the nightmares stayed away for sure. She hoped they would work better than the ones from Urgent Care.

She could smell smoke! Looking around she could make out the interior what seemed to be a warehouse. People pushed past her trying to get out of the fire's path. Carol heard a cry of pain and turned to see a woman's figure lying on the floor a few feet away. She pushed through the panicked crowd and knelt on the floor next to the woman.

"Are you all right?" Carol yelled to be heard over the crowd and the now raging fire. "Can you stand?"

The woman did not answer.

Carol turned her over. It was Sarah!

"Wake up! It's me, Carol. Please wake up."

Sarah's eyes were closed, her breathing labored. Carol tried hard to keep her panic down, but all the screaming people made it difficult. She located the door everyone ran towards. Perhaps she could pull Sarah to safety. She stood and grabbed her friend under the arms. Pulling her was harder than she thought it would be. Too slow to get them both to safety.

"Please, someone help," she begged. No one stopped.

A roaring sound made Carol look up. The entire ceiling was ablaze. Someone grabbed her from behind pulling her away from Sarah's limp body. Carol struggled to free herself and return to Sarah. The ceiling collapsed. She watched in horror as a fiery beam fell on Sarah, her body consumed by flames. Carol's legs could not hold her. Her sobbing would not stop. The noise would not stop. She turned to the person who had grabbed her away from Sarah and started pounding him with her fists in an attempt to hurt who was responsible for Sarah's death. The man dropped her and ran away into the smoke. Carol just lay where she was, unable to control the emotions that crushed her.

Another hand reached out of the smoke and grabbed her by the hair, yanking her body across the floor back towards the flames. The pain made Carol gasp. The smoke she inhaled made her cough and her eyes to water.

A raspy voice assaulted her ears. "You are nothing. You deserve to die."

Carol felt the invasion of another mind pouring into hers, consuming her will to live. "No!" she screamed and grabbed the hands that grasped her hair. "I will not die!"

The smoke became too thick to see anything. Carol could not breathe. She clawed at the hands holding her, trying to rid herself of the torment. Blackness came.

She sat up in bed gasping for breath.

SEVEN

CAROL SLOWLY walked up and down the meandering streets of her beloved canyon, hoping to lighten her dark mood. The sky glowed with pale yellows and blues as the sun rose over the hills. The new day's air brought healing freshness; the trees embraced her in their calm, helping her return to this world. She sat for an hour on a forgotten stone bench nestled into the hillside near the road, well hidden by the trees and over-grown bushes. She had found it a few years ago, and cleared the seat of the ivy that threatened to return it to nature.

Birds flitted in and out of the branches. The dappled sunlight and the sheer quiet helped distance her from her terror. She knew she should call Dr. Cameron, but her energy, still drained from the nightmare, made it impossible. She had no will to do anything but sit here. She remembered taking more melatonin than required. She had called Sarah as soon as she could. She had needed reassurance that her friend was alive and well. Sarah had wanted to come over, but Carol just couldn't manage seeing anyone. It had been difficult, but Sarah finally agreed to wait until Carol felt better.

It was so beautiful here under the trees. Why couldn't she just stay forever? Carol's head dropped. Exhaustion claimed her and she fell asleep. She heard her name called from far off. She awoke with a start, fearful if she slept any longer it would invite another nightmare. She actually felt better. Surprisingly, her brief nap had refreshed her and she slowly started back home, relishing every breath she took.

She loved to walk here. Beyond her first impression of the Canyon five years ago, she had come to find something much older and more powerful seep into her conscious mind. The air, trees, even the earth itself felt imbued with a power that defied mere words. It did not frighten her. It calmed her. It renewed her.

Th walk down the brick path towards her front door seemed surreal. The colors were brilliant and infused vibrancy into her spirit. She stopped by the courtyard fountain and watched the water dance, sparkling in the morning light. She ws mesmerized by its beauty. The koi came over to her, hoping for some breakfast. It made her smile to see them vie for the best position like puppies wanting to be petted.

Dinah trotted up and meowed for attention. Carol happily obliged. "Where's Marguerite?"

She heard high pitched laughter coming from her neighbor's. "I see. She's visiting. Making sure we're all okay."

The koi expecting food made her think of her own breakfast. She was actually hungry. Carol went into her bungalow and headed for the kitchen. George waited for her at the table.

"Mornin'." She smiled at her roommate. "Always good to see you."

George's shadow remained as Carol put her yogurt and fruit on the table. She made extra coffee, filling the largest mug she owned.

George faded as she pulled her cell out of her pocket. She slowly dialed the doctor's home number from the card he had given her.

"Hi. I've had another nightmare, a really bad one this time. I promised to call." She hastily brushed away a tear that escaped down her cheek.

"Can you come to my office now?"

"Yes." Her voice flat.

"Are you ready to try the hypnosis again?"

She hesitated. She didn't want the feeling she had gotten from her walk in the canyon to end.

"It's important that we talk as soon as possible after a nightmare."

"OK," she said. "Let me finish my breakfast."She had to end her miserable existence somehow. "I'll get there as soon as I can."

Carol topped off her cup of coffee and took it with her to the bedroom, sipping it as she searched for something nicer than an old t-shirt and sweat pants. After putting on stylish jeans and a red silk blouse, she swallowed the last of her coffee, found her purse on the way to the door, strolled down the path to her car, and headed to Dr. Cameron's.

As she entered the office, Laurie had yet to arrive for work and Dr. Cameron greeted her. Carol was taken aback by his appearance. She had expected him to be in his usual attire, but he was dressed in sweat pants and t-shirt. His long blond hair fell loose hitting his shoulders. She remembered how early it was and realized he had hurried here too.

"How are you feeling? I hope you're ready to discover more." His blue eyes flashed with anticipation as he motioned for her to lie down.

It angered her to see his excitement. "Not as much as you seem to be."

"I feel we may be on the brink of a breakthrough."

Carol's anger turned to hope. "If we can stop my nightmares today, I'm all for it."

"Please, relax as much as possible." He pushed the record button.

Again Carol listened to the doctor's voice putting her under hypnosis. When she awoke his face held concern, but his eyes held hope.

"What happened this time?"

Dr. Cameron hit play. His voice asked, "Carol, can you take me back to the before time when you were waiting to be born?"

Carol's voice sounded childlike. "Why? I like being here."

"Where are you? Can you describe what you see?"

"I see Teddy on my bed."

"How old are you?"

"Four-and-a-half. Mommy says I'm a big girl now."

"Think back to before you were born. Can you do that for me?"

Carol heard her breathing get louder then become slow and rhythmic. Her voice sounded calm and adult. "The light is strong, but peaceful."

There was silence and Carol looked at Dr. Cameron. She'd been staring intently at the recorder and hadn't noticed that he studied her as she listened.

Her voice came again. "The Master Spirits are with me. They know so much."

"Are they speaking to you?"

"They always speak to me."

"What are they telling you?"

"It's sad, but I'm not afraid."

"Can you tell me what they are saying?"

"They tell me I have been reborn many times but the ability to know myself from the before times has been taken from me."

"Who took this knowledge away?"

"Because of the one who now attacks, a lover must act. The attacker believes that what he seeks is worth much pain and sorrow."

"Who attacks?"

"He should know better."

"How does he attack?"

"Like dreams but not dreams."

"Why does he attack?"

There was a pause until Carol's child-voice answered, "They only say there are many gods because god is in each of us."

The doctor reached over and turned off the recorder. "After that I couldn't get you to go back before you were born again."

Carol glared at him. "What's all this?" she demanded.

Dr. Cameron reached for her hand. "Are you okay?"

"Ah. Not sure." She pulled her hand back.

"I can tell you where your nightmares come from, if you're ready."

"If you have an answer I want to hear it." She sounded small, like her four-and-one-half year old self.

"You're not dreaming, you're going to the astral plane," he announced as he leaned back.

Carol just stared in confusion.

"Plato talks of the astral plane as one of the levels your soul must travel before reaching its final destination. It's another dimension. It has many levels that vary in complexity and concept." He hesitated searching for words to better explain. "The least complex level is comparable to your normal dream state."

"You can't be serious."

"I know how this must sound, but I assure you, I have made a lifetime study of this phenomenon. Throughout history you will find

42

references to the astral world or astral plane. Physicists are currently exploring the idea of many planes of existence. The astral plane is one of many."

Carol thought he sounded a bit anxious. She stared at him trying to pull herself together. Ridiculous! I'm not an idiot.

"The fact you remember every detail of every nightmare, told me this could be the case. You said yourself you've never had dreams like these before."

"Yeah, but—"

"The level of terror and the fact that there seems to be someone trying to control you also tells me you are travelling to the astral plane." He reached for her hand again.

Carol calmed at his touch. "This astral plane: is that where the Masters are?"

"No, they're from one of the other dimensions. Some refer to them as angels."

"How can they know where my nightmares come from?"

"The Masters understand all dimensions. But it is the astral dimension they are referring to when you said 'like dreams but not dreams'. And the astral dimension is only terrible if you wish it to be."

"You believe this is what's happening?" Carol couldn't understand how her session had led to such outrageous conclusions.

"Yes, I am certain. And I can help."

Her heart beat so fast it hurt. Dr. Cameron squeezed her hand and her heart slowed. The pain lessened.

He watched her closely. "It is possible to travel unaware to the astral plane but only to the lowest levels."

She liked the way his voice sounded. The calm tone drew her to him. But what he was saying made no sense! At times he seemed to fade away into a gray fog. She struggled to listen.

"By your descriptions, you've been to some of the highest levels. That takes a lot of hard work and determination from someone devoted to astral travel. I know where your dreams come from, but I don't know why. Yet. The way your trips to the astral dimensions happen is very unusual. I have concerns about the person you always meet there."

43

"Wait. You're telling me I'm not dreaming. I'm actually experiencing this...this horror?"

The doctor's blue eyes pleaded. "Understand. Your perception of reality is not reliable. No one's is. If your unconscious trips to the astral dimension continue, after a while you may not be able to discern this world from the astral world."

Carol's hands began to shake. "None of this makes any sense! I can't believe it. You're positive there's no other explanation," she pleaded.

"Yes, I'm positive."

"I need a moment." Carol closed her eyes, her breathing was hard and fast.

"Would you like some tea?"

"Yes," she answered dully. "No. Do you have coffee?"

Carol sat up as the doctor left. His theory was farfetched. She could have been saying strange things by being in a dream. Maybe she actually went to sleep during the session. But it wasn't that she had said strange things, it was the doctor's explanation that unnerved her. How could she live with the knowledge that her nightmares were real? How do you fix that?

"How do you take your coffee?" he called from the office kitchenette.

"Black, thank you."

He came back and handed her a mug. She didn't even notice the cardboard bitterness that can only come from office coffee.

"Dr. Cameron, if what you're saying is true, who's trying to hurt me?"

"I don't know yet. But it answers the question of your headaches and nosebleeds. In order to travel to the astral dimension, your life force creates an astral twin or spirit that leaves your body."

Carol just stared back. Her brain felt as though it was physically twisting in her skull in an effort to understand. Things were getting weirder by the moment.

"If for some reason your astral twin returns to your body too quickly, too violently, it can give you a bad headache. Nosebleeds are not uncommon."

Carol rebelled. "Doctor, this is all too out there for me to even consider. It's been wonderful meeting you, but I don't think you can help me."

"I've studied the astral dimension for many years. I know what I'm talking about. I can help you."

Carol handed him her empty coffee mug and stood. "Thank you for your concern, but I have to go now."

He faced her. His eyes held genuine concern. "You will be having more nightmares. And you will continue to be attacked. We must discover who is doing this to you."

She took a sharp intake of breath and sat back down.

"You are in serious trouble. Please consider what I have said before you reject my diagnosis. I will help you. I will not give up hope. If you have another nightmare please call me anytime, day or night, I'll be here for you."

EIGHT

SITTING IN HER CAR in the doctor's parking lot, Carol's mind whirled. Overwhelmed, she grabbed her cell and called Sarah. "Can I come over? I really need to talk."

Sarah opened her door at Carol's knock. "I have a pot of coffee ready."

"I'm going crazy with these damn nightmares!"

"What happened?"

"Just saw Dr. Cameron. He put me under hypnosis, said a lot of things that sounded like a bad script from the Twilight Zone!"

"Awesome. I've heard hypnosis can really work. But you don't sound happy about it."

Carol blurted her frustration, "It all sounds crazy to me. I heard the recording of me under hypnosis. I went back to before I was born! How could that be? He says I'm running off to some astral place or dimension or whatever! Says that's causing my nightmares. Wait, no, he said that I am not having nightmares; that all this horrible stuff is really happening to me! He actually believes that you leave your body and go running off to some other dimension. It's all just stupid if you ask me. I think he's a fake."

"I'm worried about you. Your call this morning needing to know I was still alive was spooky."

Carol turned to Sarah. "I'm afraid. He doesn't know what he's talking about. I want a rational explanation! I don't want—"

"But this is all so amazing." Sarah tried to calm her friend. "You actually went back to before you were born. How wonderful is that! Perhaps Dr. Cameron has something here."

Carol glared at her friend. She didn't want to think about it any more.

Sarah brightened.

"The astral something. Astral plane. I've only read fictional stories about the astral plane. Let's check it out on the Internet. Maybe we can bring some reality to all this."

"What reality?" Carol spat. "I don't see anything real about any of this!"

"Well then, I need to understand if I'm going to help you. Please. Try to calm down."

Carol started to cry.

"Come on. Let's see if we can make any sense out of all this."

Although filled with shelves of computer books, Sarah's office looked organized and tidy mainly due to all the sleek brushed-nickel office furniture. The wide desk that dominated the room had multiple monitors and keyboards all easily reached from an office chair that rivaled any space ship command seat ever created. The two friends spent hours looking up the astral plane on the Internet, finding far more information than they expected. Much of it corroborated Dr. Cameron's theory.

"Look, Carol, even Freud and Jung accepted this. It says, 'Jung saw the astral journey as a paradigm of modern man's search for a soul.' Freud's idea of the astral was to draw a parallel between it and the unconscious mind. This is fascinating."

"Can we take a break? My head's spinning."

Sarah leaned back in her command chair. "This astral plane stuff is incredible. And we found that it is one of many dimension physicists are studying. I'm going to look for more about it later and fill you in on anything I find. You have to go forward with Dr. Cameron's therapy."

Carol was irritated with Sarah's enthusiasm. In spite of all the evidence to support Dr. Cameron's diagnosis, it couldn't be the rational answer. But was she just being stubborn? Damn, there's all this evidence that the doctor's right. He'd been nothing but kind and helpful in his way.

"I give up. I see your point." Carol was exhausted. All the disturbed sleep was taking a huge toll. "I promise to give this serious thought. I did hear my own voice talk about having lives before this one; that I talked to these Master Spirits."

"I'm sorry it's so painful and confusing. I'm with you no matter what." Sarah's eyes misted up.

"I'd better head home. I need to get ready for tonight. I'm taking Darren to the Film Club." She hugged her friend. "You always make me feel better."

"You sure you should go?"

"I need to escape all this for a while."

Darren picked her up promptly at seven. Carol was dressed in a simple blue dress that complimented her dark hair and brown eyes. She was determined to have a normal evening devoid of fantastical ideas of astral travel.

"You look fabulous," Darren said.

"Thank you." She liked being complimented when it was sincere. "I totally forgot I volunteered to make the popcorn tonight. We have to go straight to the club."

"Not a problem. We can't have a movie without popcorn now, can we?"

"Here's the address. You have GPS?"

"Wouldn't go anywhere without it. Couldn't, much of the time."

The Film Club met at the home of Evan Pleger in the West Adams Historical District of Los Angeles, a stunning 1912 Craftsman house. Evan was a young aspiring producer who had worked on a couple of independent movies over the past five years and was actually beginning to make a name for himself.

Carol introduced Darren as they entered. "Evan, this is my friend, Darren. He also works in the film industry."

"Welcome to our movie night, Darren. Please come in, find a seat." Evan smiled, delighted to have a new person join them. Then to Carol. "You're popcorn tonight?"

"Yes, I am." Note how puffy and yellow I am."

48

"Never, darling," Even responded as he turned to greet the next comer.

Carol took Darren into the large living room. "Here. This is the best seat in the house. Just save the seat next to you. I'll go make the popcorn."

"Bring some back with you, and I'll save the seat."

"You're holding my chair for ransom? Remember, I'm the one making what you are about to eat."

"In that case, could you put extra butter on it?"

Carol gave a fake evil glare. "You think I jest?" She laughed, "Okay, you'll get butter. If you're good, I'll bring napkins too."

"You drive a hard bargain. Your seat is reserved. Just hurry back."

Carol bustled into the kitchen, rolled out the club's antique movie popcorn machine and starting making a large batch. As she oversaw the process, the doorbell chimed many times as members filed in to enjoy the meeting of like minds over a rare movie.

As she put popcorn into circus-striped bags, she couldn't stop thinking about her nightmares. Was she making a mistake dating Darren? What if no one could help her? What if she ended up committed to an asylum, never to get out? How would he respond? Turn away in disgust?

Many members came to claim their bags. When she felt there were enough filled bags of popcorn, Carol hurried back to her seat next to Darren, relieved to escape her thoughts for a while.

"Hope I wasn't gone too long," she whispered, handing a bag of buttered popcorn to Darren.

"No, this is a great group. I'm a social type. No problem making friends."

"Good, I was hoping you'd enjoy this."

Evan walked to the front of the room. "Welcome. Tonight we have a treat. George Méliès *The Merry Frolics of Satan* released in 1906 in its original hand colored glory."

A pleasurable murmur ran through the group.

"Without further ado, please run the film, Dave." Evan pointed to the back of the room. He hit the light switch and the movie began to flicker on the screen before them.

Starting with a carriage which changes from ordinary to satanic complete with a skeletal horse, then is pushed into an active volcano. The travelers are tormented by Satan as they travel in Hell from inn to demon-infested inn. All magical fun, albeit strange to today's eyes. Carol tried hard not to make any comparison between her nightmares to the movie.

Afterward there was a lively discussion on every topic from the techniques that were ahead of their time to the historic period in which the movie was made. Darren joined the discussion and brought up the fact that Méliès started making films because he was a stage magician who fell in love with the magic a film camera could do.

Carol was thrilled that Darren fit into this part of her life so well. As they drove back to her place, she turned to him. "How about I make you dinner tomorrow night? My place." She really liked Darren. Maybe this could turn into something worthwhile for a change. Maybe she didn't want to face what was happening to her.

Darren looked like he'd just won the lottery. "What time?"

"Would seven be good?"

"Perfect."

Carol was impressed when he escorted her to her door instead of just dropping her off at the street. She didn't want him to leave but did not have a good enough reason to ask him to stay. Not after asking him to dinner tomorrow night.

Darren held her hand. "Thank you for inviting me to your film club."

A thrill went through her as he held her hand. "You're welcome. I'm glad you enjoyed it. We can be a very nerdy bunch at times."

"I think everyone is a little nerdy about something. I'm glad we share a love of films." He reached up his other hand and touched her cheek.

She knew he wanted to kiss her. Carol tilted her head back as he leaned forward, softly touching her lips with his. His kiss sent waves of longing through her.

He straightened up. "See you tomorrow night."

She watched as he walked back to his car. How wonderful everything had been tonight. Such a welcome relief. She refused to think about her bad dreams; it would break the lovely spell she was under. She turned to her door and let herself in. George's shadow filled the corner by the fireplace.

"Hi, George. Had a great time. Darren's coming for dinner tomorrow, so I need you to be on your best behavior."

George faded away.

"I mean it. No sudden appearances or anything spooky. Okay?"

Slipping out of her clothes, Carol got into bed, the sheets cool against her skin. She thought about Darren's kiss and smiled.

Was she blind? She could hear. People in extreme pain moaned and cried out their misery all around her. Lying amongst them, the smell of death and decay was overwhelming. She struggled to sit up. A body slipped from top of her. Now that she could see, she closed her eyes in terror. She lay in a large deep pit, filled with rotting corpses and those near death, struggling to stay alive in spite of the horror around them. Carol looked up at the red glowing sky. She saw dark human forms standing around the edges of the pit, silhouetted against the bonfires behind them. She could barely discern the smell of smoke over the reek of corpses. A shot fired. Carol jumped. More shots came and she glared with loathing at the figures that ringed the ridge firing into the mass of misery below them. A baby cried but the next shot silenced it. Carol stifled a scream, fearful a bullet would find her as well. Fear gripped the remaining living victims, freezing their bodies and minds, keeping them incapable of saving themselves or anyone else.

Carol felt the presence of her tormentor again. "You can be free, if you want. Just let me into your mind."

"No", she yelled.

A bullet screamed towards her but missed. Fearing another shot, she pushed herself under the corpse next to her.

"Don't you want to be free?" the male voice purred.

Carol awoke screaming, "No!"

NINE

IT HAD TAKEN LONGER for the nose bleed to stop and the headache still pounded. Carol couldn't face calling Dr. Cameron. Should she cancel having Darren over for dinner? She sat in a ball of misery on her couch wishing it would all go away. If the nightmares, or whatever the hell they were, would just stop, she could enjoy her growing relationship with Darren. She wouldn't call Sarah, either. She'd just tell her to call the doctor immediately.

Carol slowly disengaged herself from the couch, showered and dressed in jeans and blouse. Zombie-like, she plodded into the kitchen to make a pot of coffee. She felt alone and afraid; it seemed even George had deserted her this morning. After a couple of sips of hot aromatic coffee, she felt more capable of functioning on a near-human level. Not calling Dr. Cameron loomed over her, but she still could not bring herself to act. She made a promise to herself to call him first thing Monday morning. It took some of the pressure off. Carol felt as though she were still in the pit of death, incapable of feeling anything but terror, unable to think past the current second, and helpless to change her existence.

She started slowly, deliberately filling the day with decisions on what to serve Darren for dinner. Carol just wanted one day of pleasure before she had to face the inevitable. Perhaps Darren would want to spend time over Sunday too and she wouldn't have to be alone the entire weekend. The fear she might have another nightmare made her rethink wanting him to spend the night.

The trip to the market occupied hours picking just the right vegetables and main course. Choosing the wine took the longest. Unloading the groceries in her kitchen, Carol's thoughts turned to Darren. She couldn't remember when she'd had such a wonderful time with a man. He was charming and polite, the perfect diversion.

In the glow of that realization, she tackled the preparation of the dinner with uncharacteristic verve. She finished by setting a table for two near the fireplace in the living room. Carol doubled-checked everything. Her olive-colored walls complimented the dark woodwork. The fireplace had a small fire that reflected in the beveled glass doors of the built-in bookcases on either side. Stained glass windows glowed with the last rays of daylight. Comfortable antique furnishings completed the charm. Carol lit candles on the table, making the room even more warm and inviting. Darren arrived on time and with flowers. Carol hurried to the kitchen to find a vase. Coming back, she placed the flowers on the table.

Darren stood before the fireplace. "Your place is amazing."

"Thanks."

"Can I help with anything?"

Carol shook her head. "This is my treat. Have a seat at the table and I'll bring in the first course."

After the endive salad then the main course of salmon over rice with asparagus on the side all with Béarnaise sauce, they sat eating lemon sherbet for dessert.

"I've been telling you my funny stories; you surely have a few moments of insanity in your life." Darren raised an eyebrow encouraging her to share.

"Being an accountant does not generate interesting stories unless you're another accountant." Carol took a sip of Chardonnay. "Hmmm… Oh, wait, I know. I was asked to help out the regular accountant at the Art Directors Guild several years ago. They set me up in a small room on the first floor next to their archives."

Darren leaned back listening to every word.

"I was deeply involved in some complicated figures when suddenly my office door opened and in popped this wiry little guy maybe in his sixties. 'Is this the ADG Archives?' he asks. He was smiling from ear to ear and he was so energetic, I was taken aback. Before I could redirect him down the hall he asked me if I was an actress. I smiled, shook my head and told him where the archive was. He bounced out of my office. About twenty minutes later, he bounced back into my office and said 'You should be an actress. I've been a camera man for forty years and I know a great face when I see one!' Then he bounced out of my office and was gone before I could say a word."

"Wow, was he the actor's good fairy?" Darren chuckled.

"Possibly a leprechaun. I never saw him again and no one at the Guild knew who he was. You could be right!"

"But you didn't follow through?"

"No. I didn't believe him. The story of my life."

After dinner, Darren helped her carry the dirty dishes into the kitchen. Coming back into the living room, she poured them each a glass of sherry. They stood together before her fireplace.

He tipped his glass into hers. "Here's to a great dinner."

"Thanks. And here's to a great eater." She laughed.

Darren took her glass and put both down on a side table. He looked at her and she stood in fascination, mesmerized by him. He tenderly reached for her. His long deep kiss sent waves of lust through every nerve in her body. What a delicious thrill! She slowly disengaged herself from his embrace. Desperately wanting more, she abandoned all caution. Taking his hand, she led him into her bedroom. Self-conscious of her own body, she felt more confident in the darkness. At least the first time. As she threw off her dress, Darren pulled off his sweater revealing a well-muscled upper body that took her breath. The dim light that fought its way into the bedroom made enticing shadows on his ripped abdomen. She leaned back onto the bed as he approached. With one skilled movement he removed her bra. He cupped her breast in his hand and lowered his mouth onto her nipple. Utter delight seized her, and she threw her head back with a moan. She wanted more.

She removed her panties as Darren undid his jeans. They slipped from his narrow hips as if responding to their master's wish. He lifted her farther onto the bed, mounting her body as he moved her. She felt like a feather in his arms. He entered her in one fluid movement. Carol moaned with ecstasy as he made love with long luxurious strokes. She pushed her hips to meet his thrusts and was rewarded with deep groans from him. The moment came with great passion as they both rose together, releasing their joy in one wave that left them both helpless and heaving to catch their breath.

Exhausted, physically and emotionally, they fell asleep, awaking only once for a reprise of rapture. Then, wrapped in each other's arms, they slept deeply for the rest of the night.

TEN

CAROL AWOKE first. The late morning sun caressed them as it slowly illuminated the bedroom. Though small, Carol had furnished it with an antique bed and matching bureau. The robin's egg blue walls soothed. She looked over and saw Darren sprawled naked beside her. Asleep, his breathing deep, he looked like a dark angel. Carol smiled as she took in the gorgeous man in her bed. What a night! And no nightmare!

Not wanting to wake him just yet, she slowly slipped from the bed, threw on an oversized t-shirt, and tiptoed to the kitchen.

When she turned to grab the coffee pot, she saw George's shadow in the kitchen doorway. "Mornin', George," she said, turning to the sink. Glancing back, she noticed George's shadow still stood in the doorway. "Not here to scold me for last night, are you?" she said over her shoulder.

Darren's naked figure walked straight through George's shadow. "Who you talkin' to?"

"Myself." She didn't want to share George with Darren yet, afraid he'd think she was some loony. Sarah knew, but she couldn't see George either. "I live alone so usually I'm the only one I can have conversations with." She laughed as she filled the coffee pot with water.

"Would you believe me if I said you are irresistible?" Darren reached for her, pulling her close, kissing her lips gently.

Carol blushed, unsure how to answer. She returned his kiss. "How about grabbing a shower while I finish making coffee?" She wanted to believe she was irresistible, but it had sounded like just a line.

Smiling, he headed off towards the bathroom.

Carol prepared a tray of coffee and toasted bagels with butter and cream cheese to take into the living room. She hoped Darren would drop the flippant line type of talk and go back to being the person she wanted to be with. When he came in from his shower, he only wore a towel tucked around his waist.

"Is this your idea of formal breakfast attire, sir?"

Darren laughed. "Don't you like my tailor, madam?"

"Very much," she answered slowly.

She stood and gave him a quick kiss. "Go ahead and get some coffee, I'm going to jump in the shower. Be back in no time."

After her shower, she joined Darren for breakfast dressed in nothing but her towel. Sitting together on the couch, they luxuriated in the butterscotch colored sunlight that filtered through the small stain glass windows high on the wall to either side of the fireplace.

"I love your place." He looked around the room. "You've done a wonderful job of recreating… 1913, wasn't it?"

She cuddled closer, flattered that he remembered the year of her home. "Thank you. I really enjoy living here."

He put his arm around her. "When I sat at your table in the Hollywood Canteen, I was drawn to you. You fascinate me." He kissed her quickly on the forehead.

"You missed."

"What?"

"You missed." Carol pointed to her lips.

"*Elf*," he said, and kissed her again, full and hard.

"Nice catch," she murmured.

He looked deep into her eyes. "I may be a bit lame telling you sometimes, but I really do think you're very special."

She could feel his sincerity this time and believed him. Carol didn't want the glorious day to end and Darren showed no sign of wanting to leave. "Want to do something? Maybe go for a walk or watch a movie?"

"Movie. I want to be alone with you."

She walked over to her vintage armoire in the corner and opened it to reveal the TV and some of her movie collection. "I'm thinking a comedy. Oh, I know, *Singing in the Rain*. Gene Kelly is great, and Donald

O'Connor won the Golden Globe for Best Actor. They released it in 1952 but it's all about Hollywood history. When talkies changed everything."

Darren chuckled. "No wonder you're the popcorn girl at the Film Club. Perfect choice. Haven't seen it in years."

After the movie, Darren noticed the time and reluctantly got up to put on clothes to go home. "It has been the best two days I can remember having," he said after a lingering kiss. "I'll call you tomorrow."

After he left, the bungalow felt empty and lonely. Carol made herself another pot of coffee, and without enthusiasm gathered her client's accounts together. She started organizing the figures to keep ahead of her work now that she had taken two days for the job Darren had gotten for her. She felt guilty about not getting the work done she'd intended. Priding herself on being responsible, she usually went to great lengths to meet deadlines as well as provide excellent work. Even though her client would understand if she needed more time, she didn't feel good doing that. She opened a cabinet in one of the built in bookcases next to the fireplace and revealed a pull out shelf, which served as her desk. Pushing a small but comfortable antique chair up to it, Carol opened her laptop, hit the on switch, and keyed in her passcode. As she waited, her mind drifted back to Darren. She had never experienced such intense and satisfying sex before. It had been intoxicating and she wanted more. Sighing, she tried again to concentrate on the figures, but her mind refused to let go of her time with Darren. Her cell rang, and she saw Sarah's name pop up.

"I'm dying to find out how it went with Darren," her friend declared.

"I'm surprised you didn't call earlier."

"It was hard not to. I figured I'd give you some time, but I just can't wait any longer. Did he spend the night?"

"He just left."

"Oooo, I knew it," Sarah gushed. "I'm so happy for you." There was a pause. "You're okay, right?"

Carol giggled. "Best sex I've ever had."

"So, you gonna see him again?"

"Yes." Her immediate response came before she'd thought. She added, "Maybe, I'm not sure."

"But—"

Carol cut her off. "What if I start having more nightmares?"

Sarah spoke cautiously, "Did you call Dr. Cameron?"

"Not yet." Carol's voice lowered. "Couldn't face another appointment. I just wanted my date with Darren."

"I understand but don't wait too long. Just remember I'm here for you."

"Didn't have a nightmare last night."

"That's great but are you sure sex with Darren is the answer to your problem?"

"No, not sure at all, just find it curious, not to mention a relief."

"Give the doctor a chance before you go judging what will help you."

"You're right. I promised myself I'd call him Monday."

"See, you must have felt something was right about Dr. Cameron. Sure you should wait that long?"

Carol didn't feel sure about much of anything. "No, but it's what I'm comfortable with. I just hope I'm not making a mistake."

"If you don't like what Cameron does after this next visit, I'll help you find someone else. You need help. You have to start somewhere."

"I'll call Dr. Cameron first thing Monday morning. Now, I need to get back to work, too much playing this weekend."

"It did you good. Stop feeling guilty. Okay?"

"Okay. See ya soon."

It was late by the time she closed the books and put them away. Wishing Darren were there, she headed to bed. She took the melatonin Dr. Cameron gave her in spite of having little hope it would help.

Carol floated in midair. The ground seemed very far below. She wondered how she could be suspended here. She looked around her for some meaning, some answer. A slight breeze blew her gently sideways and she smiled at the sensation of floating. She leaned slightly forward and flew a few yards before straightening. What a wonderful sensation! She experimented, learning how to hold her body to move straight forward, sideways, or even up or down.

A sudden gust knocked her off balance. She started falling. Carol screamed as the ground rushed towards her at a terrifying speed. Struggling, she tried to regain the balance she had felt floating. Laughter, again the mocking laughter! Her fall suddenly stopped. She hung suspended, still high above the ground. She put her arms out to the side and clumsily moved her body into a stable position. The feeling of someone intruding into her thoughts through her fear made her panic. Again she fell. Out of control, she grasped at the thin air trying to stop her descent. He was toying with her! Anger vied with fear. Again she stopped falling. "Why are you doing this?"

"You must learn you are under my control, not your own."

She fell. The air rushed past her and her attempts to stop her descent failed. Laughter assaulted her as she rushed towards the ground. It was mere feet away. She was going to hit the ground. "No!"

With a loud gasp, Carol woke up. Her head was splitting with the pain. Blood dripped down her face.

ELEVEN

SUNDAY MORNING. Carol tried to calm herself. I should call Dr. Cameron. But she couldn't make herself pick up her cell. Still confused and doubtful about his bizarre diagnosis, she did not know how she wanted to proceed. Darren had not been with her last night. Could he really stop the nightmares? Her mind twisted from diagnosis to Darren.

After a shower and an attempt at breakfast, Carol sat alone in her living room. Nothing could motivate her to do anything but stare at the blank screen of her computer. It was frustrating. She needed to get work done. Her cell rang.

It was Sarah. "How did last night go?"

"Won't lie. Another nightmare."

"You don't sound good. Did you call…"

Carol interrupted, "I'm calling Dr. Cameron tomorrow morning."

"Whoa, sounds like you need a break. Let's go antique shopping."

"When?" Even antiquing didn't motivate her.

Sarah laughed. "Right now."

"Not sure I've got the energy. Maybe I should stay home."

"And what? Sit and feel sorry for yourself all day. No. I'll meet you at Second Hand Rose. We can have a drink at Maxie's after. See you in an hour."

Carol arrived at Second Hand Rose to see Sarah waiting for her out front. She felt better now she was out and about. Carol smiled as she approached her friend. "I want to make a deal. Let's not talk of nightmares or anything related for the rest of the day. Okay?"

Sarah frowned. "You sure? I thought we could talk over drinks."

"I'm sure."

"What about tonight?" Sarah worried. "Stay with me tonight in case you—"

"Sure. That's a great idea. Now, no more. Let's go shopping."

The little bell over the door tinkled as they closed the heavy leaded glass door behind them. They greeted Liz, the owner.

"Hey. How've you been?" Sarah asked.

Liz came from behind the counter to give the girls a hug. "I was just thinking about you two!"

Carol smiled with pleasure. Liz had helped find most of the antiques she had in her home.

Sarah grinned. "Any new tea pots come in?"

"Just got three last Monday," Liz said, pointing to the left side of the store.

Sarah wandered off to see if any were suitable for her collection.

"Carol, I've just received a piece you need to see." Liz took her to a back corner of the shop. "Just came in yesterday. I was going to call you today. You have to see this candlestick."

Carol picked up the large ornate candlestick. What she assumed would be a cherub was actually a beautiful women draped in flowing robes holding the candle up in one hand, very Art Nouveau. Upon further inspection she noticed around the bottom of the piece, snakes writhed in an entrancing pattern. "Can you tell me anything about this?" she asked with fascination.

"Isn't it an unusual piece?" She grinned at Carol. "You're going to love this. It's from the early 1920s and it came from a silent era star's home in Briar Cliff Canyon." She paused and a gleam came to her eyes. "Rumor has it that he held many orgies during his lifetime. There's supposed to be a second candlestick, a mate, but no one's ever found it. I have the provenance for it at my desk."

Carol murmured, "I wonder what happened to the other one?" The information enthralled her. What a great piece to have in her Briar Cliff bungalow. Part of Hollywood history, it belonged back in the Canyon, she rationalized. Carol looked at the bottom of the candlestick and saw it was solid silver. It would be expensive.

"You still have layaway?"

Liz laughed. "I knew this piece was for you. Yes, there's still a layaway plan."

Together they went to check the books. Liz found the page. "This is a consignment piece. Let me see if he's given any room for some price breaks." She turned a page. "He wants eight hundred but gave consent for a twenty percent discount. That makes it six hundred forty dollars." She handed Carol the envelope containing the candlestick's history.

Sarah noticed Carol standing at the counter with Liz and wandered over to see what her friend had found. "Not cherubs, please don't tell me you're thinking of cherubs," she moaned as she approached.

Carol laughed and handed the piece to Sarah. "Do you see any cherubs? It belonged to a silent star that lived in Briar Cliff Canyon."

"Whoa, now that's a candlestick." She handed the silver treasure back to Carol. "Ya gonna get it?" she asked with fascination.

"It's expensive even with a discount." Carol turned back to Liz.

Sarah said, "I know how much this means to you. How about I pay for half as a gift?"

Her offer would make it possible to own this amazing piece without layaway. Stunned, Carol whispered, "Are you sure?"

"Positive. Call it an early birthday present. A very good birthday present. Maybe even Christmas presents for the next five years."

"But I don't feel good about so much money."

"It's perfect for you. I want to help you get it. I'm good, just got a bonus last week for finishing a job early. Besides, after all those... you should have it." Sarah shrugged.

Carol hugged Sarah. "Thank you!"

Liz smiled at Carol. "It's a deal then?"

"Of course!" She looked at the candlestick with the pride of ownership.

After all the details of the purchase were taken care of, Carol turned to Sarah. "Mind if I call Darren and invite him to join us for drinks?"

"Sounds good to me."

Darren met them at Maxie's' just around the corner from Second Hand Rose. The bar had a long history of serving Hollywood's finest, or at least most interesting, for over seventy years. Its rich mahogany-paneled walls and red-leather-upholstered booths immediately transported patrons back to 1950. Carol always expected to hear the Rat Pack having a party in the back room. The autographed pictures of Hollywood stars that adorned the walls ran from the early 1940s to the present.

Carol took her candlestick out of all the tissue Liz had wrapped it in and showed it to Darren. "You've got to see this. I haven't read its history yet, but Liz said it was owned by a silent actor who used to live in Briar Cliff Canyon."

Darren took the antique and frowned as he looked it over. "I wonder…?"

"Wonder what? You know about this piece?" Carol asked.

"Not sure. What do you know?" Is there any provenance?"

Carol opened the envelope, pulled out the yellowing piece of paper and read out loud.

Edward Blair, leading man of both stage and silent movies, commissioned a pair of silver candlesticks in 1918, Art Nouveau in style with a woman in ancient Greek clothing holding up an unfolding lotus. The bases are decorated with snakes. Although many attempts have been made to find the matching candlestick, it remains unfound. The silversmith mark on the bottom of each candlestick reads "Parrish Brothers 1918." The Parrish Brothers went out of business in 1932 but no records remain due to a fire in 1931.

As the round of drinks came to their booth, Darren said, "Let's see." He paused, taking a sip of his scotch. A smile crept across his face. "My grandfather told me some things about Edward Blair. He had a wild life."

Sarah leaned forward. "Oh do tell all."

Darren stared at the candlestick. "Let's see, Blair had a short career as one of the first leading men for Centaur Film Company when they transferred their movie business to Hollywood in, I think, 1913. Blair's house is still at the top of Briar Cliff Canyon according to grandfather."

Carol put down her four-olive Martini. "And now I own a piece of that history." She said in awe. "Where exactly is Blair's house?"

"Grandfather said it's the two story mansion directly at the top of the canyon. The one with castle turrets. Oh yeah, the front door has a stone carved frame that makes it look like the huge mouth of a demon." He leaned forward with a smile. "I guess you were to be swallowed up in its luxury as you entered."

"I've heard people talk about that house," Carol said excitedly. "But I've never seen it. Not yet, anyway. It's a lot further up the canyon from me."

Darren's voice lowered. "It's a dark history. Drugs were mostly legal and cheap. My grandfather said that Blair himself didn't use drugs, he bought them to lure the young starlet hopefuls."

Sarah frowned. "Pervert!" She took another glass of wine from the waiter.

"When the girls wanted more drugs, Blair would "ask" them to entertain at his parties. Blair became infamous for providing his male friends with only the youngest and most beautiful girls. Orgies were rumored." Darren looked at Sarah then back to Carol. "There were allegations of rape and other sadistic sexual practices too."

Carol looked at the package holding her silver treasure. "Were any of the girls hurt?"

"No one knows." Darren shrugged. "Besides, there were loads of girls coming and going from Hollywood trying to make it in the movies at that time. If anyone even noticed they were missing, they passed it off as running back home." Darren took another sip. "But rumor has it that several decades later, new owners discovered hidden chambers dug into the hillside in back. They also found two skeletons. Police never identified the bodies."

Carol shivered and turned to Darren. "Would you like another drink? You've earned one for all this great information."

"Are you trying to get me drunk and take advantage of me?"

Carol only gave him a comic leer. "Why don't you come home with me and help me decide where to put the candlestick?"

Sarah interrupted, looking at Carol. "So you won't be coming home with me then?" She smiled her approval of the new arrangement.

"Personally I think it should go on the mantle."

Carol poured two glasses of Sherry then placed the candlestick center stage in a place of honor. They both stepped back to admire it. Darren stood near her and put his arm around her waist.

He raised his glass into the air. "Let's toast to history."

Carol saluted the candlestick. "May you rest in peace," she offered, thinking of the possible pain and horror the candlestick had witnessed.

"A bit odd, but I suppose it serves the purpose." Darren drank the toast.

"Works for me." Carol drained her small glass.

Darren turned to her. "I'm so glad you called. I was hoping I could see you again." His face held only honest hope.

Carol felt herself blush. "I feel the same way about you."

Darren kissed her. "How about tomorrow night? I'd love to take you to dinner. Are you busy?"

"What time."

I'll pick you up at the usual seven." Darren pulled her closer. "I can't help thinking this was all meant to be." He kissed her again and the passion between them rose.

They didn't even make it to the bedroom. Darren gave her another long deep kiss that left her weak. Pulling off their clothes, he picked her up and carried her to the couch and gently laid her down on the cushions, lightly kissing the tops of her breasts. She groaned with need, unable to resist him. Closing her eyes, she delighted in how he touched her. Their sex was raw and passionate, leaving both sated and happy.

Later Darren started a fire in the fireplace. He had slipped back into his jeans and Carol joined him on the rug after retrieving her tee shirt. They watched the flames lick at the logs on the grate. He reached for her and she snuggled against him. Being with Darren felt so real, so far away from her troubles. She relaxed. She couldn't remember being so happy.

"Carol," Darren hesitated, "I need to say…well I want to say that I'm really enjoying our times together. All the times together not just the…"

"Oh, but the sex is wonderful, don't you think?"

He smiled and held her close.

Calling Dr. Cameron flashed through her mind. Darren wanted to be close to her, maybe even take it further than just friends. Was she being fair to him?

He kissed her. Her mind flew from her problems. She wanted to always be here and now with Darren at her side. They remained holding each other staring at the hypnotic flames for some time, neither saying a word. Carol felt warm and deliciously happy. Why couldn't it be like this always? Why did the other side of the coin have to be so horrifying? But could she make this relationship work?

Darren shifted, and Carol sat upright. He put his hand under her chin and kissed her gently. "Should we go to bed?" he murmured.

The next morning Carol delighted there had been no trip to nightmare land. What a wonderful relief. Perhaps Darren would be her cure and she could forget Dr. Cameron. But reality intruded, and she knew it couldn't be that easy.

After a shower and a quick breakfast, Darren left early to meet with his agent. As he paused at the front door, he gave Carol a kiss.

Nodding to the mantle he smiled. "Take good care of our candlestick."

She like the way he said 'our'.

"And please take care of yourself. I'll see you tonight."

TWELVE

CAROL PICKED up her cell to call Dr. Cameron but couldn't dial the number. She'd promised herself and Sarah that she would call him today, but she put the cell down, unable to face her fear of his theories.

She spent the rest of the day working on the month end reports for Brown & Associates. As she saved the last spreadsheet and closed her computer, she again glanced at the clock. It was five pm and her thoughts fled to Darren. The two nights they had spent together had been the only two nights without nightmares. She felt safe with him. Smiling, she lingered on memories of how his clean manly scent drove her to heights of passions she had never known. But there was more than just the sex. They shared similar passions about show business and he was easy to be around; he was fun. Good friend fun. Not demanding or condescending like some of her other dates had been. Tonight she would see him again. Possibly it would keep the horrors away. She had to admit Darren had become quite an addiction, one that she didn't want to be cured of.

Determined to forget her troubles and enjoy the evening with Darren, she took pleasure in putting on her makeup. Her hair behaved beautifully. George's shadow appeared as she spun in front of the bedroom mirror in a red silk dress, delighting in how the red made her skin and hair glow.

"Hello, George. What do you think? Too much or just enough?"

As she slipped her feet into red high heels, the doorbell chimed and George's shadow faded. Opening the door, the look on Darren's face rewarded her efforts to look special.

"You are the loveliest woman I have ever seen!" His dark eyes drank her in.

She laughed. "Don't just stand there gaping, come on in." The flattery felt good and her confidence grew.

He gathered her into his arms and gave her a passionate kiss. She returned the passion.

He released her. "Are you ready? My favorite restaurant has the best steak in town." Lowering his voice he added, "We can come back here for dessert."

"Dessert's the best part of any meal," she answered, knowing what he meant by dessert. A thrill ran through her in anticipation.

Before he could catch hold of her again, she grabbed her beaded bag and a light shawl and headed out. As she locked the door, he took her arm and pulled her to him. Not to kiss her this time but to lead her into a few graceful steps around the fountain. He hummed the song, "Lady in Red" as he danced her back to the pathway. They both started laughing.

He whirled her under his arm. "I just had to try the Fred Astaire approach at least once in my life. How was it, Ginger?"

"Dreamy. Now feed me, I'm hungry."

He laughed. "I see. The real motive for this evening is revealed."

He offered her his crooked arm and, clicking his heels, played the part of a prince escorting his princess to the carriage. Carol took his arm, her nose in the air. They remained in their roles all the way to his car. Opening the door for her, he helped her into her seat.

Near downtown Los Angeles, the restaurant glowed with warm outdoor lighting, and its façade, painted with murals in red, green and yellow brought a festive air to the building. At dinner, conversation fell to how Darren had gotten another commercial.

"A fluke really. I was hurrying down the hall on my way to a production meeting. I'm finding some film sites for this independent movie company. Well, I walked into the wrong office. A lady looked up, said I looked perfect and asked me to sign a contract."

"Well you are perfect, you know."

"Thank you." He bowed his head to her with a smile. "When I explained that I hadn't come for her commercial, she asked if I would be available Friday to film. When I said yes, she said I was hired anyway. Just a standard contract, so I signed on."

"If anyone else told that story, I'd never believe them. What did your agent think?"

"Pretty crazy, huh?" Darren laughed. "Agent's good. He'll get his commission."

"What's the commercial for?"

"Some new shaving cream. She asked me not to shave. I'll find out more Friday."

"Congratulations." Carol beamed, holding up her glass of Merlot, saluting him.

"Thank you." He saluted back. "Even better, I also got the go ahead to scout locations for the film I actually went in for."

"Wow, what a day you've had. Did you rub a magic lamp or something?" Carol felt relaxed, the wine beginning to take effect.

"I'm just a lucky guy. I met you and got two lucrative jobs." The fire in his eyes traveled to the tops of her breasts. "Hmmm, are you ready for some dessert?"

"Starving."

Once more the night had been free of nightmares. Perhaps she was over them and she could go back to a normal life. Carol made a quick breakfast for her and Darren since he had to leave and try to get some location scouting done before he started the shaving cream commercial. Carol felt elated about her growing relationship with Darren. She breezed through her work, knowing that she would see him again soon.

That evening, she pulled out Buster Keaton's Seven Chances and curled up on the couch to enjoy the silent movie. She wished Darren could be here to share it with her.

Darkness had crept into the living room by the time the film ended. She yawned, feeling exhausted. Carol giggled aloud, figuring lots of good sex made for a very tired girl. She gratefully slipped into bed thinking she should sleep well.

The candle lit ballroom echoed with strange minor key violin music but the whirling dancers did not seem to notice the maudlin cacophony. Their faces were grotesque and their clothing ragged, torn and filthy. There were many others watching the dancing from the shadows that clung to the walls. Carol stood at the entrance to the ballroom not sure where to go. Looking down she saw her dark red silk gown flowing to the floor. Her hands were jeweled with ruby and diamond rings. Her low-cut bodice shimmered in the candle light.

The music disturbed her. Perhaps leaving would be the best choice but when she turned the doors were closed and locked. Laughter assaulted her and she turned to see the entire assembly howling in uncontrollable guffaws at her dilemma. A hand grasped her arm and she was pulled into the arms of a tall man whose black velvet mask covered the top half of his face. His lips were full and too red to be real. His long black hair curled snakelike over the sides of his mask, around his shoulders and down to the middle of his back. A crown of steel spikes seemed to spring from his forehead, blood flowing freely down the mask and onto the black velvet of his doublet.

Carol shrank from him and tried to wriggle out of his grasp. He nodded to the musicians and the minor key waltz began again. Unable to free herself from his arms, he pulled her along like a rag doll. She screamed to let her go, but the music drowned her out. Grasping her tighter, he shoved her painfully against his chest as he whirled around the dance floor. The others watched silently as their macabre king danced with her. Numb with fear Carol tried to keep up with the eerie waltz to avoid the pain of being dragged. As she regained some composure, she noticed the king's subjects were jostling to see them better. She saw the blood on their clothes and it dripped from their hands. She understood in a flash that she would be devoured by them at the end of her dance with their king.

The music stopped and he pushed her away. Carol fell to the dance floor. He removed his black mask. She cried out. The black king was Darren! She reached to him, hoping he would save her but his face became cold and compassionless. He turned from her and walked off the dance floor. Carol had never felt so betrayed. Crushed by his cruelty, she sobbed her anguish as the crowd of famished dancers closed in upon her.

THIRTEEN

SCREAMING, Carol awoke on the couch, the TV still on but blank, dutifully awaiting the next DVD. She had not gone to bed, it had been part of the nightmare. George had disappeared. Wet with sweat and panting to catch her breath, she stood looking around in confusion.

Carol started to cry. Fear flooded all her senses. Insecurity descended, and she rushed to the kitchen then her bedroom making sure Darren was nowhere in her bungalow. When she entered the bathroom, she caught her image in the mirror. Her pale face still held terror. Blood smeared her face. The nightmares were back and getting worse. Get a grip! She commanded herself.

It took time to settle down enough to think clearly. Carol glanced at the clock on the mantel and shivered as her eyes caught sight of the silver candlestick next to the timepiece. It made her remember Darren as the cruel dark king. She forced herself to check the time, five-thirty in the morning, too early to call Dr. Cameron in her opinion.

Carol went to the kitchen unable to go back to bed. George sat at the kitchen table. She thought his shadow seemed deeper, as she nodded in his direction. "You're up early. Did my screaming frighten you?" she asked sarcastically. George's shadow remained seated at the table.

"Glad you're here. I need some company this morning."

She prepared toast and jam while the coffee pot dripped her favorite blend. Pouring a mug, she took a welcomed sip before sitting down at her table.

"Had another horrible nightmare and I can't shake it loose."

George listened.

Carol took a mouthful of toast. Swallowing quickly she looked at him. "What's causing them? Dr. Cameron says it's because of the astral dimension, but why that?" She realized she was raising her voice and stopped. "Sorry George." She shuddered. Whatever the cause, it was terrifying. Isn't that what Dr. Cameron had said would happen? He also said that soon she may not know what is real. Now she'd met Darren she had been so hopeful he would make the nightmares go away. She amended that to going to the astral dimension. How could Darren stop that? Now he'd been in her nightmare. If her dreams were real, what part did Darren play now? The thought brought chills. She shut it out of her mind.

The first rays of dim sunlight began to remove the shadows from the corners and birds were beginning to sing. At first their song irritated her. Carol took another sip of coffee. The hot liquid ran down her throat, the caffeine coursed through her veins. More birds joined the chorus outside her window. She began to find them soothing, a reminder that life had started a new day. The gentle dawn breeze parted the curtains as though the breath of life had come back to her and Carol filled her lungs with its healing spirit. She glanced over to George, still there, although the morning light made him more transparent.

She gave him a shy smile. "Thanks for being here, George."

His shadow slowly faded away.

Finishing her coffee, Carol decided to shower. Afterward, she threw on a simple t-shirt over jeans. Glancing at the clock, it was only six-thirty, still too early to call. Besides, she didn't feel ready to jump in the car and go anywhere. Calling his private number made her nervous. She knew she was making excuses not to face the reality of her situation, but she couldn't help herself. Hearing the birds again and seeing the shaft of sunshine through the window, made her decide to go into the courtyard. Perhaps she could find peace sitting beside the fountain. As Carol closed her front door, Dinah's meow greeted her.

"Hello, your highness."

Dinah graciously accepted her appropriate title and sat down next to Carol's lawn chair by the fountain to luxuriate in the morning sun. Licking her paws, she washed her face. Stroking Dinah's long gray fur, Carol kept her mind on the fountain, the plants, and a beautiful yellow butterfly bent on drinking nectar from every flower in the small garden.

Carol heard the shuffle of feet, then the call of "kitty, kitty". Dinah concentrated on bathing, ignoring the voice of her owner.

"Marguerite, over here," Carol called.

The landlady huffed around the corner and into the courtyard. "There you are, you little demon." She glared at her cat then turned to Carol. "Thanks. Hope Dinah isn't bothering you."

"Never," Carol said honestly.

"You look tired. You okay?"

"Just had a long night with a client's books is all," she lied. "How's Dan's plumbing?"

"The plumber comes today. With any luck he won't be here during my wrestling program."

Carol smiled at her landlady. Marguerite had attempted to become a nun in her youth but when that failed, she'd joined the Roller Derby; sort of explained why the nun part hadn't worked out.

"Good luck with the plumber."

Her landlady waved dismissively as though she just knew she would miss her favorite wrestler today. She plodded off toward the next courtyard. Dinah decided to follow. Carol didn't have the heart to tell her the wrestling was faked. Or maybe she knows. How could she not?

Carol's eyes drifted back to watching the water dance in the fountain. Life isn't predictable. People lull themselves into a false security by thinking they know what their lives are all about. But it's just an illusion. Her life felt like an illusion now. She couldn't face that her nightmares were real.

There were many things she knew about and there were many things that defied explanation. This reincarnation and astral dimension creepiness belonged to the latter. Carol knew she couldn't always add up life's experiences like her ledgers. She had to come to terms with her inability to make Dr. Cameron's ideas fit comfortably into some easily understood equation. Her last session had not gone well. She still did not see how he could help her, so why was she still considering going? Where else could she go?

As her thoughts became more rational, the heaviness in her heart lightened a bit. Darren had been so wonderful to her, why had he been so cruel in her dream? She reminded herself that it was the person in her nightmares she feared. It wouldn't be fair to judge Darren one way or another. He was not the demon she had met last night.

Carol turned and headed back into her bungalow. It was time to call Dr. Cameron.

"Have you been crying?" Dr. Cameron sounded concerned.

She hesitated, uncomfortable calling the doctor at his home. "More nightmares."

"Would you like to come to my office?"

"Honestly, I'm still not convinced you can help me, but I don't know where else to turn."

"I can and will help you. Can you come to my office as soon as we hang up?"

"Sure. Should take me about an hour."

It was 8:30 before Carol walked into Dr. Cameron's office. Laurie was just putting her purse in the bottom drawer of her desk when she sat down to wait.

Laurie smiled at her. "You can go right in. He told me you were coming in early."

Carol entered the doctor's office slowly. Her anxiety rising with each step.

"Carol. I'm so glad you have come back." He motioned for her to sit.

"Thanks." Her apprehension made her want to demand what he was going to do to her now, but she remained rational. She'd try to give him a chance.

As though he read her mind, he said, "First, I would like to address any questions and issues you have in regard to my diagnosis."

Surprised, Carol had assumed he'd want to put her under hypnosis again. It made her realize how much she dreaded another session. "I'm having difficulty believing that my nightmares are more than just bad dreams. Why do they have to be real? Why do they have to be in some astral dimension? Why..." She looked away because tears threatened.

Dr. Cameron offered her a small box of tissues. "Why? Because it's the truth. I'll explain more, if you will allow me."

Carol could only nod.

"This person you always encounter seems to have developed a way to control minds. Perhaps he's using the astral dimension as his testing grounds."

Carol stared at him blankly. "Under someone's control? What's that supposed to mean? Please get to the point."

"It's never been possible before. It goes against the laws of nature."

"I don't see anything natural about any of this. All I know is I heard my own voice speaking from some place before I was born. All my instincts yell 'run away'!" Carol crossed her arms, avoiding eye contact, as she attempted to control her frustration.

"I know how strange this must sound to you." His voice remained calm. "May I continue?"

Carol reluctantly nodded again. She'd come here to understand.

"The astral dimension is part of nature and subject to its laws. This person in your nightmares is breaking those laws. Someone can attempt to convince or trick you into believing or doing something, but they can't force you to do it."

Carol cleared her throat, trying to focus on understanding what he told her rather than her fear and anger. "So, it's kinda like hypnosis."

"Close enough for now," he acknowledged. "And you need to understand that the astral dimension is only horrible if you want it to be."

"You'll have to prove that one to me. I've only seen the worst."

"It's my theory that this person, this Entity, is very close to trying to control the minds of others in our physical world as well."

"If what you say is true, I see how dangerous this is. My nightmares prove that." Realization struck and fear surfaced again. "That's why you're convinced I'm going to the astral dimension and not having nightmares!" Her breathing came hard and fast. "This has to stop!"

"Yes, it does. I have every intention of stopping this from ever happening to you or anyone ever again."

Her fear calmed but her anger surfaced. "So, I've been a guinea pig for some weirdo?"

"Yes, I believe so."

"That's not creepy at all! It's like being stalked!" She shuddered.

"Now you are beginning to understand my concern."

Carol felt desperate. "But what can I do? How do we stop this? Do you have any plan at all?"

"I do, but it's going to take all the courage you have."

Carol just stared at Dr. Cameron. Suspicion colored her tone. "What do I have to do?"

"Call me the moment you return from your next trip to the astral dimension. I don't care what time it is."

"But how will that help?" Carol stood. "I don't want to go to the astral dimension ever again, if that's even where I'm going!"

Nothing seemed to be making sense again. She did understand that someone was trying to hurt her by controlling her mind, but she couldn't completely believe in the astral dimension. That part of the equation eluded her still.

Dr. Cameron also stood then came around the desk. "The only way to explain is by telling you the truth. I can help you." He held out his hand.

Carol backed away, tears coming to her eyes again.

"Do you want to stop being the Entity's victim?"

Carol shivered. "Of course I do."

The doctor took a step closer and reached for Carol's hand again. This time she allowed him to touch her. A sense of comfort calmed her as his hand closed over hers.

"Just call me the moment you have returned to your body. I promise to have a plan of action at that time."

"Why do I have to take another trip before you have a plan?"

"It's best to start finding solutions as close to your return as possible."

Carol's mind spun. She had to stop this creep. Had to stop this misery. Carol lowered her head. "You're sure this is the only way?"

"Yes."

She looked him in the eye. "You're right. This will take all the courage I have."

Carol sat curled on her couch thinking about her promise to Dr. Cameron. She had seen all the information in the astral dimension at Sarah's. Sarah had even sent her multiple e-mails giving her more astral information, all making the doctor's diagnosis more of a reality. Her nightmares were not like anything she had ever experienced before. Why was she so afraid to accept Dr. Cameron's conclusions? Her mind turned to George and how she was always careful who she told about him. Not everyone would believe her, yet she knew he was real. Why couldn't Dr. Cameron's theories be real? She jumped when her cell rang.

"Hello, lovely lady." Darren's voice was low, seductive.

Carol actually felt weak-kneed with fear. She had not expected his call any more than her reaction to his voice.

"Hi." She tried to make it sound casual.

"Hey, anything wrong? Did I call at a bad time?"

"Of course not, I'm just extra tired today. Loads of work."

"Good." He sounded relieved. "Speaking of work, I have the night free. Would you want to have a drink with me tonight?"

She hesitated. But she knew she wanted to see him again. "Sounds great. What time?"

"I'll pick you up around seven as usual."

"Perfect. See you then."

FOURTEEN

DARREN had just left. Although their date had only been a drink, the night had been more great sex. She didn't have another trip to the astral dimension either.

Carol forced her way through her client's accounting. She could not keep her mind off Dr. Cameron's offer to help. Her life had turned upside down and she found coping difficult. She managed to push through a few more hours of work before she put it all away and had a small supper.

Carol tried watching television but kept nodding off. She realized how tired all her nightmares made her. Getting up to prepare for bed, she opened her medicine cabinet. The sleeping pills she had gotten from Dr. Cameron were there. She knew since Darren wasn't here, chances were high she would fall victim to the Entity. Grabbing the pills, she downed a triple dosage. Maybe they would keep her earthbound tonight.

Carol stood on a plateau in a rocky mountainous area. A meager campfire sputtered, almost out, the only light in the deep darkness that smothered her surroundings. A stone rolled loose and she whirled in fear. A pale gray horse stood a few feet behind her, saddled and ready to ride. He seemed too perfect to be real. His mane and tail were long and wavy and his head held high and proud. His ears pricked forward as he looked at her. Fascinated, she walked towards him. He allowed her to approach and she touched his neck softly. The stallion did not frighten her. Together they waited in the cold darkness for the source of the fear that seeped into her bones.

Thunder rolled in the distance, such a lonely sound in the darkness. The wind that tore through the ravine below moaned like tortured souls in Hell. She stared into the night, shaking. The horse tossed his head and Carol moved closer to him as a menacing cloud passed across the sliver of moon. The night got even darker. She felt calmer being near the beast, but she knew he couldn't stop the terror from coming. Nothing could.

He turned his head, nostrils flaring as though he had caught a scent. From the corner of her eye, Carol caught a sudden flash of light and jumped making the horse dance sideways. As the light streaked towards them from the mountaintop, Carol panicked and grabbed the horse's reins. Perhaps she could escape before the light could reach her. She knew it brought terror. The stallion stood still and allowed her to climb into the saddle, but instead of following her frantic urgings to flee, he turned and headed straight for the oncoming light.

The stallion's speed terrified her almost as much as the descending light. Wind tore at her eyes, sending tears streaming down her face. She held onto the saddle afraid she would be thrown before she could escape. Wiping her eyes clear she tried to make out where they were heading. They had covered the width of the little plateau in seconds. She could see the light rushing at them from the mountain as the wind howled angrily.

They reached the edge of the plateau and stopped. Carol desperately tried to turn the horse around but he refused to obey the yanking of his reins and the pumping of her legs. Carol felt helpless. Any second the horrible light would be there. As though this thought brought the evil upon them, the light whipped around the edge of the mountain and stopped just beyond the narrow ravine in front of them. The gray trembled as Carol looked at the shaded figure bathed in the hellish light. Another horse stood before them, pure black and pure evil. On its back sat a darkly hooded rider. Sparks leapt from the devil horse's hooves as it nervously pawed at the stone. Its rider leaned back and laughed with an empty sadness that chilled Carol's soul.

The gray screamed a challenge and reared to fight the devils before him. He came down with a jolt and Carol felt herself slipping from his back.

FIFTEEN

AS SHE FELL she woke in her bed, drenched in sweat and thoroughly exhausted. As soon as she felt able, Carol turned on a light and looked at the alarm clock. Three A.M.! She could vividly remember the dream and her head throbbed painfully. Thankfully, the nose bleed was not as bad. She turned over and sobbed her agony into the pillow. Crying drained her and she still felt the effects of the triple dose of sleeping pills. She was groggy and disorientated. She got out of bed and, after putting a cup of milk in the microwave, sat down with her Mom's 'bad dream remedy' and watched old movies until dawn. The sun made her feel safe enough to go back to bed. Carol would call Dr. Cameron later. She had to get some sleep. She slid back into bed and immediately fell asleep.

The phone awakened her. She glanced at the screen as she picked up her cell, eleven am.

Daren's voice greeted her. "Hi, couldn't get you out of my mind so I called. Did you get caught up with your client's books?

Carol sat up and leaned back against her headboard. Hearing his voice made the night's terror seem very far away. "I think of you all the time too. Finally got the books done, thanks. I feel much better now."

"Good! I don't want my girl unhappy."

"Your girl?"

"Of course. And my lucky charm."

Carol wished he could be next to her in the bed. She could feel his arms pulling her closer. She snuggled down into her pillow. "Thanks. You're special too, you know."

His voice deepened, "I'm glad you think so."

"When will you have time to get together again?"

"Soon." His voice brightened. "I've found most of the locations already and after Friday's commercial shoot, I'll have loads of time to spend on you."

"Can't wait."

After hanging up, she lingered just for a few delicious moments thinking of Darren. He intoxicated her. She remembered his sensual lips touching hers and the thrill that flooded through her body as he kissed her. Carol Jane Knight, you are in deep. But she smiled just the same.

After talking to Darren, it seemed more like a commitment to call her doctor than a necessity. She dialed Dr. Cameron's number.

"Carol, how are you doing?" His voice sounded restrained.

"Had another nightmare, I mean trip. I promised to call."

"Of course. How soon can you get here?"

"Hour, give or take."

As she came into the office, the receptionist, Laurie, greeted Carol with a big smile, "He's waiting for you in his office." And she announced Carol's arrival over the phone.

Carol stepped into the doctor's office with a smile, but it soon faded as he looked up from his desk. She could almost see the storm clouds churning over his head.

"Why didn't you call me earlier?"

Carol felt defensive. "I fell back to sleep. I didn't wake up again until I called you."

His features softened. "Forgive me."

"What's this all about?" She sat down in front of his desk.

"I must give you my apologies."

"What for?"

"I promised a plan to stop your trips to the astral plane so I took some liberties that, I assure you, were taken wholly in your best interest." It sounded rehearsed.

"What's that supposed to mean?"

"I went with you last night."

Carol looked at him hopelessly confused and frustrated. "Just tell me what you mean! If this is a new type of therapy, I don't like it."

Dr. Cameron turned from her gaze and stared out the window behind him at the ocean. Carol could see his reflection. He was smiling! What the hell?

Before she could protest, he spoke. "I must say you don't ride very well. I could hardly keep you in the saddle."

Her mind rebelled. "You mean …No! That's not possible!" She stood in alarm and took two steps towards the door. This was the last straw! "But." She spun back to face him. "How did you know?"

He looked at her calmly. "I know you're going to the astral dimension, but I needed to understand why and you needed proof that the other dimension is real."

Things were moving way too fast again. "But, how did you 'come with me'?" Carol needed to understand one simple fact at a time.

"Please sit down."

Unable to take her eyes off the doctor, she felt for the chair.

"I absorbed some of your astral energy when I held your hand during our last session. I used it to monitor your dreams. When I sensed you slip away, I followed you onto the astral plane. I tuned into your vibration."

"You did what?" Carol leaned back as her mind raced. He knows about my nightmare. Does he really mean he was that gray horse? She blushed with embarrassment as she realized she had actually ridden… No, I won't believe it! But if Dr. Cameron was there with me… There? That meant the astral dimension, didn't it? She opened her mouth to protest but he continued to explain.

"After your astral spirit left to return to your body, I also left the plane."

This was just too creepy, too personal. "I don't like your invasion of my privacy," she stated flatly. "Aren't you supposed to ask my permission?"

His eyes searched hers. "I had to take the risk to make you understand that the astral dimension is real."

Fear began to worm its way in again. She frowned at him.

"Please. Bear with me a moment. It's vital you understand that—"

"You can't blame me for being blown away. You're scaring me!"

His voice soothed, "Take a deep breath. I'm here to help. I have verified enough information to begin to understand how to stop your unwanted trips to the astral plane."

The breathing helped, but Carol's stomach remained defiant and held onto its nervous flutters. "This is beyond strange. Embarrassing to be honest." She took another deep breath when the doctor motioned. "I've got questions I don't even know how to ask. What did you find out?" Another deep breath. "Will IT help calm me down too?" she added sarcastically.

With a slight smile, he stopped the breathing exercise. "The Entity was the black horse you saw. His rider only some other soul under his control, like you are. He's performing acts that are unnatural. I confirmed my diagnosis. The Entity must be stopped."

Carol's mind spun towards panic. "He's already done harm! Call the police, I'll testify! Just lock the creep up and throw away the key!"

Dr. Cameron leaned forward, putting his hands on the desk. "What proof do we have that the police would listen to?"

This shocked Carol back to reality. "Nothing." She looked down, her hands trembled. "You promised to have a solution. Is there one?"

"Yes. I can help you. Everything we need is in my library and laboratory."

"Great! When do we start? Where's your lab?" Perhaps he could whip up an antidote for all the creep's victims and she'd be back to normal in no time. That would stop the creep!

"I work with a colleague. His name is Mr. Toga. He knows more about the astral dimension than I do."

"Perfect. Call me the minute you two have whipped up the solution."

"There's something you need to understand. There's no knowing when you'll be attacked again."

Carol knew that. "What are you getting at?"

"I can protect you from future attacks but only if we remain together." He paused, "I need you to stay with me until we've stopped this Entity."

"Now wait a minute…"

"Your life depends on it," he interrupted. "You'll be perfectly safe. I give you my word."

"But…"

"You will have your own room. Meals will be provided. Most of all you will be protected from the Entity. No more trips to the astral plane while you're with me. Just give it a couple of weeks and …"

"Two weeks!" Carol's idea of a quick antidote faded.

"It is vital that you not spend another night alone."

"How are you going to stop…all this?"

Mr. Toga and I plan to find as much information as we can. We don't know the Entity's motives. What he is doing is new, never possible before. We have ways to protect you until we stop him."

She began to cry. She felt trapped with no control over anything in her life. She was going from victim to prisoner in her estimation.

Dr. Cameron came around his desk and offered her a tissue. When she couldn't stop crying, he attempted to soothe. "I know this is difficult. In only a few days you've gone from needing some help stopping nightmares to life threatening trips to the astral plane."

"It's not fair!" Carol wiped her eyes, trying to get control of herself.

"No it's not. But you've come to the right place for help."

She just sat and stared at him.

"We have to fight together. I know this doesn't make sense right now, but it will. It's the only hope we have of stopping him and what you're going through."

"The only hope?" Carol's mind was in shock. Suddenly everything seemed so desperate. "Why…"

He held up a forefinger. "I have only one question. Do you want to help us fight this evil or do you want to remain its victim until it kills you?"

That made it simple. She didn't want to die. It had to stop. Carol calmed a bit. She squared her shoulders. "What choice do I have?"

"None I know of," he said quietly. He handed her another tissue. "There's only one more thing you need to know."

"What's that?"

"My library and laboratory are in my home."

87

"Your home!" Could this get any worse? Wiping her eyes, she sought some control over her situation. But she came back to what choice did she have. "If you ask me for anything more than helping you get rid of this Entity and my nightmares, I'll be out of there before you can blink."

"Agreed."

"You have to allow me to let my landlady know or she'll have the entire Los Angeles police force out looking for me."

"Agreed."

"And I need to call friends and let them know where I am."

"Also agreed. Anything else?" He stepped back, his face calm.

Carol looked him straight in the eye. "A good stiff drink!"

SIXTEEN

DR. CAMERON asked Laurie to reorganize his schedule. She would run the office while he was away. Carol called Marguerite, Sarah and Darren. She told Marguerite she had won a vacation to Hawaii but told Sarah the truth. She then made arrangements with her client so she could keep in touch during her absence. When she called Darren, she had to leave a message. She only said she would be gone a while, doctor's orders, and that she'd call him as soon as she had a break to explain better. She gave him Dr. Cameron's phone number.

"Carol I'll be happy to follow you home and help with your luggage. Then I'll take you on up Briar Cliff Canyon to my house."

"I didn't know you lived in the Canyon! That's convenient," she added sarcastically. "No, I'll drive my own car. But you can help me load my luggage. I'll follow you to your house."

Dr. Cameron sat in her living room while Carol finished organizing her overnighter in the bathroom, the last bag to pack. When she started calling her stay with him as her internment, he had taken it with good humor.

"Carol, where did you find this candlestick?" he called out.

"Antique dealer in the neighborhood," she answered as she threw in her toiletries next to a long flannel nightgown.

When she walked back into the living room, Dr. Cameron stood at the fireplace examining the candlestick.

"I couldn't resist getting it. It's from a house here in the Canyon. Supposedly loads of mysterious evil took place there."

"I think we should take this with us," he said matter-of-factly without looking up.

89

"What for?"

"Sometimes objects bring harmful energy with them. This candlestick could be a factor."

"But I had nightmares, ah, trips, before I got it." She blinked. "What do you mean harmful energy?"

"Nevertheless, I wouldn't want to take any chances."

"Why this and not something else I own?"

Dr. Cameron looked up. "I sense energy in it worth studying."

"What do you mean? You sound more like a Jedi Knight than my doctor."

"Hmm?" Dr. Cameron had been staring intently at the candlestick and not really listening. "Ah, yes, it's been possible for centuries to put energy into objects. Good or bad."

This made Carol pause. He'd proven to her that the astral dimension existed when he went there with her. But she felt uncomfortable taking the candlestick. Seemed ludicrous and far too occult.

"I'd rather we just leave it where it is." She shrugged. "It's rather special to me."

He nodded. "Allow me to help you load your car. Hand me that suitcase over there."

As she followed Dr. Cameron's Mercedes up the canyon and deeper into the hills, her thoughts churned. Carol worried she could be getting into something so beyond her control she'd be trapped. Could she trust Dr. Cameron? She reminded herself that he knows what's wrong. He said he could help her, save her from this creep who has control over her. Could she actually die or is this the best lie she'd ever heard? Carol realized she had to cut the next curve tight, or not make the turn. Pay attention to the road!

After her nerves settled, she decided to take things one step at a time. If she kept her wits, she could decide if all this was going to help. If not, she'd figure out what to do then. She could always leave.

After several more winding turns Carol saw him pull into a garage under an older home that nestled into the side of the hill. Through the trees she could barely see turrets and stained glass windows that told her the house must have been built in the early twenties. It had the popular

Moorish castle look of that time. She couldn't wait to see the inside. Pulling in after the doctor, she parked her VW next to his Mercedes. Dr. Cameron came around to help retrieved her bags. A few stair steps ended at a door that led directly into the house from inside the garage. As Dr. Cameron set down a bag to reach for the doorknob, the door opened seemingly by itself.

"Ah, Mr. Toga." Dr. Cameron said with a smile.

Carol looked around the doctor and saw a very handsome Asian gentleman in an impeccable black three-piece suit helping with the bags. He did not smile.

Once they were all inside, Dr. Cameron turned to her. "Carol, meet Mr. Toga, my colleague. Mr. Toga, this is Carol Knight, my client."

Mr. Toga gracefully bowed to her. He reminded her of a sleek black cat as he straightened. Although looking near the same age as the doctor there was an air of calm assuredness that usually came with age or perhaps difficult times.

"Very glad to meet you, Miss Knight," he said in a calm level voice. There was no trace of an accent. His deep black eyes seemed to be taking her measure.

"Please, call me Carol."

Mr. Toga nodded his assent. Intrigued, she hoped to get to know him better over the next two weeks. Right now she felt apprehensive. It was like meeting a new professor who had the reputation of being very strict. She couldn't help wanting to see him smile at least once during her stay. She bet it would even make him more handsome.

"May I take your bags to your room?" Mr. Toga offered pleasantly.

Carol nodded and entered the house. She watched Mr. Toga take her bags up a graceful staircase to the second floor.

Dr. Cameron turned to her. "My library and lab are this way. I would like to get started as soon as possible."

Carol felt pressured. "Sorry, but I'm not quite ready to rush into this. I do understand the urgency but just give me a few moments. May I have a cup of coffee?"

"Of course. My apologies. I'm often too focused. I'm afraid I totally forgot how to be a proper host."

"Could you take me on a tour of your house before the coffee? It must be from the early twenties."

"Great idea. I've lived here so long, I take it all for granted."

She followed Dr. Cameron through the house. She realized it was much larger than her view from the street below had allowed. Their footsteps echoed on hardwood floors. She was astounded by its unchanged architecture and antiques. But it all seemed cold, without personality as though no one lived here, except there wasn't a speck of dust anywhere. Still furnished in the popular heavy dark style of the early twenties, the living room had blackened wood beams holding vaulted ceilings aloft. The floors were covered in strategic areas by silk oriental carpets. Carol noticed the gray stone fireplace that dominated the far end of the living room. It had carvings of dragons, griffins and other mythical beasts around its grate and an opening so huge you could actually stand upright inside it. Carol was reminded of the remake of The Haunting and the gigantic fireplace with its lion-head shaped flue that beheaded Owen Wilson.

Dr. Cameron sounded like a tour guide. "The house was built by my grandparents starting in 1920 and finishing in 1923. My family has always owned the house and lived here. I was never here much. I spent most of my time as a child in boarding schools before college."

Walking into the formal dining room, Carol caught her breath at the sight of the large crystal chandelier that showered down from an ornately carved medallion in the center of the ceiling.

"Oh, the chandelier. Grandmamma Alise had it shipped from her ancestral home in Vienna seventy-five years ago. It doesn't really go with the rest of the room. I've just never considered redecorating."

Carol noticed the same heavy Moorish influence of the rest of the house in the dark table that sat twenty guests comfortably. The hutch that held the dishes and silverware matched the table and chairs, with one other cabinet stretching all the way to the ceiling. A deep burgundy oriental rug filled the space under the table adding the only warmth to the room. Another stone fireplace, smaller but still impressive, stood at the other end. It too had carvings – birds this time.

"Do you have dinner parties here?"

The doctor laughed. "No, I'm far too busy and not very social, I'm afraid. Never wanted the life my parents had. After they died, I just moved in."

When they reached the solarium off to the left of the dining room, Carol heard running water. A fountain dominated the large room. A life size statue of a beautiful woman draped in diaphanous Grecian robes held an orb where water bubbled forth into the basin below her feet. Plants of many species filled the rest of the solarium.

"Oh." Carol murmured. The solarium was magnificent. "This is beautiful."

"Glad you like it. It's one part of the house I actually use. It has doors to the kitchen and my lab as well."

"May I have my coffee here?"

Toga brought them coffee. The fresh air, the glorious plants, she felt she could stay here forever. The mostly-glass walls from floor to ceiling brought in the warm yellow tones of the afternoon sun. They sat at a black wrought iron table that seated four near the fountain. She knew she would have to have her breakfast here every morning. Maybe two weeks wouldn't be so bad after all.

She turned back to Dr. Cameron and realized he had been watching her, a smile evident in his clear blue eyes. "Thank you," she said quietly. "I think I could do some work now."

"Good," the doctor said excitedly. "Follow me to my lab. It's just over here through this side door."

Carol became overwhelmed all over again as she stepped into the doctor's lab. The largest room in the house by far, she'd never seen anything like it except in the movies. More library than laboratory, it rose two stories high. Bookshelves stuffed with thousands of volumes lined the walls all the way to a balcony that ran around three walls of the room. More shelving reached to the ceiling from the balcony floor, also crammed with books.

More volumes occupied antique tables, stacked in overstuffed leather chairs or lay on the floor, multiple bookmarks in all. Glancing around the room she noticed odd-looking sculpture and paraphernalia that looked like it had come from an archeological dig.

"This must be where you spend all your time."

"Yes, unless I'm at the office."

Carol's eyes were drawn upward by a ray of sunshine. Most of the ceiling formed a dome in the center. Its intricately carved dark wood interior held mysterious shadows in the soft light. Around the bottom edge of the dome, small stained glass windows glowed, the late afternoon sun shining through their red and blue hues. Carol stepped to the nearest bookcase and looked with amazement at the volumes in many languages.

"You belong here."

She turned, unsure what he meant.

"You love books."

Carol eased. "Yes. I've never seen a private library like this. This is amazing."

"Thank you. It will go a long way in helping us stop the Entity and keeping you safe." He motioned towards a large dark wood desk with two heavily carved chairs in front of it. "Have a seat and we'll get started."

Mr. Toga entered and quietly sat in the chair beside Carol.

Dr. Cameron smiled at him. "Thank you for joining us."

Carol smiled too, hoping to get one in return. "Thank you for helping me, Mr. Toga."

Toga only acknowledged her with a nod. His eyes seemed to hold secrets. Nothing sinister, Carol decided, but this man knew a lot.

"Mr. Toga is more adept at solving your problem than I am, Carol." Dr. Cameron moved some books out of his way. "Now, I think it would be best to go over some basics. It will help you understand what Toga and I plan to do."

Carol held her hands to keep them from shaking. "I'm still trying to come to terms with my trips to another dimension. This all sounds like something occult and not—,"

"Something normal?" Cameron finished for her.

"Yeah. I don't believe the supernatural is real, so how could it play any part in what I'm experiencing."

Dr. Cameron leaned back. "It is real and as much a part of nature as the trees in this canyon. The word 'occult' carries too many bad connotations these days. That's why I've never referred to the astral dimension in relation to the occult and it is why I do not call it the astral plane as is customary in more occult beliefs."

Unsure, Carol wrinkled her brow. "All I know is the astral dimension sounds like it belongs with crystal balls and Ouija boards. All I've seen so far is terror. Makes it hard for me to understand."

The doctor was patient. "True. I understand. Let's address your issues with the occult. When you look up the word 'occult' in the dictionary it comes from a Latin word meaning 'to conceal' and the definition is 'pertaining to unexplained phenomena or knowledge beyond human understanding'. If you study the occult, you begin to understand it as the quest to understand the secrets of the Universe, just like physicists are doing today.

Carol became intrigued. "So, the occult sounds like it was the physics of the old world?"

Mr. Toga answered. "Since we are only looking at the basics, yes." His face remained calm, unemotional. "Physicists today theorize that many planes or dimensions exist in the Universe. They see nothing supernatural in any of their theories."

Carol still felt uneasy. "I bet they don't call their planes or dimensions astral."

Mr. Toga explained. "No, it is an ancient term. Perhaps we should just refer to it as the other dimension until you understand more," he offered.

Dr. Cameron nodded. "I have no problem with that. Would it help you?"

"Maybe it will make it more real for me." Carol thought a moment. "All I know is that it's the most horrible place I've ever been."

Dr. Cameron shifted in his chair. "The Entity is making it appear horrible to frighten you, keep you under his control."

Carol needed a moment. She stared into the corner where a fire crackled in a large stone fireplace, somehow making the enormous room warm and friendly. A computer, nestled into the dim recesses of a dark wooden cabinet near the fireplace seemed out of place but not unexpected.

Her eyes began to tear. Why is he doing this? Carol swallowed hard. "Tell me more about this other dimension."

Dr. Cameron looked pleased by her interest. "It is the next dimension above the physical one we live in.

"But how do you get there? I know you said we can leave our bodies, but how is he forcing me to leave mine?"

"Another puzzle we hope to solve. No one's done this before. A person can allow their own astral double or soul to explore the other dimension, but they can't force another to go.

"You promise to keep me safe?" Carol felt hopelessly out of her league. She glanced around hoping some of the information would sink in a bit deeper. She was so tired after so little sleep the past week. "How do you plan to stop this mad man?"

"I will be teaching you as much as I can about the other dimension. The more you understand and become familiar with it, the better chance we all have of stopping the Entity."

"What? Wait." Carol fumed. "You want me to travel to the other dimension?"

"I don't know what you or I or Toga will have to do in order to stop this Entity yet, but I'm certain we'll be going to the other dimension before we're done. The more you know the easier you will be able to stop him from taking you there against your will."

She stood and approached him angrily. "I'm guessing you know all this stuff because your trip with me in my dream wasn't the first time you've been to this other dimension. You go there all the time just like the creep that forces me there. Am I right?" she challenged.

"Yes," he answered calmly. "That's why I know I can help you."

She turned her back, unable to look at him. "You're crazy. Why didn't you tell me this when you offered to help me?" she demanded.

"Would you have understood? Your life is in danger. I can't stand by and watch you die."

Carol calmed down. "Okay, okay. I don't want to... I just thought there might be some antidote or you'd teach me ways to block my mind. Something. Anything but...this."

Dr. Cameron's words came back to her. 'Do you want to help me fight this evil or do you want to remain its victim until it kills you?' She felt physical pain in her chest. She'd been afraid before. She knew it was better to face it and be done with it than remain in the hell indecision brings. Tears threatened as she confronted her dilemma. She must face the fear to save her own life. So be it! Her back stiffened. She would do what had to be done. When she looked at Dr. Cameron again, he watched her anxiously, waiting for her to decide what to do. She glanced to her left. Mr. Toga remained still.

"Okay. Fine. I understand." She tightened her jaw. "I'll do whatever it takes." Carol could see the relief in Dr. Cameron's face and Mr. Toga's hand relaxed on his chair arm.

Dr. Cameron walked over to her. "Are you all right?"

"No." She looked up at him. "I understand what I must do. I'm terrified, but..." her throat tightened. "I just need some time to get used to the idea."

Dr. Cameron looked at his wrist watch. "It's already five-thirty. How about dinner?"

"Great. What do you have in mind?" She did not feel hungry. "I might be able to eat something. Not easy after all this."

"Italian sound good? We can have some of Toga's special spaghetti then go back to work. We have a lot of ground to cover still."

"Heaven," she answered flatly. "Just promise no more talk about the other dimension until after dinner."

"Done." He ventured a laugh. "After dinner, I'll show you what protection we have devised to keep you safe." He held out his hand to escort her back to the kitchen.

While Toga prepared his spaghetti, Carol wandered back to the front of the house. Its atmosphere gathered around her, feeling like a draft but thicker somehow. It did not feel sinister, just full of memories and deeds of the past. Wondering if the doctor had any ghosts, she found herself looking out the large diamond paned front window. It occurred to her that she had not really seen the front since the garage entrance had not allowed a view of the entire house. She reached for the tall heavily carved double doors that served as the main entrance. Stepping outside she gazed at the lovely dappled sunshine upon the quiet narrow street. The sun had begun its descent into the west and the filtered light calmed her. Taking a deep renewing breath, she walked across the balcony-like patio that defined the front entrance, noticing stone steps to her left that led down to street level and the garage. Leaning upon the balustrade, Carol watched the birds flit in and around the huge trees that gracefully draped their branches over the street.

Her mind returned to the first time she had experienced Briar Cliff Canyon. She had gotten lost winding through the hills. When she stepped out of her car to calm herself and figure out what direction to take, the quiet energy that surrounded and comforted her made her decide to live here.

A slight breeze refreshed her and brought her to the present. She became aware of yet another impression now, something much older seeping through, a barely perceptible feeling, both ancient beyond comprehension yet vibrantly fresh. A compelling concept entered, captivating her core on a level that she just understood without being able to explain, an ancient power and wisdom beyond conscious meaning, a power beyond mere words. She simply felt it. Closing her eyes, she breathed in the thrill of this deeper understanding. She still felt safe in Briar Cliff Canyon in spite of all the things happening to her.

Thinking of all she had learned in just the past few hours, her mind compared what she had known with what she knew now. Here, away from the doctor's presence, doubt crept unwelcome into her mind. Could this really be the right thing to do? Were her nightmares just that and nothing sinister at all? But she knew. They were evil and they were not dreams. She decided to go back inside and have something to eat before she talked herself out of what needed to be done.

Turning around, she stopped. Every nerve in her body tensed as she stared with disbelief at the doorway. Putting her hand on the railing behind her to keep steady, she let the meaning of the intricate stone carving around the front door sink in. The eyes and nose of a Demon glared from over the door and the doorway became its gaping mouth. The house of Edward Blair! The house Darren had said the candlestick had come from, the house where so much evil had taken place.

SEVENTEEN

PANIC consumed her. She must leave! Run away! But the only way was back through the demon's mouth. Closing her eyes, she rushed inside. Her heart pounding, she grabbed her purse and tip toed to the inside door to the garage, she slipped through noiselessly. Car keys in hand, she checked the garage doors, finding them unlocked. She nearly let panic consume her again when she realized that pushing the old folding doors to one side would be very loud. She put her purse in the back seat, started her car, left its door open then shoved the garage door. The old door scraped to one side. The noise seemed deafening. Hoping she hadn't alerted the doctor and Toga, she rushed to her driver's seat, hastily backed out of the garage and took off leaving the door open. Driving down the canyon, Carol slowed as curve after curve put her in danger of losing control of the car. When she felt far enough away, she pulled over and reached for her cell phone.

"Sarah, I've just left Dr. Cameron's."

"I thought you were there for the duration?"

"I was." Carol tried to sound calm not wanting to alarm Sarah. "But I need a break. Can I come over?" She knew if she went home, the doctor could find her quicker. Maybe he'd think to call Sarah, but it was farther away than her place. All her thoughts were focused on getting as far away as fast as possible.

"Of course you can. You okay? You sound stressed." Concern colored her voice.

"That's why I need a break. I'll tell you about it when I get there."

"I'll have glasses of wine ready."

Being with her friend tonight would be the best medicine she could ask for right now. She put her phone in her purse and continued down the canyon out into Hollywood and off to Beverly Hills. The drive began to relax her. Her mind replaying the information she had learned, which led to the reality of how concerned Dr. Cameron had actually been for her well-being. She began to feel foolish that she had panicked at the site of the front door. Why didn't she just go ask him about it? Those stories Darren had told her happened over ninety years ago. Dr. Cameron had nothing to do with that. Then the candlestick came to mind. He had insisted it come with them. Did he know about its history? Did he actually have some connection? Pulling into Sarah's driveway, she didn't understand any more than when she'd left the doctor's. But she felt calmer.

Nestling into Sarah's couch, Carol caressed a glass of chardonnay as she looked around the familiar surroundings of her friend's living room. Unlike her office, the room had warm dark rose walls filled with walnut bookcases that held her vast science fiction collection. The furnishings were a beautiful blend of vintage pieces and very comfortable classic pieces. It felt good to be here. Now things could be simple, easy and, best of all, far away from her problems. But her thoughts turned back to Dr. Cameron. Now what would happen? She owed him an explanation, she realized. Her panic had completely consumed and confused her

Sarah refilled her wine glass. "So Dr. Cameron thinks he can stop this, ah, um, Controller, from taking over?"

"Oh, I like that. The Controller. Sounds like a comic book villain, or perhaps the head accountant of a large firm." She grinned at Sarah. The wine had done its job and she was much calmer now, even tipsy.

"If we knew his name we wouldn't be struggling with nicknames for him, would we? Give me a solid Tom, Dick or Harry, every time." Sarah put her wine down as if to punctuate her sentence. "Seriously though, he must be stopped and, if what you say is true, the doctor is the only one who can do it." She frowned. "So, why are you here?"

Still haunted with doubt about the doctor's theories, a more horrible thought flew through her mind. Could he actually be causing her nightmares? That would be another way to explain why he knew she'd had the nightmare about the horses, but why such an elaborate plot? Why would she be his target? Her mind flashed to the film The Collector starring Terrance Stamp. He had played a disturbed young man who kidnapped a woman hoping she would fall in love with him during her captivity. That elaborate plot hadn't worked and she'd died.

Carol answered Sarah. "The doctor has ideas about stopping the Entity, as he likes to call him. I started to understand what he was explaining, well some of it. I really believed that an outside force could be attacking me by using the astral dimension. But something happened that terrified me."

"What?"

Carol sipped her wine. "Remember the story Darren told us about all the orgies at Edward Blair's mansion in the Canyon?"

"Yeah. Creepy stuff."

"Dr. Cameron lives in that house."

Sarah stared at Carol a moment. "Are you sure it's not just a coincidence? You live in a complex built in 1913, but you don't have anything to do with stuff that might have happened in the past there."

"He said it was his ancestral home and his family had always lived there.

"Well, we've got to find the truth before you go crazy between your doubts and your nightmares. I feel awful. I'm the one who suggested you go to him."

"You didn't know. You're time with him produced great results. I don't blame you."

"Thanks, but we need to figure out what to do."

"You're right, but I don't want to talk to Dr. Cameron until I find more information.

"Maybe we can start by finding out about his house?"

"Great idea. I'll call Darren. He does location scouting. I bet he knows how to find out all sorts of things."

"Does Darren know about all this…, I mean your dreams?"

Carol put her phone down. "God. No. I had to leave a message. I told him I'd call him back when I had a break. Guess this is it." Things were getting serious between them and she knew it. She had to tell him about her dreams before they got even closer. It was only fair. He had no idea what he was getting into.

"I'll call him from the bedroom. I'll try to find a way to tell him."

Sarah winced. "Over the phone is bad. Be careful."

Carol nodded. "No choice." She rose to find some privacy. She sat down on the guest bed and dialed Darren's number.

"Hi Darren, its Carol."

"Hey sweetie, what's up?" There was a pause. "You don't sound good."

"You're right. Things aren't good. I am so sorry to have to tell you what's happening over the phone, but there isn't time to get together."

"You're breaking up with me."

"No! There's things going on for me and I need to fill you in." Carol's voice broke.

"Tell me. How can I help?"

"The reason I'm seeing a doctor is because I'm having horrible nightmares. Dr. Cameron is trying some unorthodox treatment, but it scares me. It's occult type stuff.

"What's he doing to you? Where are you? Let me come get you."

"I'm okay. I'm at Sarah's house. But I need some help before I decide if I should go back for treatment."

"Tell me what you need."

"The doctor lives in the house you said Edward Blair lived in. It makes me worry that he may not be all that straight forward with me. I need to know if I can trust what he's suggesting. Do you know how to find the chain of owners that house has had since 1923?"

"Shouldn't be a problem. But I wouldn't go back. There has to be other ways to stop nightmares," he pleaded.

"I'll fill you in on more details about my treatment when you call back. I just need to have enough info to decide if I go back or not. He has helped me."

"You sure you're okay?"

"I'll be fine. I'll stay with Sarah, and I don't plan on going back home until I talk to Dr. Cameron and make a final decision. If he's not being honest with me, I'll find another way to deal with the nightmares."

"That's my girl. I'll help however I can."

"Just a thought, if I don't go back to the doctor, could I stay with you until I find a way to stop the nightmares?" Carol hoped he wouldn't think she was pushing their relationship too far.

"Great idea! Stay with me instead of Sarah. I have a late flight to San Francisco tonight. I'll leave my key over the door. I'll be back in a couple days."

Carol bit her lip. "I need to explain something. I have a nightmare every night except when I'm with you. I will take you up on your offer when you get back, unless I decide to go back to my doctor. If I have another dream tonight, Sarah will be here."

"Oh." He sounded disappointed. "I'll work on the information you need the minute I get to San Francisco. I'll call as soon as I know anything. Just please be careful!"

"I will. And thanks. You're a life saver."

"Wait. Just a thought. Where's the candlestick now?"

"It's at home. How'd you think of that?"

"Well if this is Blair's house, I kinda put two and two together. I suppose that's okay. Better at home than with the doctor I guess, if you believe his occult angle."

After saying her goodbyes, Carol came back to Sarah. "He'll help us."

Sarah frowned. "How'd he take your nightmare problem?"

"Wanted to come to my rescue."

Sarah smiled. "Good!" And she poured Carol another glass of wine.

They sought diversions on the SciFi channel for a while until Carol announced, "I'm done in. I'm ready for bed." She yawned.

"Stop that. It's contagious." Sarah said through her own yawn.

Standing, Carol realized how tipsy she was. She giggled. After half a bottle of wine, getting a good night's sleep shouldn't be difficult. Also actually doing something about her situation made her as giddy as the wine. She felt in control and what a relief to have Darren on her side.

Deciding a shower would relax her even more, Carol slipped under the hot running water, her mind turning to the question that plagued her most. What should she do about her nightmares if Dr. Cameron proved untrustworthy? He'd seemed honest and straight forward, why would he want to do her harm? Putting her face into the spray of water, she knew she would just have to wait to see what tomorrow brought. She was simply too tired to think anymore.

Smiling as she walked into the spare bedroom, Carol looked at the cookies on the end table. A note read 'I'm just in my office if you need me. Have a nummy.' Sarah's thoughtfulness made her feel good, but she left the cookies and burrowed herself under the blanket.

The ancient stone ruin loomed silent, cold, waiting. Carol looked back. Only darkness lived there, crouching, ready to snatch and swallow her whole. Fear grew, clawing at her inside. Cautiously heading into the ruined structure, she prayed salvation could be found in its depths. But she had no hope that it would really be there. Dripping water echoed from somewhere in the dimness before her. Crumbling mortar fell from over-head and skittered across the floor, echoing through the structure. Cold damp air crept deep into her bones. She shivered.

Footsteps! Standing still, listening hard, staring, straining into the dimness for any sign of human life, she waited. There! A shadow moved. A long low misery sodden wail came from the dimness. It did not sound human. Carol took a step forward. The wailing stopped. Deathly silence descended. Her nerves stretched to their limit. Gathering every ounce of courage she took another step. The ragged wail came again, rising to a shriek that pierced the silence ripping it like claws tearing through flesh. Carol fell to her knees, her hands over her ears. She saw it again! A dark mass huddled in the corner. As it rose from the ground, Carol struggled to stand. A black ape-like beast rushed towards her, its long hair hanging like dread locks from its arms, its red eyes glowing with hate. Jaws opened wider and wider revealing needle teeth seeking to rip her apart. Its shrill screaming became unbearable. There seemed nothing in the world but the rending cry of this monster. The jaws reached for her throat. She turned, raising her arm to defend. The creature became smoke and simply drifted away.

Harsh laughter assaulted her. Carol whirled around, seeking the En-tity. "No!" she screamed. Tendrils of thick fog reached for her and the ground beneath her feet felt wet and slippery. The damp air became unbearable and she couldn't stop another shiver. This one came from a deeper place than mere cold alone could cause.

"You escaped me last time, little one." His deep voice penetrated her entire being.

Carol's mind filled with all the fears suffered at the hands of this monster. A tiny spark of anger ignited enough courage to demand, "Who are you!"

"You need to understand that you belong to me. No amount of help will change that."

Another wave of fear threatened to put out the tiny spark. "Go play your silly games somewhere else," she shouted defiantly.

Invisible hands grasped her and forced her to the wet ground. Carol struggled, but failed.

"Kneel before me!"

"Why should I?" She was beginning to lose the battle against her terror, tears flowed down her face.

A hand struck her across the face. Her scream told of her agony as pain sliced through every nerve in her body. Pain that chipped away at her resolve to escape. Her moans acknowledged defeat.

"You deserve to be punished for leaving me." His cold voice cut her. "You know that."

Carol defiantly raised her face, only to receive more pain as an unseen force beat her to the ground.

Awaking with a start Carol heard Sarah frantically calling her name. Sobbing uncontrollably, she looked around in confusion. Sarah sat next to her on the bed, Carol fiercely hugged her friend.

Tears streamed down Sarah's face too. "They're getting worse, aren't they?"

Carol let go of Sarah. Unable to speak through her sobs, she only nodded.

Sarah grabbed some tissues and handed them to Carol. "First your cell phone rang and woke me up. Then you screamed like Hell itself was after you."

"It was." Carol managed. Her cell phone rang again. Grabbing it, she saw Dr. Cameron's name on her screen. Letting it ring, she leaned back exhausted.

"What are we going to do?" Sarah whispered.

EIGHTEEN

DARREN CALLED early next morning from San Francisco. Carol put him on speaker so Sarah could hear too.

"Well, ladies, it seems that your doctor's telling the truth. His family has owned that house since it was built in 1920."

Carol asked, "No mention of Edward Blair? Maybe they rented it out for a while?"

"No, there are no records regarding renting, but it was common for the wealthy to allow movie people to stay with them. Mary Astor's parents insisted that John Barrymore live with them at Moorcrest during the time Mary and John were engaged." There was silence and they could hear papers rustling. "Moorcrest was built in 1921 and is only a few streets away from the doctor's house. The Astors were the trend setters of their day."

Looking at Carol, Sarah asked, "So we still don't have any real evidence that Dr. Cameron's house was ever involved in the Blair rumors?"

"No. Nothing I can find so far. It's possible someone thought the doctor's house would make the perfect setting for Blair's life and the lie stuck. Or perhaps the doctor's family was ashamed and never handed down the story. I just started digging into Cameron's life history. There are some tidbits that make me worry about his motives, though. I want to help you. I feel bad about telling you the story. I think you should stay with Sarah until we find more information. I'm going to continue to search and see what I can find. I'll be home tomorrow night, you can come stay with me then."

"Thanks. You didn't know the story might be a lie. When this is all over, I at least owe you a drink at Maxie's'," Carol said.

"If I can have dessert with that, you're on! Seriously, please stay with Sarah. I want you safe until I can get home."

Quickly taking her cell off speaker, Carol turned from Sarah's look of 'I bet I know what dessert really means' and said her goodbyes to Darren. Blushing, she faced Sarah again. Her friend only gave a 'honey, I-know-what's-going-on' smile of approval.

Carol was disappointed. She had hoped something would surface that made the direction she should take clearer. She wanted to call Dr. Cameron today, get things resolved, especially after last night's horrific trip to the other dimension. She didn't want another trip tonight. Good solid information and a good night's sleep would have gone a long way in helping her explain her panic after seeing his demon door. Her exhaustion would be a handicap. She needed help ending the horror, but she didn't want her only hope of finding the road out of nightmare city to fall to its mayor. But no evidence that Edward Blair had ever been in the doctor's house existed. That was something, at least. Perhaps meeting him in some neutral place would help her manage the energy and the courage to face him.

"If I arrange to meet Dr. Cameron today, would you go with me?"

Sarah frowned. "Are you sure you should meet him? Darren said…"

"If I don't, it feels like I'm just running away. He's offered to help. I'll never find the truth if I just leave. I don't even know if there is a real reason to run. And the forced trips to the other dimension won't stop. I don't see an alternative."

"But this could be really dangerous. I think Darren's right."

"I've been trying to be logical and bring things back into perspective. Not easy after last night's horror, but if I just look at the facts, I can keep my panic under control.

"Yeah, I see your point. We've been jumping at shadows that have no basis in fact or reality. At least not yet."

"My trips to the other dimension don't help the jumping part either, actually made it rather easy.

"I worry about you. We need more information."

Carol nodded. "So far, even though I don't completely understand his entire theory, I believe that this other dimension does exist. And I believe someone is forcing me to this dimension. I have also been shown that this evil is happening to other people as well. I willingly agreed to help stop the Entity. I think if we are careful, we can make some sense of it all, don't you?"

"Sure. I'll go with you. Two heads are better than one. But make it a public place. In broad daylight."

"You read my mind."

Feeling better after taking some control of her situation, Carol thought being exhausted, confused and afraid could be the main reason she'd panicked and fled in the first place. She shuddered as the unbidden voice of the Entity condemning her for leaving him echoed in her thoughts. She straightened her shoulders. Nonsense! How could that be Dr. Cameron? But if he was involved, perhaps her trips to the other dimension and the threat the Entity posed were only lies. In that case, she'd just break off their relationship and seek help elsewhere.

Sarah left the room to make them some coffee.

Picking up her cell, she called Dr. Cameron. "I owe you an explanation."

"Carol! Are you okay? Where did you go last night?"

"I'm okay. Can we meet today? I'll explain."

His voice became calmer. "My office?"

"No, let's meet at the Rose Café in Venice Beach. Noon all right?"

"Perfect. Lunch will be on me."

"I'm bringing Sarah with me."

There was hesitation. "That's not a problem."

Hitting the hang up button, she realized how tight her shoulders were and stretched her neck to relieve some of the tension. Sarah walked in holding two mugs of steaming brew and handed one to Carol.

"So, are we on for today?" she asked.

Carol nodded, trying to smile. She didn't succeed.

NINETEEN

ENTERING the Rose Café, Carol felt warmed by its bright and welcoming interior. Dr. Cameron had arrived early and waited for them in a booth by one of the stained glass windows that added color to the eatery's atmosphere.

As they approached the booth, he stood, waiting for them to sit on the opposite side. Then seating himself, signaled to the waitress. Carol hardly glanced at Dr. Cameron as they quickly ordered lunch.

When the waitress left, he asked her calmly, "Do you have any idea what a foolish thing you have done?"

Carol managed to look him in the eye. "Somewhat," she said just as calmly. "Panicking is always foolish."

"What did I... What made you panic?"

"First, I need to apologize for leaving without saying anything."

"Thank you." His eyes darkened. "I thought you'd been abducted."

Carol hadn't thought about that. Guilt seeped into her heart. "You know the candlestick you insisted we bring along?"

He nodded.

"The provenance said it belonged to a silent actor name of Edward Blair. Allegedly he enticed young starlets to orgies, possibly their deaths at his house – your house."

Dr. Cameron just stared at her. "My house? If this bothered you, why did you agree to come?"

"Didn't know. The story only said that the house was at the top of Briar Cliff Canyon with a front door that looked like the mouth of a Demon."

His brow wrinkled. "I've never heard of this rumor. Are you sure someone didn't just make it up?"

"No." Carol looked at him straight in the eye. "In the light of day, this all seems completely absurd, but last night I was tired and confused. I needed to sort things out. When I walked out your front door to watch the sunset, I panicked when I saw your demon door. The panic was over-powering. All I could think to do was run."

"I see." He leaned forward. "I understand what happened. You were..."

Sarah intervened. "Carol told me everything about last night, doctor, and you two can sit here all cool and calm, but she was really upset. I don't think you understand how it was. She even..."

"Had another trip to the astral dimension?"

"Yes, but how..."

"Please, listen to me. Carol you are in a great deal of danger. Your panic was so overpowering because you were mentally prepared to panic before you even got to my house. This Entity must be skilled in this form of attack." His eyes pleaded with her.

"If you knew about my trip last night, why weren't you there to help me like before?"

The doctor's face softened. "When it seemed you trusted me, I severed our connection. I'm so sorry."

Carol heard sincere regret in Dr. Cameron's voice.

He turned back to Sarah. "About knowing Carol'd had another trip, it goes to follow."

Sarah took the offense. "How do you figure that?"

He looked at Carol. "It's not like you to panic. The Entity doesn't want you seeking help. He made you panic."

"But how did you know about my trip?"

"After getting you away from anyone who could help you, he would make sure to strengthen his hold by using another attack."

Sarah interrupted. "It seems to me that you know a lot about this psychic attack stuff. How do we know you're not the one doing the attacking?"

Before Dr. Cameron could respond, their food arrived. After the dishes were sorted, he continued, anxious to address Sarah's accusation. "You're right. I do know a lot about it. I've studied it to help patients who suffer from similar problems. I can only tell you that I would never use this skill to do harm."

"You said my life was in danger. If what you say is true, and he's stepped up his attacks…"

Dr. Cameron rushed in. "Carol you have sought help. You have defied him and hope to learn what he is doing. If he cannot bring you back under his control, you are no longer useful. You know too much. He may try to kill you."

Sarah reached for Carol's arm. "You didn't tell me anything about being killed!"

The doctor leaned forward. "I'm begging you to come back! We need each other to stop him."

Sarah turned to Carol. "What are we going to do? If you are in that much danger, you need help now."

Carol looked from Sarah to Dr. Cameron. "How do I know I can trust you?"

"I've had you under hypnosis."

Sarah interjected. "What does that prove?"

"If I meant any harm, why not gain the control I wanted over Carol then?"

Carol sighed. "Perhaps you were waiting for the right moment."

"I saved you from him on the other dimension."

Carol realized that she'd only viewed the gray horse as a friend and a comfort.

"I only hope you can believe that I do not possess his passion to control other people."

Carol's heart and thoughts raced. Could she find help somewhere else? Did she have time to get help before the Entity tried to kill her? Dr. Cameron had the skill and knowledge she needed. Everything she'd experienced made her believe him. It made sense to go back.

"If I come back, you have to promise to keep me safe."

Sarah stepped in. "And I'll be coming with her. If you do anything suspicious, we're out of there! I'll help if I can, but she's not going alone."

"Thanks." There was a relieved tone in his voice. "I will do everything in my power to keep us all safe." Dr. Cameron signaled the waitress for the bill. "I'll meet you at the house?"

Carol stood. "Just give us time to pack a few things for Sarah. We know we have to hurry."

TWENTY

TWO HOURS later, Carol pulled her VW into Dr. Cameron's garage. Mr. Toga helped Carol and Sarah take the luggage inside. Sarah looked around in awe as she followed Mr. Toga and Carol upstairs to their room.

Sarah had insisted that she stay in the same room with Carol. "Carol, this is like taking a step into the past. It looks like no one's changed a thing since it was built."

"I don't think anyone has. Dr. Cameron admitted that he has no interest in interior decorating."

"I want a tour as soon as possible."

"You'll be able to see most of it on the way to the doctor's library."

"I thought my parents' house was grand, but this place has real character and a quality I can't explain."

"I know what you mean. It feels like it's been here since the beginning of time."

"Yeah, that's it." Sarah paused. "Ah, what do you know about this Toga character?"

"Handsome, isn't he? Sorry, he's been too aloof, at least around me. Just know he's as skilled and capable as Dr. Cameron."

Coming down after unpacking, they found Dr. Cameron in the living room, standing in front of the huge fireplace, waiting for them. Carol went over to him, and Sarah headed for the wine-red velvet couch, obviously impressed by everything in the room.

The doctor smiled. "Toga will be joining us in a moment."

"What all does Toga do here?" Carol asked, knowing Sarah would like to know too.

"He's my assistant, my teacher, my researcher, my friend..."

"Sounds like you've known him all your life," Sarah said.

Mr. Toga entered the room pushing a teacart laden with sandwiches, cakes and large teapot. His graceful movements made it all a work of art. His dark eyes fell on Sarah as he offered her a cup and saucer. Dr. Cameron and Carol walked towards the cart and helped themselves to the welcomed refreshments.

"And the cook." Dr. Cameron helped himself to a piece of sesame seed cake.

Carol sat on the couch next to Sarah, balancing her plate with cake on her lap. "What are we going to do?"

"First, I thought we could set some ground rules so everyone knows what to do."

"I like that." Carol was glad of some order to the chaos she felt.

Dr. Cameron shifted his weight. "I would like to make clear that there are some things you can do to help, Sarah, but in the interest of time, it will be restricted to helping Mr. Toga in the library."

"I hoped to be with Carol."

"You will be, as much as possible, but we need to move fast and there will be times you simply cannot be with her."

Sarah objected, "Why can't I be with her all the time?

"I'll be instructing Carol on the vital things. She needs as much information as well as experience on the other dimension as possible. We simply cannot afford the time to teach you about these things as well. You will not be able to go with her to the other dimension."

Carol seeing her friend's distress added, "I see Dr. Cameron's point. Right now the other dimension is not a pretty place and we need to make it safe again." She turned to the doctor. "What can Sarah do?"

"There will be a great deal of research as well as organizing information for the battle ahead. I understand you are very good with computers. We could use the help. Our library and computer are at your disposal."

"Okay. At least that's something. I can help there." Sarah did not seem entirely satisfied with her role.

Carol sympathized with her friend's feelings. She only hoped that more ways Sarah could help would surface as they went along. "At least you will be here. That means the world to me."

Sarah smiled but Carol could still see the disappointment in her eyes.

"We should get started as soon as possible." Dr. Cameron motioned for them to follow him.

Walking through the house, Carol watched Sarah take in the dining room and solarium. She was delighted to see her friend's mood brighten a bit. Carol smiled when Sarah agreed that they should have breakfast in the solarium every morning. When they entered the library, she laughed when Sarah stopped and openly gaped at the huge expanse of books.

"What did he do, transport the entire Library of Congress here?" Sarah said trance-like, looking around.

"Incredible, isn't it?"

"Yeah. You could say that."

Sarah followed Carol to the doctor's desk. He was already seated almost hidden by a stack of books. Carol glanced over at Mr. Toga who stood on a library ladder pulling down even more volumes.

"What are we doing first?" Carol asked as she sat in front of his desk.

Before answering, Dr. Cameron turned to Sarah. "Would you mind taking this book over to Mr. Toga? Just ask, he'll be happy to show you what to do."

Sarah's mouth tightened but she reached for the book. "Not a problem," she said curtly and hurried over to Mr. Toga, her arms wrapped around the large leather-bound book.

"I want to explain a couple of things about the other dimension, so you will have a deeper understanding before we begin, since we missed this lesson last night."

Carol nodded. A shiver of guilt ran through her as she remembered running away the evening before. "Go ahead. I'll try to keep up."

The doctor smiled. "When you were forced to the other dimension it was always a place. The illusion felt and looked real because the structure and substance of the other dimension are fluid. Each participant

117

shapes their own environment allowing their own experience with imagery to support their intellectual and emotional needs. Their astral twin or inner being or soul, as you like to say, creates easily without the restrictions of our normal physical dimension here."

"Create what, a chair? People? Clouds?" She was being flippant. She still didn't completely comprehend everything yet and some of it sounded downright silly. "I'll be honest with you, it's beginning to sound more and more like a bad science fiction movie." Carol tried to be more serious. "So that's why it's so easy for this creep to give me such horrible nightmares."

"Yes. It takes considerable skill and practice." Cameron stood and began to pace.

"We will be going to the other dimension to investigate the Entity's situation. You will not have to create anything. I'll always be with you."

She stood and took a couple of steps away from him, her fear rising.

"We have to work together." He stepped towards her.

Carol crossed her arms over her chest to stop her trembling, as if that could protect her from the task ahead.

"Toga and I have prepared protection for us while we're there." He took her gently by the arm. She saw the concern on his face about the look of panic on hers. "Here, let me show you."

Looking where the doctor headed, she noticed a raised dais the width of the room. At first, it reminded Carol of a stage, but it was only about a foot high. It remained free of books, bric-a-brac, even furniture and the balcony that stretched around the other three walls, did not touch the wall above the dais. As she got closer she saw that a large circle had been drawn on its floor. Within the circle, lines and strange symbols intertwined and, in the center of it all, stood a clear multi-spire crystal at least three feet high. Carol had never seen a quartz crystal this large before and never one so perfectly clear.

Wondering what this beautiful yet bizarre artwork had to do with the other dimension... it suddenly hit her. "That's what you mean by our protection!" She had seen this type of thing in the movies, but she had never really believed a few lines drawn on the floor could protect anything or anyone.

"It's the best protection anyone can have."

He reached out and took her hand. Carol's focus became Dr. Cameron's incredible blue eyes and nothing else. She experienced a strong surge of connection to the doctor and understood this connection would stay while danger remained. She instinctively fought him. It felt too close to what the Entity tried to do.

Dr. Cameron put his hand tenderly on Carol's shoulder. She closed her eyes as the feeling of safety and comfort flooded through her.

Acknowledging what they were about to do, Carol straightened her shoulders, deciding she must face whatever it took to get through to the end. Realizing the doctor had started speaking again, she turned her attention to his words as the rest of the room swam back into focus.

"There are symbols in the Universe that, when properly applied, form bands of energy that can be controlled creating walls that counteract harmful energies. Toga will guard our circle from any harm while we're there. If the designs are disturbed or altered, its power can be lost or changed, even reversed."

Mr. Toga started down the ladder carrying yet another large leatherbound book. He crossed the room and handed it to Dr. Cameron. He glanced at Carol.

"Thank you." The doctor turned back to Carol. "Toga and I have studied for many years and I assure you, you will be as safe as we can make you."

Carol looked at Mr. Toga with skepticism as his dark eyes looked back at her with calm reassurance. She turned to stare at the circle as though it could somehow help her understand more. When she turned back, Mr. Toga had gone.

The doctor's face softened. Carol felt the warmth of security that radiated from him fill her again. Turning her gaze back to the circle, calmness infused her soul. How curious, the circle seemed more intricate now, more solid; safer. With amusement, she suddenly thought of Alice. Although she couldn't be thrilled about this rabbit hole, she couldn't help wondering if the doctor would be her White Rabbit, or her Mad Hatter.

Knowing that they were not completely powerless brought the confidence she needed. "Thank you, at least I don't feel so absolutely terrified at the thought of going on this little trip."

Dr. Cameron put down the volume Mr. Toga had given him. "Good." He took a step closer. "Now I wish to try a little experiment before we go to the other dimension. Come into the circle and lie next to me."

Carol felt heat rise in her as he stepped closer. She took a deep breath and turned, trying to calm her beating heart. Dr. Cameron's inner strength overwhelmed her senses making it impossible not to be attracted to his power. He stared at her with such tenderness. It made Carol aware that her relationship with Dr. Cameron had changed from doctor and patient to comrades in arms.

Sarah approached, loaded down with books, breaking the grip of the moment. "Dr. Cameron, Mr. Toga asked me to bring you these." She set the books on the desk with a smile. "Toga's wonderful!" There was a happy gleam in her eye. "He's been telling me about the other dimension. I understand more now. I'm even more determined to be here for Carol, and for all of us too. So I will help. Gladly. I know you didn't have to allow me to come here."

"Thank you, Sarah. Perhaps after this is over Toga can continue your education."

Sarah flashed a smile then hurried back to see what Mr. Toga might want next.

Carol appreciated the interruption. It gave her the moment she needed to bring her senses back in line with her priorities. Her attraction to Dr. Cameron surely had to be some form of hero worship and not serious. She visualized her goal to stop the Entity and the doctor's powerful attraction diminished.

Carol slowly walked to the indicated place on the floor inside the protection circle. "What are we going to do?"

"Practice. Please lie down here." Dr. Cameron touched her on the shoulder to reestablish the mental contact they had shared before. "I want you to close your eyes and when you start to feel a falling or pulling sensation, flow with it. Don't fight it or you'll never make it out of your body. I'll be there to help you."

He lay beside her and took her hand. A tingle went through her and she understood that a physical connection had been made as well as the mental one he already had. He could teach her like a flight instructor, he had control as well. She closed her eyes, cautious but curious to see what his experiment would do. Finding it difficult to flow with the sensation of the floor suddenly dropping out from beneath her, she made a few false starts, but stayed with it. Soon, the falling sensation lessened then stopped.

"You can open your eyes, but slowly."

Carol hovered within the dome in the library ceiling. The stained glass fascinated her. The colors were amazing. Carol became attracted to the glorious blue light in one pane, wanting to meld with it and understand what blue truly meant.

"Don't let what you see frighten you. All that's happened is you've left your body for a little while."

Dr. Cameron's voice sounded near and she reluctantly looked away from the mysterious blue to see him hovering right beside her. He glowed like an angel. She reached towards him, drawn by his radiance.

"Look down," he said gently before she could touch him.

She saw her body lying next to the doctor's on the floor of the platform. A slender pale blue string of energy connected her to her body. This was not like her nightmares. It was gentle almost loving. A deeper understanding rushed through her. She almost fainted, but the doctor's soothing voice brought her back.

"You are a very fast learner. I congratulate you. Not many can accomplish this in so short a time."

His calm voice helped her control the elation that rose to unbearable heights, filling her soul with a great and horrible longing for more. What an experience! The freedom from her body heightened her senses almost beyond endurance.

The doctor's voice sobered her. "Perhaps being pulled out of your body against your will on several occasions has helped speed the process."

"I'm not afraid," she said in amazement. "I can't even explain the sensation!"

"Take me by the hand. We are going back to our bodies, slowly and gently."

Together they floated downward. Nearing the floor she felt sucked towards her body, the pull getting stronger the closer she came. This time instead of slamming back into her body, Carol merely slipped into herself. No headache, no bloody nose.

"You are the best pupil I've ever had." He smiled at her as their eyes met.

Carol couldn't help thinking he was the most exciting teacher she'd ever had. Then she realized she just stared at him and quickly looked away.

Sarah's excited voice interrupted. "Wow, you guys actually went to the other dimension? I didn't see a thing, just you two lying on the floor."

"Not yet, just practicing leaving my body. It's kinda like flying!"

Dr. Cameron added, "We'll start your flying lessons as soon as this is all over."

"Wow! I'll tell Toga." She hurried back to the bookshelves where Toga pulled more books.

"So, doctor, what's next?" Carol's eyes bright with the excitement of her out of body experience. This was amazing. Not scary at all and how wonderful not to have the pain from reentering her body too fast.

"I think it's time I take you to the other dimension."

Fear started to swell. "It's safe, right?" She gritted her teeth to keep the terror away.

"Just a short trip to a very low level so we don't attract any unwanted attention. You'll see that it doesn't have to be horrible, when you know what you're doing. Do you feel up to the trip?"

Carol slowly nodded.

He motioned for her to lie back down. "Then let's go."

The sky shone softly with the pale blue of summer and the trees whispered with the gentle breath that came from the cool deep green lake before her. Long grasses and wildflowers wove themselves together as the breeze played in the lush greens, reds and yellows of the thick blanket of life growing at her feet. Embracing the enchantment, Carol raised her arms into the warm air to experience its vibrant living pulse and attempted to understand its place in the Universe. Feeling a soft touch on her elbow she turned to see Dr. Cameron standing next to her.

"Ready for some adventure?"

"Yes." Had she actually spoken the words or only thought them? There was still a lot to learn about being out-of-body.

Dr. Cameron's face appeared smooth and carefree. Vibrant blue eyes glowed with childlike wonder. Carol could still feel the inner energy he possessed. His long blond hair flowed around his shoulders and he moved with a self-confident grace that stirred feelings in Carol she did not think appropriate.

The doctor's voice interrupted her thoughts. "Carol. I realize I should tell you that it's extremely easy for me to read your mind, especially here."

Blushing, Carol could only stare at him, horrified.

He gently touched her cheek. "I should have told you sooner, but honestly it slipped my mind with all that's going on. Forgive me." His eyes pleaded for her understanding.

Carol didn't like that he could read her mind, but she accepted that he had merely forgotten to tell her. She couldn't deny she liked his touch on her cheek. Realizing she needed to be careful, she resigned herself to locking these feelings safely away.

"There are ways to block your mind from others," the doctor explained. "The best way is to concentrate on each moment. Even when you think you're completely alone, you may not be."

"That's a scary thought. What does that mean?"

"There are many who travel to this dimension. Some are out of sync with others on a particular level. Sometimes you can see them but they are completely unaware of your presence. You can also wish to be invisible."

She had to know. "Is this here all the time for people to visit?"

"Think of this as a dream state except you are very awake and aware of what you are doing. I'm creating this environment for us in my mind.

I come here often. It's my special place. Only those I invite here are allowed to enter."

"I'm beginning to understand." She was flattered that he had taken her to his special place. Carol turned her thoughts to what it must take to create something like this. But she only became overwhelmed by the difficulty of what Dr. Cameron was showing her. If the doctor can do all this... Suddenly, fear knotted her stomach. The Entity could control her at his slightest whim. How could she possibly fight that kind of power when she couldn't even control her own thoughts or surroundings?

Dr. Cameron took her hands in his. "Please do not be frightened." His touch calmed her. "Fear is a far greater enemy than this Entity."

She wanted to fall into his arms. For a brief moment, she knew he wanted her in his arms. But before she could move, he turned and walked away. Carol stared after him, disappointment surging inside her. Shame blazed through her and she became determined to get her head straight. Concentrate on stopping the Entity and not these new feelings for the doctor. Closing her eyes, she began analyzing what she wanted to learn from being here.

"Carol, come here. I want to show you something."

She saw Dr. Cameron at the edge of the lake. She walked toward him, steeling her emotions. She smiled as she approached but clenched her teeth in the great effort to keep her mind in a moment-by-moment state. Easier said than done, but it made her even more determined.

He held a stick in his hand. "This will help you understand what I mean by creating your own environment."

He raised the stick to the level of her eyes and before she could blink it had become a small brown snake. Carol gasped and involuntarily took a step back. The snake curled around the doctor's hand poking its little tongue out to taste the air.

"Simple really," he said as he bent down to let the snake slither away into the tall grass. "You could do it with a little practice." He stood and gave her a look that asked if she wanted to try.

"Sure, but can we try something other than a snake?"

Laughing, the doctor picked up a fallen brown leaf almost the size of his hand and gave it to her. "Perhaps a butterfly?"

124

She took the leaf. "How?"

"Look at it and imagine what it would look like as a butterfly."

Carol concentrated on the leaf in her hand. As she began to relax she actually could visualize the colors and shapes that might be wings. Then she knew exactly where the insect's body and antennae should be. The leaf transformed into the butterfly of her mind's eye, right in the palm of her hand.

The butterfly spread its huge brown and gold wings revealing black edges. Each upper wing held an iridescent green and gold splotch reminiscent of large eyes. "Wow," she whispered as she allowed the butterfly to flutter away on the summer breeze. She could not suppress a giggle as she watched her creation softly land on a flower too small to hold its weight.

"Well done."

She barely heard him as she watched the graceful butterfly, her butterfly, slide then flutter through the air. Not only did she understand she accepted this new reality. Turning she reached out and gave Cameron a jubilant hug.

Carol remembered herself and dropped her hands to release the hug, but Cameron held her a moment longer. His eyes locked onto hers. An aching far stronger than any before gripped her and she inhaled sharply. He let her go but Carol sensed his reluctance to release her.

Cameron's voice was husky. "We should go back to our bodies now. You've done quite a lot today."

Slowly, the lovely summer landscape dissolved and the doctor's library began to take shape. Returning, Carol could see her body still lying on the floor next to Cameron's. The blue strands that tethered their essence to those bodies glowed bright as they slowly descended. Slipping back into her body, she lay there a moment before sitting up, remembering how the lake had glimmered in the afternoon summer sun. I made a butterfly!

Sitting up, she saw that Cameron already stood beside her. "Thanks," she said softly. "That was incredible."

He smiled. "You must get some rest before we practice anymore." He held out his hand to help her stand.

"I'm starved. How about dinner?" Carol announced as she stood. "I promise to stay this time."

Cameron laughed.

Sarah walked up to Cameron's desk and put a book down. "Did someone say dinner?"

TWENTY-ONE

WHEN TOGA announced that dinner was ready, they all headed out of the library. Carol envisioned eating in the cold dark dining room, but happily they followed Toga to the kitchen, the only room in the house that had been remodeled. Remodeled yet keeping the style of the house intact. It provided the comfort and informality the dining room lacked. The original terra cotta tile floor remained but the dark wood cabinetry and stainless steel appliances streamlined the kitchen to user-friendly perfection. French doors connected the kitchen to the solarium, which would bring more light into the room during the day. A single door connected to the library.

Carol watched as Toga lowered long strands of spaghetti into a pot of boiling water and smiled, remembering that Toga's famous spaghetti had been promised the night before. Mr. Toga stirred his sauce then started to arrange the dishes for the café style booth which served as the kitchen table. Sarah and Toga were talking and smiling while they sorted the plates and wine glasses.

What a flirt. Leave it to Sarah to break the ice. Carol still wanting to get to know Toga better, walked over to offer help.

He turned to her and nodded slightly. "You may take those plates and silverware to the table." Then he turned back to the stove, dismissing her without further conversation.

Cameron arrived with Chianti in hand from his cellar. He popped the cork and began pouring, looking at Carol, as she placed the plates and silverware on the table. "What a great way to have a meal, everyone pitching in to prepare the feast."

Carol enjoyed his boyish delight in pouring the wine, how his blue eyes shone with excitement as he took their glasses to the booth's table.

He still wore jeans, topped by a T-shirt with a picture of Einstein on it. His long hair fell loose onto his shoulders. The formal doctor had disappeared, before her stood a man and a friend. She couldn't help liking what she saw.

"Carol. I have a favor to ask."

"What doctor?"

"Call me Michael."

Carol's face got hot and she knew she must be blushing. "Of course …Michael." She smiled. It sounded a bit strange after calling him Dr. Cameron for so long, but she liked Michael. It suited him.

Carol tried again to engage Mr. Toga during dinner, but although he smiled and politely answered her, he remained elusive. She often caught him looking at her, studying her. It made Carol uncomfortable. But Toga seemed more curious than creepy.

Michael refused to allow Carol or Sarah help with clean up after the meal. "You are exhausted and you both need your rest for tomorrow."

Sarah got up from the booth. "Toga's been keeping me up on what's happening. I don't think I could sleep a wink."

"I know what you mean." Carol felt the same excited energy as her friend.

Michael sounded like a doctor again. "We plan to stand guard through the night. Mr. Toga has prepared a special tea that will make you sleep. He's taking it up to your room now. There will be no unscheduled trips to the other dimension."

As Carol and Sarah entered their room, Toga had just set down a tea tray.

"Mr. Toga, how long have you known Dr. Cameron?" Carol asked, still determined to make a friend.

He turned slowly his black eyes emotionless as he answered softly, "Long enough." He must have caught the exasperated look in Carol's eye. "I have been with the doctor for a considerable time. I have every confidence he is capable of helping you." His back stiffened. "Will that be all for this evening?"

"Yes, thank you." She did not push. She only watched as he gracefully left the room, closing the door without a sound. He acted the loyal servant, but Michael had said he was a teacher and an associate. She knew there was much more to this quiet man.

Carol turned to Sarah. "Have I done something to offend him?"

"Not that I know of."

"You seem to be getting along great."

"True. Toga's been wonderful. He loves telling me about the library, the other dimension, and things that he does," Sarah said dreamily. "He spent his childhood in a Buddhist monastery. He said he cooks and serves to remain humble."

"You like him."

"Yeah. He's not like any man I've met before. Not my type really, but he fascinates me. And so handsome! Believe it or not, he's very funny at times. But he's so intelligent. If I didn't know better, I'd think he was a hundred years old, he knows so much. He's made me understand how important it is to stop the Entity."

Carol looked around. Although the bedroom had a masculine décor, its Art Deco luxury made it comfortable. More wood beams arched over the ceiling and thick oriental rugs softened the hard wood floors. A huge diamond paned window dominated one wall and Carol realized that the house's front windows were all paned in this fashion. She stepped towards a dark heavy bed with a rich plum velvet spread.

Sarah sat down on the other bed just like it. "This is the most incredible time I've ever had in my life. I'm glad I'm a part of helping you. It's the most important thing I've ever done."

"Thank you for coming with me."

"Couldn't let you have all the fun," Sarah declared. "So, do you think we're doing the right thing now?"

Carol sat down on her bed. "I think so. Feels right. I've been shown the other dimension. Something I doubted only a few hours ago."

"This is big. Toga filled me in on a lot of things. I'm just beginning to realize what the Controller's power can do to people. Catastrophic only touches the surface."

Carol nodded in agreement.

Sarah continued. "No one is safe. Free will is gone. We're merely puppets to be used at a whim. Terrible."

"Only a few hours ago I ran away from here in terror." Carol took a contemplative sip of tea. "Things are happening so fast. My life's changed completely in just a couple of days. I believe the doctor, ah Michael, can defeat him. I can't go on without thinking he can."

"When he took you to the other dimension, what happened?"

Carol considered how to explain all the wonders she had experienced. "The first trip just gave me practice at leaving my body. He said I learned fast because the Entity had taken me out of my body so many times before. But the second time..." She couldn't find the words. "It was wonderful. Just wonderful."

"Come on. Details, I want details." Sarah took a sip of her tea.

"I saw a beautiful lake and all these incredible trees. He taught me that you create what and where you want to be in the dimension. It was Michael who made up where we were, said it was his special place. Then he showed me how to create things. I made a butterfly! It was so beautiful." Her mind drifted into her memory. "I hugged him for showing me this amazing... thing." She stopped, worried she'd said too much.

"I heard him ask you to call him Michael." Sarah gave Carol a curious look. "And...?"

Carol couldn't look at Sarah. "He didn't want to let go of me any more than I wanted to let go of him. I... Well, we...." This would be difficult and staring at the ceiling wouldn't help. She looked her friend in the eye. "Okay, I'm attracted to Michael but I'm keeping it under control." She said wanting to end the discussion.

"That's the last thing I thought I'd hear from you."

Carol took another sip of tea. "Am I out of control?"

Sarah shook her head. "No, please. I'm just surprised, that's all." She reached for more tea. "What about Darren? I thought that was getting serious. Boy, when you decide to come out and play you really go for it! You go girl!" She glanced at Carol's stunned expression and toned down. "I thought you had a strict policy not to mix business and pleasure."

"I do. I feel infatuated with Darren, perhaps in love. He's fun and sexy and smart. He doesn't scare me." She hesitated. "Michael makes me feel safe, confident, maybe truly connected or grounded? But, I can't be sure of anything because being in the other dimension intensifies all my senses. Perhaps that's all there is to this connection I feel for him."

"Dr. Cameron only helped me for about a month. Have you found out much about him?" Sarah asked.

"Mysterious character, huh?" Carol shrugged. "Don't get me wrong, I think he's a capable and professional man."

"I hear a 'but' coming."

"When you realize the other dimension is for real, it opens all kinds of questions. Who is he really? Where did he learn all this stuff?"

"You never asked?"

"Not yet. Plan to," Carol said with determination.

Sarah scoffed. "I think you should stay with Darren. At least he seems normal."

"Michael says the occult is normal too." The tea, beginning to fuzz her thoughts, made her take a left turn. "He can read your mind! Did you know that?"

"Who? Darren!"

"No, Michael. He told me he could."

"That's not fair!" Sarah slurred.

"No it's not! I tried to control my thoughts like he said, but I couldn't." Carol curled her feet under her.

"Yet another reason to lean toward good old normal Darren." Sarah closed her eyes.

Carol poured more tea. So much had happened all at once. What were these feelings she had for Michael really? Probably just a bad case of hero worship or Stockholm syndrome! That's all. She shouldn't go thinking there's more here than there really is. And it wasn't fair to Darren!

"You don't think the doctor's from another planet, do you?" Sarah asked suddenly.

Carol stopped in mid sip. "No," she answered flatly. "No!" she said again as if to reaffirm her decision. "He's not that strange."

"Tell me more about what happened between you and the doctor."

It felt like old times talking to Sarah and not this new world. "I think it started after the nightmare about the horses. When I realized he'd

131

actually been in the dream with me, I mean in the other dimension. He saved me from the Controller."

"And...?"

"Things are getting more.... Well, today on the dimension, I sensed that he feels the same way about me."

"Whoa!" Sarah's words slurred even more. "You're sure?"

"No. Told you. Can't trust my feelings." Carol thought back to the embrace she'd shared with Michael and again felt the all-encompassing thrill. She straightened her back and attempted to get control of herself.

"What are you going to do?" Sarah asked attempting to keep her eyes open.

"Try to keep to my policy, I guess. I shouldn't be having these feelings. They get in the way. Nothin' but trouble." Carol's eyes started to close. "I'm done in."

Carol and Sarah undressed, put on oversized T-shirts and climbed into their beds. Pulling the soft quilt up to her chin, Carol's mind drifted to Michael. What had led him to study and travel in the other dimension? He seemed ageless to her now, a delightful combination of youthful enthusiasm and the kind of wisdom that only comes with years of experience. Like Sarah had said about Toga. She thought about his long sandy colored hair and blue eyes, eyes that held deep pools of knowledge far beyond her own. So, she would stay here under his protection. That felt good. He had been a gentleman so far. She only hoped she could remain a lady. Stop it, she chided herself. She'd always been attracted to intellect. Drawn to the brainy types. Right now it would cause nothing but trouble.

She forced her thoughts back to Darren. The way his dark hair dropped across his forehead when he leaned forward. How his dark eyes lingered over her naked body...

Toga's special tea had the final word.

TWENTY-TWO

WHEN CAROL awoke, the sunlight beaming through the beveled panes of the window made rainbows on the opposite wall. She lay there a moment entranced by the dance of colored light. She knew she had slept later than usual, and Michael's promise came true, no trip to the other dimension! Carol rose and woke Sarah. They quickly dressed and hurried downstairs, eager to learn the plans for today, and to find breakfast. Carol wanted to see Michael again too. She forced her mind back to thinking about what new things she might learn today. But it made her worry about how long before they went after the Entity.

They found Toga in the kitchen, fixing toast and scrambled eggs. He glanced at Carol and then smiled shyly at Sarah. "Good morning," he said with quiet dignity. "Please go to the Solarium and I will bring your breakfast."

"Good morning," Sarah purred back.

"Is there any coffee?" Carol could kill for a cup.

"It's already in the Solarium."

Carol and Sarah headed into the indoor garden. Carol felt her tension slide away as they sat down at the wrought iron table by the fountain. "I could spend my whole life just in this room," she said dreamily.

Sarah put her mug down. "Be careful what you wish for."

"I promise not to throw a penny into this fountain." Remembering the Fountain of Wishes at The Hollywood Canteen and how her penny seemed to bring Darren into her life.

Sarah laughed. "Perhaps we could wish this was all over and we are safe at home in our little beds. I'd throw every penny I could find in that fountain."

"Somehow I don't think all the money in the world could accomplish that wish."

After breakfast, they hurried to the library.

"Come in," the doctor greeted them enthusiastically. "You've arrived just at the right moment."

His enthusiasm made Carol wince. It felt forced. Made her wondered what was up.

He paced while he collected his thoughts. "I'm sure you're ready," he mumbled to himself.

"Ready for what?" Carol asked as she came to his desk.

"We need to work fast."

"Why? What's happened?" Sarah asked, stopping next to Carol.

"Toga went to the other dimension last night and learned that the Entity plans to make his move very soon."

Mr. Toga entered the room. "I spoke with some trusted friends who use the other dimension regularly. They have all felt a presence there, one that pushes boundaries and seeks control over the natural course of things. They all fear something will be happening very soon and it will not be for the good."

Michael rubbed the back of his neck, frowning. "Carol you need to be the one who lures the Entity to us."

"What do you mean, exactly?" Apprehension crept up her back bone.

"It will be easier for the Entity to find us than for us to find him."

"I don't understand! Just explain this all to me."

Toga turned to her. "He'll know you are on the dimension. He'll be curious and hopefully come to find out why you're there when he didn't send for you."

"I see. So I'm the bait."

Michael frowned at the word 'bait'. "Toga and I've tried. There's no other way to get fast results."

Sarah stepped between her friend and Dr. Cameron. "Sounds dangerous. How can Carol be ready after only one training session?"

He shook his head. "We must risk it."

Carol moved up beside Sarah, her mind racing. "But I don't know enough if he attacks us. I can't even keep my thoughts hidden or…" She grasped for words. "Disguise myself if I had to."

Toga answered, "We don't expect you to. That's why it will be easy for him to find you."

Sarah interrupted, addressing the doctor. "Are you disguising yourself then?"

"Yes. He can't know I'm with Carol. It could give him an advantage over us. I need to understand him, not let him know I'm checking him out."

"But what if he finds out about you through me?" Carol's brow furrowed.

Toga stepped forward. "Thought of that, I will place a temporary block on your thought patterns concerning Dr. Cameron." He made an attempt to smile but failed.

"I'm afraid." She stared at Michael.

Sarah grabbed Carol's arm, closing in on Cameron. "You're sure there's no other way?"

"I'm sure."

Sarah looked at Toga who nodded his agreement, then at Carol. "What do you want to do?"

Carol frowned. What choice did she have? "I'll go," she whispered.

"Is there anything I can do to help?" Sarah offered. "Toga filled me in on this creep. I'm for stopping The Controller as soon as possible. Please give me something to do."

"I'm sure we can find something," Michael answered, then with a dubious grin looked at Sarah and raised an eyebrow. "The Controller? Catchy."

Carol asked, "When do we go?"

"Now."

"Wait!" Carol's heart pounded.

"I'm very familiar with the part of the dimension I'm taking you to. Toga will be protecting the circle and keeping an eye out while we're there."

"But, I'm… Let me catch a breath."

135

"I will be with you every moment." He put his hand on her arm.

Carol looked at him, her mind spinning with fear. His touch soothed. His eyes radiated confidence. She felt a calm descend and she knew it had to be coming from Michael. She also remembered her purpose for being here. Help stop this Entity.

Michael did not look away. "Sarah, be here for Toga in case he needs something while we're gone."

"Sure." Sarah's tone told Carol she was still uncomfortable about what they were about to do.

"Are you ready?" Michael asked.

Carol took a deep breath. "No. Let's just get this over with."

Michael escorted Carol inside the circle. Her stomach knotted. She must trust him. He motioned for her to lie down in the middle of the circle with her toes at the edge of the huge crystal. He lay down beside her. Carol looked over to Sarah.

"I'll be here when you get back." Sarah attempted a smile.

Toga stood at the top end of the protection circle. He looked down at Carol. "I will be able to see where you are every moment. I will keep the circle safe." He sat down in lotus position, falling into a trance.

Carol could sense his presence surrounding her. She could feel a barrier develop in her mind that made it difficult to think of Michael. She closed her eyes. Michael gently put his arms around her and they began to fall away.

TWENTY-THREE

THE SUN felt gloriously hot. Beautiful green trees shaded the forest floor. The person walking ahead of her was a stranger, a man with short brown hair, black eyes and sturdy build. Turning he waited for her to join him. Dressed in simple shirt, pants and walking shoes, he looked as though he only wanted to enjoy a pleasant walk in the country. She only regarded him as a friend.

Amazingly, her mind held no doubt that they would succeed. The thought felt so powerful, she instinctually understood what positive thinking could truly accomplish, especially here. She at least had this power to help her through this task.

At the end of the forest trail, two marble pillars stood to each side. On the top of each, a dark blue ceramic Foo Dog stared out like sentinels over the trees. Large vines wrapped themselves around the pillars and small birds of varying colors flitted in and out of their dark leaves. As they walked slowly between the pillars, Carol felt a calm descend upon her spirit. Just inside, a large brass Japanese Temple Bell hung suspended within its sturdy wooden framework. Her friend swung a thick wooden striker that hung from ropes next to it and lightly tapped the bell with its end, causing a low calm melodious note to swell through the lush garden. As the tone fell, the man's body changed. He became wrapped in the black silk robes of a Samurai warrior. A red sash tied a long bright blade to his waist. The euphoric feeling Carol had experienced at the lake came to her and gave her strength.

Together they entered the magnificent Japanese garden of another world, another dimension. Flowers bloomed in every imaginable color, a red painted bridge arched over a stream that meandered through a rocky bed, ending in a large pool filled with lily pads in bloom.

He chose a path to their right and before long they neared an ancient teahouse. Entering, Carol felt calmed by its simple grace and beauty. They knelt by a small fire in the center of the main room where a pot of tea waited to be served. As Carol reached for the steaming pot, her friend raised his hand and signaled for her to remain still. She watched in anticipation as he sat frozen, listening. She heard nothing.

He stood and with one fluid motion pulled the sword from his sash to swiftly stab the blade through the thatched roof. A figure clothed in black crashed through the ceiling and fell to the floor dead.

Ninja! Carol had seen her share of action films. She ran for cover into the corner. A razor-edged shuriken streaked from nowhere across the room straight for her friend. He skillfully parried it to one side then, whirling the blade around, stabbed through the shoji wall behind him without turning. The paper grew red as blood soaked it. He pulled his sword back and another Ninja fell through the wall, his eyes glazed with death.

All fell quiet.

Carol shook. She stayed still, waiting to be told when to move. As she stared at the two dead Ninja on the floor, their bodies shimmered then disappeared. The house returned to the way it had been when they first entered. Her knees felt weak when she tried to stand. Her friend rushed to her side and helped her to her feet.

"Are you okay?"

"I'm fine, just wobbly."

His mouth curved in a sheepish grin. "I think we have the Entity's attention."

At those words, a cold chill brought all the horror back. Her friend vanished. Terrified at being left alone, she turned to see a warrior in full Japanese feudal armor appear in the corner. She knew she had been good bait.

The warrior laughed cruelly. "Carol, why are you here? Did you miss me?" His voice was cold, cruel. "I can't have you coming here without my permission." He peered at Carol through the slits in his helmet's mask. "Pity you had to defy me."

The warrior raised his arm and pointed at her. A tremendous wave of fear engulfed her. Carol could only cower in the corner as he came towards her. She knew he was going to kill her and she could do nothing to stop him. The air between them shimmered and her friend reappeared still in Samurai guise. He moved swiftly and smoothly as he brought his sword to bear on the advancing horror.

"Dr. Cameron," The Entity said calmly, lowering his arm. "I thought I recognized you. But I'm not ready for you yet." He raised his hand and made a dismissive gesture.

The Samurai image faded away and, exposed, Michel stood defenseless.

Carol screamed.

The Entity laughed at her. He disappeared as suddenly as he had appeared, leaving her and Michael alone in the teahouse.

Michael murmured, "I've never seen such...."

Carol was in shock. What had just happened? Where was she?

Michael touched her shoulder.

TWENTY-FOUR

INSTANTLY they were back in the protective circle in the doctor's library. Mr. Toga took a deep breath as he came out of his trance. Carol felt the barrier that kept her from knowing Michael lift.

Sarah ran over. "You guys okay?"

Carol and Michael slowly stood. He reached out and pulled Carol to him and held her tightly in his capable arms. Carol caught Sarah's frown.

Michael let go of her and led her to a chair. "I almost lost you. The Entity had protection shields so strong, I had trouble getting back through."

"Why didn't he just kill us? What do we do now?" Carol asked.

"I have enough proof to know that my theory is correct." He looked back at the protection circle.

"How come he said he wasn't ready for you yet?"

Michael murmured. "I have never experienced a mental force such as this."

"Okay, what do we do now?" Carol asked, realizing he wasn't listening to her.

He didn't answer.

Carol tried another question. "How did he know who you are?"

"He recognized you!" Sarah said in alarm. She looked at Toga for any reassurance. He came to her and put his arm around her.

Michael stepped to his desk. "I wonder…"

Carol raised her voice in frustration. "Doctor, how did he know who you were?"

"It should be impossible?"

Sarah stepped forward. "What's impossible? From where I stand there's a lot of impossible going on right here."

Sarah's words brought Michael back from his thoughts. He looked up. "I'm sorry. Our little trip was quite an eye opener."

Carol demanded, "Just tell us." Then added in a softer tone, "Please."

"There were occult masters thousands of years ago with incredible powers." He turned to Toga. "Perhaps we had better look into it. You know where to look in. I believe we have a tablet on powers of the Guardians. It will be in Babylonian."

As Toga hurried towards the stair leading to the upper level of the library, Michael continued to explain. "I could catch fragments of his thoughts but his power is so great I couldn't risk digging deeper into his mind."

Carol tried again. "What did he mean he wasn't ready for you yet?"

"Not sure. Can't be good"

Sarah leaned forward in her chair, deciding to try for an answer as well. "Dr. Cameron, how did he know who you were?"

He looked up. "If I'm correct we are facing a Guardian occult master. He would have seen through my disguise as though it wasn't there."

Sarah sat back. "This is getting out of control. What the hell is a Guardian?"

"At least I have more power than he bargained for. I was able to sense his immense hunger for something that would help him gain control." He suddenly stopped. "I picked up something else."

"What?" Carol asked, hoping it would be good news this time.

He asked urgently, "Who told you the stories about the candlestick?"

"A friend of mine, why?"

"What's his name?"

"Darren. Darren Campbell."

"Darren is part of all this somehow."

"That's not possible." Carol glared at Michael.

Sarah blurted, "I can't believe that."

"Do either of you really know him that well to be so sure?"

141

Carol stood. "No, I haven't known him a long time, but I think I would know if he'd...!" She turned and walked away from Michael. Her pride refused to believe Darren had just been using her.

"Please. What's wrong?" Michael asked with concern.

"You can't possibly believe Darren's a part of this!" Carol accused.

Sarah tried. "Why would he want to hurt Carol? He only offered to help us."

Michael frowned. "I only want to make sure we know who we're dealing with. Our lives depend on it. Darren may be on our side, but the fact he was on the Entity's mind makes me worry."

Carol whirled around. "Okay, I hear you. So, what do we do about it?"

Michael paled. "Please sit down. I need to show you something."

Carol did not like how Michael sounded. She slowly sat down. "You look like you're about to tell me some really bad news."

"I have a confession that you are not going to understand at first. I ask only that you bear with me as I explain."

Sarah leaned forward. "Get on with it! You're making me nervous."

"I took your candlestick." Michael reached into the drawer of his desk and removed the silver antique Carol thought was safe on her mantle. "If Darren had something to do with you finding it, he may have used it to help the Entity. I know a way to neutralize its power if it's been given any. If I'm wrong, nothing will happen."

"Nothing will," Sarah stated.

Michael looked at Carol. "You've been through a lot in a very short time..."

"Just stop there. You better know what you're doing! You make me suspicious. You stole that from me!" She felt her anger rise. Seeking help was supposed to make things better not worse! Darren had made things better. She didn't have nightmares when he was with her. This thought made her realize how suspicious that seemed now. Damn it all to Hell!

He looked at her. "I have reasons for taking the candlestick. I don't have time to explain now. We need to find the truth and this is the only way to know for sure."

"Fine. But I don't have to like it."

Toga walked over and handed Michael the Babylonian tablet he'd asked for.

"We need to perform a cleansing ritual. See if we have what we need." Michael ran his hand through his hair.

Toga nodded. "I'll get what we need."

Carol just sat, too stunned to even think.

In minutes, Toga returned, his arms full of cloth bags, candles and a bowl, a sword. Michael and Toga began to arrange the table that stood behind Michael's desk.

Sarah came up to Carol. "It'll be okay. You'll see. Darren's innocent."

"I'm going crazy!" Carol whispered, not wanting Michael to hear her. She hoped he wouldn't eaves drop on her mind. "What if Darren's in on this?" Tears threatened. "He'd better be on our side. And the doctor had better have a very good reason for taking my candlestick."

Sarah tried logic. "Hang in there until we know for sure, okay?"

Carol took a long shuddering breath and sat straighter, she could only nod.

"Let's see what their up to," Sarah held out her hand to Carol. "Don't know about you, but I want to see how there're going to do this."

Sarah and Carol brought their chairs nearer to the square table that had served as a reading area behind Michael's desk; its surface now cleared of books and papers. They watched as Michael and Toga arranged items on the table. Carol felt a charge in the air that increased as the simple arrangement became complete. Four tall white candles were placed, one at the middle edge of each of the four sides and a large crystal bowl sat in the center of the table. After filling a censor with incense, water was poured into the bowl. As Toga added pinches of various powders from the cloth bags, the water sizzled or turned red or blue after each ingredient before clearing again. Carol could see the yellowed and elaborately illustrated labels on the bags. They all seemed to be written in a variety of languages, mostly either Asian characters or Celtic runes.

Sarah fidgeted. "Doctor, can you explain what you're going to do?"

Michael straightened. "We will be cleansing the candlestick of any elements that are not inherent to its original state. If foreign elements are found, we will know who put them there."

Sarah frowned. "But how? All you have are some candles and a bowl of some weird herbs. And, if there's something in the candlestick, how will you know it was Darren who put them there?"

Michael smiled. "Toga and I know how to use the chemical properties of these herbs, as you call them. You'll see."

Sarah looked at Carol with more questions in her eyes. Carol tried. "Perhaps you could explain how you use the powders or what you are going to do with them."

"Toga and I will be using both chemical infusions and verbal chanting or vibrations to induce the elements that are unnatural to the candlestick into the atmosphere where they will dissipate and become harmless. There will be a signature essence that will be released with the foreign elements that will tell us who put them into the candlestick. It's hard to explain. This kind of science is not taught in school, so you may find it all very unusual, but I assure you, it's very effective."

After putting in the last candle, Michael straightened. "Toga and I ask that you remain silent until we have finished." Michael raised his hand and the lights dimmed.

"How did he do that?" Sarah whispered.

Frowning Carol shook her head and motioned for Sarah to be quiet.

Sarah shrugged, embarrassed that she had spoken just after being told expressly not to.

Michael immersed Carol's candlestick into the crystal bowl of empowered water. Toga snapped his fingers and the incense in the censer lit; fragrant smoke filled the room as he swung it over the table three times.

Carol wanted to scoff. This looked like magic that only happened in the movies. But she had seen a lot of incredible things so far and she could feel the effects of the incense in the room. The air grew thicker, warmer and somehow infused with an intelligence of its own. It reminded her of what she felt from Briar Cliff Canyon.

Michael stood at one side, Toga the other. They both took deep breaths and their figures began to glow with a subtle golden light that grew stronger with each breath. Touching their foreheads they both chanted, "Atoh."

The deep tones of their voices pulled Carol into the ritual.

The men put their hands on their chests chanting, "Malkuth."

The notes filled Carol with well-being.

Both men touched their right shoulders and chanted, "ve-Gevurah."

Carol became entranced.

Michael and Toga touched their left shoulders chanting, "ve-Gedulah."

Carol felt the vibration in her very core.

Toga swung the censer over the table again. Carol breathed in the scent of perfumed earth with delight. Her senses became fine-tuned, completely absorbed in what was happening before her.

Michael made a circular motion over the nearest white candle. At first there was a trickle of smoke then the wick flared with flame. Toga continued to swing the censer over the table.

Michael turned towards the east. He picked up the sword and drew a five pointed star in the air.

As he pointed at the pentagram he chanted. "Yod-Hah-Vahv-Heh."

His voice sounded so beautiful to Carol's ears, she felt a growing awe in her chest.

Michael turned to the south. Again the candle lit with a wave of his hand and again he drew the pentagram, keeping his hand pointed at it chanting, "A-Don-Nai."

Michael lit the candle and made the pentagram after turning west, chanting, "Eh-Heh-Yeh."

Again for the north, "Ah-Glah,"

Carol held her breath as she watched the silver candlestick begin to glow red in the watery mixture. The air became charged with power she knew came from the bowl.

"You cannot do this." The guttural rasp came from the candlestick.

Carol looked at Michael then Toga to see if they had heard too. Michael nodded to Toga and they both turned back to face east. They

145

extended their arms out from their sides and recited together, "Before me, Raphael. Behind me, Gabriel. On my right hand, Michael. On my left hand, Ariel."

The candlestick began to glow a hotter red and the water in the crystal bowl began to boil.

"For about us flaming the Pentagram." The men proclaimed. The golden aura around them became tinged with purple.

The candlestick roiled violently in the water.

Michael and Toga continued, "In the Column of the Six-rayed Splendor." Their auras were now totally purple hued.

The candlestick stopped moving. "You shall not remove me!"

It was Darren's voice.

Carol stood. Anxiety tensing her body.

Michael and Toga turned and pointed at the candlestick. Michael yelled, "Pure and impure, inner and outer, soul and body. Cleanse the evil. Bring the light. Go! Or be cast into utter darkness."

The candlestick rocked back and forth.

"Go, or be drowned in the watery abyss. Go, or be burned in the fiery pit."

A blue light emanated from the water, weaving its glow around the candlestick.

"Go, or be ripped by the whirlwind of eternity."

The blue light erupted like a beacon and leapt to the ceiling with a roar. The candlestick screamed as though in excruciating pain. Complete silence fell. Carol looked at the candlestick lying still in the water. No longer glowing red, it remained quiet.

Carol barely heard Toga thank the powers they had called and end the ritual.

"They're wizards." Carol whispered. She had seen it with her own eyes. Then she glared at the candlestick.

Sarah looked at her oddly.

Toga placed his hands over the candlestick. "It is pure." He extinguished the four candles. "Go with peace." He finished.

Michael waved his hand and the lights in the room brightened.

Anger consumed Carol. Her stomach lurched. She began to pace. "So, Darren deceived us!" she blurted. "Bastard! Why didn't I see it? I've seen ever dirty trick in the book! And I had to jump in bed with him. How stupid was that? He was sooo perfect! Creep!"

She glared at Michael. "Okay, you were right! I hope you're satisfied! Damn, I'm such an idiot!"

Michael looked alarmed. "Be calm. Let's think about this."

Carol grabbed a deep breath and tried to calm herself. "I'm sorry. I'm just so angry!" She couldn't keep control. Tears came. "Nothing is right anymore. Nothing! Why is this happening to me? What did I do to piss off the Universe? Why can't I have my life back the way it was?" Carol abruptly turned and stormed out of the library.

"Carol!" Sarah shouted.

Carol felt a hand on her arm and whirled around, furious that someone had stopped her attempt to escape from Hell. "Let me go!" She wrenched her arm free.

Michael pulled his hand back. "Please stay," he said calmly, looking into her eyes with a tenderness that tried to break through her rage.

"Why?" she snapped.

"I need you."

"I'm useless. I can't even take care of myself!"

"Come with me. I'm still your doctor." His hand gently reached for her forearm. Warmth spread from his touch and Carol walked with Michael into the Solarium. He motioned for her to sit at the table.

"Let me help," his voice still calm.

"How?"

"Tell me what you feel."

"I feel broken. Betrayed. Stupid."

"Have I betrayed you?"

"Yes. No. I don't trust anyone."

"What don't you trust?"

Carol struggled. "Men. No, more than that. I don't trust myself. I let myself be betrayed!"

"I think that's what makes you so angry. You blame yourself more than Darren or me for that matter."

"I swore I'd never let a man fool me like this!"

"Carol you're in the middle of a new world you don't understand."

"Then I'd better start learning and fast. My nightmares started all this. We're risking our lives all because I'm a victim of this damned Entity. Now I've been a victim of Darren too!" She wiped the tears from her face. "Teach me," she begged. "Show me how to end this!"

"You have to trust me."

"Fine! But let's start by not pretending anymore. You know I have feelings for you from the time at the lake in the other dimension."

"Yes."

"I'm not sure I should trust you on that level." Carol stood and started to pace.

"What do you want?"

"Tell me the truth. Who are you? How do you know all this ...stuff?"

"You're not ready to know."

"Damn it! How do you expect me to trust you?"

"Have I misled you so far?"

Carol whirled around. "How would I know?"

"You're right. Search your feelings. I was as open to you in the other dimension as you were to me. You've been my patient and now you are becoming my friend, more than a friend. I could never hurt you."

"God, you're frustrating. You want me to accept you on faith alone. That's not enough. Haven't you heard anything I said?"

Michael lowered his head. Carol felt an incredible wave of sadness descend upon her. Michael spoke without raising his head. "I heard you. I understand. I will do everything in my power to earn your trust."

Michael raised his head and looked at her, his gaze steady, but his blue eyes held the sadness she had felt. His jaw was set and strong as though that alone could make her understand he spoke the absolute truth.

Carol felt it to her core, but she could not relinquish the specter of distrust. She sat back down. "Then teach me. Show me how to stop him. Let me be a part of this fight."

He reached for her hand. She did not pull away. His hand was warm and reassuring. "You are stronger than your past. You are able to deal with waiting."

"Answer me. Will you teach me more?"

"Yes, it has been my hope to teach you about all this since I brought you here."

Carol wanted to believe him.

"Shall we go back to the library?" he asked. "I think our friends are wondering what happened."

Carol knew she could get nothing more from Michael. She nodded.

When they stepped through the library door, Sarah rushed to Carol. "Are you all right? I've never seen you so angry."

Carol took Sarah aside. "I'm calming down."

Sarah's eyes narrowed. "But…"

"I'm struggling to trust anything right now."

"What happened to you?"

Carol's eyebrows knitted. "The candlestick. You saw it release the foreign element. Darren betrayed us."

"I heard you say that before you stormed out, but I saw nothing happen to the candlestick."

"What?"

"I saw them mumbling something I couldn't understand. Oh, and the lights dimmed. Didn't see how that would help anything, but if it's what you're supposed to do, I guess…" Sarah shrugged.

"That's all you saw? You didn't see the candlestick fight back?"

"No." Sarah frowned.

"I don't understand why you didn't see what I did."

"What'd I miss?" Sarah demanded.

"The candlestick struggled until the element was pulled out of it by what Michael and Toga were chanting. And the powder they put in the water."

Sarah looked at Carol stunned. "So Darren isn't a good guy?"

"No."

"I really thought he was great, perfect for you! God, I encouraged you."

"We both fell for his act."

"I understand why you're angry. Damn, what an idiot I am. I should have known. Lord, I feel awful!" Sarah turned away.

Carol felt the sting of Darren's betrayal all over again and struggled to stop the anger that began to rise. "At least we know. That's good. We could have lost any chance of stopping the Controller."

"But why didn't I see what you saw?" There were tears in Sarah's eyes.

"I don't know. Maybe my experience with traveling on the other dimension caused me to see it? There are a lot of things I have no answer for. Michael promised to teach me more. Sarah, I'm determined to find out as much as possible. I'm through being a victim!"

Sarah only nodded. She wiped away her tears. "I'm with you."

Carol and Sarah headed toward Michael and Toga who were clearing the table of the candles from the ritual. Michael smiled shyly as they approached. He gestured towards the candlestick. "You can have your piece of Hollywood history back tomorrow. It has to stay in the mixture overnight."

Carol sneered, "You can keep it. I never want to see it again."

His eyes narrowed. "As you wish."

"What can we do to help?" Carol asked.

Standing beside Carol, Sarah nodded her need to help as well.

"You have courage, both of you, but not the skill or knowledge to fight. You must remain here where it is safe." His eyes held such deep sadness it surprised Carol. "Until there is time to teach you more."

Carol was tired of being pushed aside. "Why can't you teach us now? Give us books, something that will allow us to be part of this."

"You need to understand I must go alone. Today. There is no time for lessons until I come back. I need to stop the Entity now." His eyes pleaded with them. "You can help best by doing only what Toga and I ask."

Sarah became alarmed. "Doctor, are you ready to fight him so soon?"

"I have many ways to fight. I am determined to stop this."

"You're sure there is nothing we can do now?" Carol asked just as determined.

"I'm sure. I almost lost you in the Tea House, I won't lose you again." When he saw that Carol was going to object, he continued. "With his immense power, I'm sure this Entity, is one of the Ancients, probably a Guardian. He must have reincarnated from the beginning of time. It will take someone with great skill to stop him." He took a breath, frowning, talking more to himself than Carol or Sarah. "He's very close to trying his skills earthbound."

Carol felt anxious about Michael's safety. "You're sure of this? If he's so powerful, why are you the only one strong enough to fight him?"

"Remember I faced him both in your nightmare and in the tea house. He was not able to stop me."

"I suppose I have to wait for a real answer until you return?" Carol didn't like that he felt she wasn't ready.

Michael nodded, his mouth a tight line. This did nothing to soothe Carol's anxiety and frustration. She understood him not wanting to put her in danger, but it rankled just the same.

Sarah put her hand on Carol's shoulder. "Let's help where we can," she offered. "Maybe something will come up." She frowned at Michael. "Wish I had a magic wand. I'd fix us up in an instant."

Michael turned to Toga. "Where's that tablet on ancient power?"

Carol found a stool under a pile of books and sat near the fireplace keeping a lid on her anger and listening to what the doctor and Toga would say as they worked. Sarah started stacking the books Carol had taken off her stool, just for something to do. Absentmindedly Carol noticed how ancient some of the volumes were, their vellum bindings yellowed and cracked. A stack of parchment scrolls stuck out from the shelf next to her. They looked original.

Carol had a thought. "Sarah, did Toga show you any books that might help us understand things better?"

Although Michael couldn't possibly have heard her, he stopped and looked in her direction.

"I think Michael's reading my mind."

"That's just rude." Sarah glared at the doctor.

"Yeah, if he wants me to trust him, he'd better cut it out." Carol said without raising her voice then stared right at him.

Michael turned back to Toga who had just brought him the tablet on Ancients from the desk. Carol assumed he had 'heard' her.

She forced her thinking toward the battle ahead. She vowed not to let her guard down until this was over.

Michael looked up. "Toga, we still need a stronger protection circle." He turned to Carol and Sarah. "Our circle almost failed this last trip."

Toga asked, "What about H. Cornelius treatise on crystal skulls?"

Carol realized they were trying to teach them something before Michael left.

Michael nodded to Toga then continued explaining. "The Entity's course of action could actually tip the balance of nature so far as to completely destroy it." Michael put down the tablet and picked up a book. He slammed it shut. "He's a fool in spite of all his knowledge and power! If he destroys the balance, all is destroyed. No one is above natural law!"

Michael asked Carol for the scrolls next to her and she brought them to him. Curious, she glanced at the tablet he'd been reading thinking it must have the information that led to his conclusions. It was in an ancient, she assumed, dead language. Her hopes of reading it vanished.

"What would make the Entity think he's above the laws of Nature?" she asked.

"I honestly don't know. Yet."

"Please tell us you have something up your sleeve."

Sarah moved closer. "Yeah, I'm beginning to worry you might not be powerful enough to stop him."

"I think the fact that I have discovered he's a Guardian will help even the scales." He rubbed his neck. He looked tired. "I have a crystal that will help strengthen the circle. It's in my safe. Be back in a moment."

Waiting for Michael to return, Carol slid a book back into place on a high shelf. The lights flickered and a sharp, cold blast shrieked through the room. The library plunged into darkness except for the fire in the fireplace. Carol froze, Toga hurried down from the ladder and came to stand ready beside her. Sarah hurried over to join them.

TWENTY-FIVE

THE FIRE in the fireplace swelled as if enraged. In the sudden brightness, Carol caught movement in the far corner. Concentrating, she heard a faint rustling sound. Mr. Toga ran to the dais and put himself between the sound and the protection circle. A loud sharp hiss escaped from the corner and Carol heard something slither towards Toga.

"Toga, watch out!" Sarah screamed.

Carol and Sarah ran to Toga. Something hissed again. The fire in the fireplace erupted, casting a hellish glow around the room.

Carol saw the monster. The size of a bull buffalo, its movements proved quick and agile. Its green polished scales reflected the light from the flames as it swayed its pointed snout from side-to-side like a huge snake. It shoved its way past a shelf and stopped a short distance from them. Its long forked tongue slithered in and out of its mouth and, with a malicious glint, it glared at Toga. Shadows made the beast even more hideous as its tail whipped and curled, sending books skittering across the room.

Carol grew anxious. Where was Michael? She took a step towards the door. Toga motioned for her to stop. The monster struck with blinding speed. It snatched Toga's shoulder in its crushing jaws. Blood spread through Toga's shirt. He fought to break the hold but the creature tossed him across the room. He lay still in a crumpled heap against the leg of Michael's desk.

Sarah stepped forward, threw a book at the monster then rushed to Toga's side.

Carol screamed, "Michael!" The creature started towards her. "Get out! Go back to Hell!"

153

Carol backed away from the serpentine monster until her back hit the wall to the left of the dais. It eyed her cautiously, then rushed past and headed straight for the protection circle. Carol swore. It was after the circle, not them!

"Stop!" she screamed as if that could work.

It stopped. Carol saw why. Michael stood silhouetted in the doorway. At the edge of the circle, the beast turned its ugly head and hissed at him.

Michael raised his arms and lowered his head, chanting in a hoarse whisper. Carol could not understand the language, but it seemed to be affecting the beast. Ducking behind an overturned table, she watched.

The monster moved to step into the circle. The doctor lowered one hand, pointed it towards the beast. It erupted into flame. Its hideous screams chilled Carol's blood as it burned, evaporated before her eyes.

The room returned to normal. The fire crackled sedately in the fireplace. Books remained on the shelves. No sign of a fight anywhere. Except Toga. Carol rushed to his still form, his face pale and gray, his shoulder badly gashed by the beast's teeth. Sarah held him, tears flowing down her cheeks. Michael knelt beside his friend.

"Let's get him to a more comfortable place." Michael reached down and gently lifted Toga. He carried him into the living room.

As Toga lay on the couch, his eyes closed in pain, Michael inspected his wounds. "Sarah you'll find bandages and some salve in a bottle with a brown label in the kitchen cabinet next to the stove."

Carol watched Michael wash Toga's wounds carefully. He then touched his friend's shoulder and murmured something. Carol figured it was another spell.

"This is my fault," Carol said.

Toga shook his head and Michael calmed him. "Please, just lay back and rest."

Sarah brought the bandages and salve to Michael.

As he applied the salve to Toga's wounds, he spoke to Carol. "You did what you thought was right." Michael reassured her. "Mr. Toga can heal himself better than anything we can do for him now. Given a little time, he will be able to protect the circle again." He stood to allow Toga to get more comfortable.

"But…." Carol didn't want him to dismiss her responsibility for Toga's injuries. Why did he patronize her?

"Please." Michael looked down at Carol's tear streaked face. "It's not anyone's fault. You don't understand most of this yet. I don't have the time I want to teach you. I'm as frustrated by all this as you are." He ran his hand through his long hair. Hesitantly, he held out his arms, begging her understanding, seeking to comfort her as well as himself.

This time, she stepped into his arms. Her anger and fear subsided. She would learn. And she would help when she knew more.

Michael said quietly to Sarah, "Can you watch over Toga until he is ready to protect the circle? Carol and I will be in the library."

"We'll be fine," Sarah's voice sounded worried. She turned to Carol. "Now that time, I saw what happened. Didn't like it!"

Michael released Carol and looked at her tenderly. "Thank you for understanding."

She managed a smile. He had made her understand. She should be thanking him.

Back in the library, Michael paced back and forth. He looked at Carol who sat on the stool next to the bookcase. "Sorry, I'm not good at waiting."

"Can we do something while we wait?" Carol suggested.

"Bring me the tablet on Ancients. It should be on my desk."

As Carol walked towards the desk she asked, "Did you get the crystal you went to get?"

"Yes." He reached into his pocket and headed towards the protection circle. He placed the six inch clear crystal spire next to the large one already in the center then rechecked the circle.

"Michael, the tablet is gone! What are we going to do without it?"

"You sure?" He walked over to her. The tablet was nowhere to be found. "I think it proves that the Entity is a reincarnated Ancient power. That's all I really needed from the tablet. He destroyed it too late."

Carol's mind flooded with questions. "What really happened? How did that monster end up in your library? It had to come from the Entity, but how?"

"The ancient powers held the wisdom to bend and reshape the various dimensions at will. This Entity, this Ancient, must have that power."

"Sorry, you're going to have to explain that more."

"Bending and reshaping dimensions allow things from one dimension to cross over into another when they touch each other."

"So the creature was from another dimension." Carol felt overwhelmed. Her new world was becoming immense and complex beyond imagination.

"It's a shame we didn't have more time for lessons before now." Michael frowned.

"That's an understatement if I ever heard one. Look, you've made me realize just how powerful the Entity is. You're scaring me that you won't come back."

"I have a better chance than you may think." He looked at the dais. "The circle must still be a threat. He wouldn't have tried to destroy it otherwise. See, we're not powerless."

"That's not good enough. I need to know if you can win this fight. You're leaving as soon as Toga is ready, right?

"Yes."

She pleaded, "You can't fail. You have to come back. Please. Let me help you. There must be something even I can do."

"Bring me that red book over by the table."

Carol found that helping Michael find chants and symbols to aid him only a small comfort. With Toga in a weakened condition, could he really keep the circle safe while Michael fought?

Toga and Sarah appeared at the library door. Carol wasn't prepared for such a quick recovery. It had only been about three hours. Toga nodded to the doctor and slowly walked to his place in the circle. He held his arm stiffly to his side, but the color had returned to his face. As Toga sat, his mouth tightened in pain. Sarah sat beside him, winding her arm around his, giving him all her support and strength.

156

Toga closed his eyes falling into the deep trance he used to focus the protection from the circle they needed. Carol felt the room fill with energy and the air shimmered as though there was a barrier forming around the circle.

Michael hurriedly stepped to the center of the circle. Lying down, he turned and smiled at Carol before closing his eyes. "I'll be back before you know it."

She sensed his essence leaving his body. Without thinking, only feeling an urge so desperate it propelled her to action, she ran into the circle before the barrier was complete. Throwing her arms around Michael's body, her astral spirit was pulled along with his into the other dimension.

TWENTY-SIX

ROCKY and mountainous, the foreboding terrain stretched before her. *Heavy billowing clouds choked the sky, putting everything into a dim twilight. On the horizon Carol saw a huge red sun. Its sanguine glow cast a hideous light over the land, making the rocks and clouds appear bathed in blood.*

Carol saw Michael walking ahead of her. His clothes were entirely black, his belt decorated with some of the magic symbols she had helped him find.

As she followed, his voice came to her mind. "You shouldn't have come. I may not be able to protect you here. Perhaps the Fates intended it."

"All I know is I couldn't let you go alone."

He stopped but did not turn. "I love you with all my heart."

Carol felt his love deep in her soul. The power of it filled her heart as she watched Michael disappear down the trail. It gave her strength. She had no fear. Carol followed, finding it unbearable to be left behind. All doubt had disappeared. She loved him too. She would rather die with him than be left alone.

When she reached the top of the incline, Michael stood on the shore of an oily dead sea. The water, no more than sludge, barely moved. It lapped at the shore leaving slimy filth behind. The stench of death filled the air.

Angry clouds boiled. Lightning webbed the sky. It cracked and sizzled, striking at the sea, the sand, the rocks, coming ever closer to Michael. A glowing light emitted from his body. The lightning struck but could not touch him.

The thunder forced Carol to cower against the rocks, holding her ears, wishing she could become one of the stones to escape the deafening explosions.

The lightning stopped. Michael faltered. The sand beneath his feet shifted. He sank to his knees. Carol froze in alarm. The ground solidified, trapping him. He struggled for a moment, then stood still, crossing his arms over his chest.

She heard laughter, derisive, gloating laughter. The air in front of Michael shimmered and something began to take shape. It appeared manlike except that huge leathery wings arched from the shoulders of its dark naked body. Long black hair fell down its back and thick black fur covered its loins.

The creature hovered just above the sand. His great wings spread wide. "To what do we owe the honor of your visit?" Long sharp teeth glinted as it spoke with a grating voice.

It was not the Entity. Carol hoped the beast hadn't noticed her. She picked up a rock the size of a baseball and edged toward it from behind.

Michael glared at the creature. "Has your master sent his dog to fetch his prize?"

"He calls me Bocan. Be as arrogant as you wish, but you have met your superior in my Master. Of that I'm certain."

As Carol lifted her arm to hurl the rock, Bocan whirled to face her. She threw it with all her might. He dipped his wings, dodging the stone with irritating ease.

A powerful force grabbed Carol and pushed her roughly to the sand. She couldn't move and her throat was paralyzed. She stared in terror as the winged horror circled in the sky above her.

Michael dislodged himself from the ground. He chanted hoarsely and fiery stones flew from the ground toward Bocan. One seared a hole through a filthy wing before he could avoid the attack. Screaming in pain and rage, Bocan swooped at Michael who leaped into the air, grabbed the nearest wing tip and yanked hard. Returning to the sand, Michael braced for a counter attack.

Bocan, unable to control himself, rotated in the air, his wings snapping in bone-wrenching efforts to stop his uncontrolled spin. After an

159

ungraceful lurch, he hovered in midair, favoring his burnt wing. His angry bellow shook the ground, "I have finished playing games!"

The force that held Carol immobile let her go. She leapt to her feet as the beast made a motion with his clawed hand causing the air itself to thicken. Michael cringed and attempted to raise his arms. She saw a glowing green light surround his body. He froze. Horrified, Carol struggled toward Michael as fast as she could in the thickening air, reaching him only to watch Bocan lift him from her grasp. She stared after Michael's raising form, tears of frustration coursing down her checks.

"It's been an interesting game." The creature laughed. "Surprise. The Master gave me many powers. Now he wishes to meet you."

With a flick of his wrist, he sent Michael speeding through the air towards the mountains they had just come from. She could see a narrow ravine in the foothills. Bocan shimmered, then disappear.

If he could capture Michael so easily, she felt certain the Entity would kill him. Carol's mind whirled. Did Michael's capture mean that the protection circle had been destroyed?

A violent earthquake shook the ground and Carol fell to the sand. Instead of causing her to panic, it focused her. The odds were heavily against it, but she did not see any choice but one. Carol needed help to save Michael and Toga was the only one she could turn to. She prayed the circle had not been destroyed. Closing her eyes, Carol's astral self, slipped away.

TWENTY-SEVEN

CAROL opened her eyes, back in her own body. Shelving lay face down on the floor. Books were scattered everywhere. She did not recognize the pungent odor that filled the room. Toga still held his position above the circle, his face strained and ashen. Sarah lay on her back beside him, but breathing. The circle remained intact. She glanced at Michael's body. The thin blue thread of energy still connect his soul to his body.

Carol touched Toga's shoulder. He took a deep breath as he opened eyes. He winced in pain.

"Toga, we have to help Michael." She sat down beside him.

"I could see what happened. I will go back with you."

She reached for Sarah's hand. "Are you all right?"

Sarah struggled to sit up. She glanced at the doctor's body next to the crystal. "Carol. Where's Michael?"

"He's been captured. I came back for help."

Toga put his hand on Carol's shoulder. "We are the only ones who can help Michael."

Relief flooded Carol. Toga would help. "What about the circle?"

"They hit us here too; it has survived the attacks."

"You two go. I'll stay and do what I can to protect the circle." Sarah's lip tightened with determination.

"This will help you." Toga put his hands on either side of Sarah's head and closed his eyes.

Carol became alarmed at Sarah's blank expression. "What are you doing?"

"Transposing instructions directly to Sarah's mind to save time." He caressed Sarah's cheek.

Sarah's senses returned. She leaned forward and kissed him. "For luck."

Carol's eyes filled with tears. Both friends knew they might never see each other again.

Toga held Sarah. "If we fail, there will be nothing here on Earth to return to."

Sarah shrugged. "Of course. But I won't be here either. Got it." She sat in Toga's place at the top of the circle. "Ready," she announced. Taking one more look at Carol, her face a picture of calm sadness, she winked at her friend. "What's keeping you?" Carol and Toga lay down. Carol reached out her hand.

TWENTY-EIGHT

WITH THE LIFTING sensation she had experienced with Michael, Carol found herself facing the deeply shadowed ravine where Michael had been taken. Without hesitation Toga hurried into the dark opening, Carol close on his heels. As Toga ran she saw his clothing remold itself into a black Jiu Jitsu Gi and belt.

As her eyes adjusted to the dim light, she could see that the path cut through the mountain, at times so narrow it became more of a tunnel. The warm and stagnant air stank of sulfur. Carol's body tensed when she heard a rhythmic booming coming from the direction they headed.

The pathway, uneven and in places broken by narrow crevices too deep to contemplate, caused them to creep along carefully. Progress proved agonizingly slow, but the booming grew louder with each step. Carol followed Toga into an even narrower section. The ground shook, sending loose rock and small boulders careening from above. Slamming her back into the wall and throwing her hands over her head to avoid being crushed; she held her breath, hoping the sides of the ravine wouldn't slam together. It didn't last long, but Carol feared they would be buried alive or the path blocked before they reached their destination.

Toga turned. "I think the quake means the Entity has gained more power."

Carol knew that meant nature had slipped farther out of balance and everything could be destroyed at any moment. To her it only meant they should hurry. She struggled down the narrowing path behind Toga as fast as she could manage.

The ringing of small bells could be heard over the rhythmic beats. Nearing a turn, Toga motioned for Carol to remain while he peered around the corner. When he turned back, she could tell that he had seen something.

"There is a guard before a wooden gate that blocks the end of the ravine. I will shoot him," said Toga as a Japanese bow and arrows appeared in his hands.

Carol's brows rose in alarm, taken aback by Toga's cold blooded statement. She saw a new Toga. Capable, quick thinking and an able leader.

"We must find Michael quickly," he said.

Carol looked around the corner. What she saw made her knees buckle. The guard stood about eight feet tall, large and muscled like the wrestlers her landlady, Margarete, loved to watch on TV. His face looked as though someone had softened the flesh then tried to knead it back onto his skull.

Toga stepped out in front of her, bow raised. She fell back, turning in time to see the giant clutch at the arrow protruding from his throat before he fell heavily to the ground. His body disappeared. It was just like the tea house when the ninja attacked.

"Wow," she managed.

Toga acknowledged her with a nod then headed towards the tall wooden gates where the guard had stood. Carol followed.

He found a small door in one side of the gate and opened it slowly just a couple of inches. The sound of drumming flowed out in a wave of primitive passion. Peering through the slit, Carol saw a landscape pocked with holes filed with steaming mud, bubbling with sulfurous gases. The ground between them was dark red in places. Shades of yellow, brown and green dust joined the red making the arena a colorful though dangerous place to hold a ritual. It was hard to see clearly through the haze of steam but she could see many figures moving. Rocks both small and large littered the ground from the earthquake. The larger boulders prevented her from seeing some of the activity, but the figures were chanting with the drumming. Small bells, attached to their ankles, jangled as they moved to the rhythm.

Carol and Toga slipped into the arena. There were no guards inside the door. Crouching and using the boulders for cover, they approached the center. Carol managed to get five yards from the chanting mob. Toga kneeled behind a rock some four feet to her right. Together they peered around their boulders.

Gray robed people swayed. Their faces made grotesque by the terrible ecstasy that possessed them. The drums stopped and the chanters all turned. Carol looked to see seven beautiful women; each holding a silver chalice approach. She noticed at least five of the huge guards stationed around the perimeter, but they watched, engrossed in their ceremony. Carol could feel the power of the ritual building.

The seven women reached a wooden dais where Bocan stood and beside him a figure clothed in a white hooded robe. She could not see his face but she felt him. It was the Entity. She was in the other dimension now, she reminded herself, and she would be feeling vibrations and hearing thoughts. So would her enemies. The women, each in turn, handed Bocan their chalice. He poured the contents into a gleaming silver bowl. Leaning out a bit further Carol saw Michael. Her breath caught. Chained to a wooden post at the edge of the dais, his body and face were covered in festering wounds and sores. His eyes stared lifelessly into space.

Carol looked at Toga as he maneuvered over to her. He motioned for her to stay. She sensed he felt shaken but she took courage from his calmness. Was Michael still alive? Surely his body would have disappeared if so but what powers did The Entity have? Carol searched her senses but could not be certain. Wouldn't she feel his loss if he was dead? The knowledge that the Entity had not tipped the balance yet seemed a good indication. She and Toga were still here. They had to destroy the Entity. Whether Michael lived or not this task must be done. She watched Toga silently reach for an arrow. She concentrated on helping Toga's arrow fly straight.

"I know you are here, both of you. You are too late to stop me." The Entity's words came lazily, as out of boredom.

Bocan stepped forward and, spreading his leathery wings, launched himself into the steam filled air. He soared higher then smoothly glided into circling the area. It did not take him long to find them. His gloating laughter made Carol's blood freeze. He hovered, wings flapping to keep him steady as he pointed his finger in their direction.

165

Toga acted. The arrow he had intended for the Entity sped towards the winged horror just as Bocan launched a spear toward them. The arrow pierced Bocan's black heart as the spear left his hand. Carol leaped behind a rock. Toga dove to his left. Bocan screamed in agony, frantically plucking at the arrow in his chest. He stopped struggling. His wings folded. Bocan plunged to the ground. Carol could not watch him hit. The sound of the impact made her sick. She leaned weakly against the boulder, thankful that one enemy had been destroyed.

The deadly calm of the Entity's voice came again. "You leave me no choice."

Guards ran towards Toga and Carol with deadly intent. Toga armed his bow and stood to get a better shot. He fired five arrows in rapid succession but two of the guards were smart enough to dodge to one side the second Toga stood. The other three fell dead.

Carol moved farther back behind the boulder. Toga crouched beside her. She nodded. They both understood that the two remaining guards were still a threat.

Toga pulled a samurai sword from his belt and placed the handle into Carol's hands. "Wait here." He grabbed another arrow.

She nodded. Carefully she tried the balance of the blade as she watched Toga leave. Things were simple now. Stop the Entity. There could be no fear.

As Toga made his way toward the dais, Carol peered over her rock. The Entity seemed unconcerned that Toga had just killed three of his guards. He stood before the doctor's body and calmly conducted the ceremony as the chanters swayed in the sulfurous steam. The bubbling mud seemed on the verge of erupting. Carol glared at the tormentor who had caused her so much pain in her nightmares. How much pain was he causing Michael? She wanted to run up, yank the hood off his face and rip his eyes out!

Carol checked the scene. Toga had managed to reach a loose pile of rock to the left of the dais. She looked around, then cautiously hurried after him. As she approached, Toga armed his bow to try another shot at the Entity. Carol saw one of the surviving guards step out from behind the dais and raise his ax to throw at Toga. Carol ran at the giant guard.

Her blade entered his back with such ease that Carol did not realize it until the guard toppled over away from her. It seemed to happen so slowly. She heard nothing of the ritual as she gazed at the dead creature at her feet. It disappeared. Something dripped down her arm. When she looked blood ran off the blade then down her hand and arm. Part of her felt satisfied that she had saved Toga; the other part wanted to run away from the death she had caused. She watched Toga release his arrow but with a mere flick of his finger, the Entity destroyed it in midflight. He hadn't even looked in their direction.

Carol heard the doctor's voice.

"Keep distracting the Entity."

Startled, she glanced at Toga. He concentrated on the Entity. Had he heard? Could she be imagining things? She looked at Michael. Nothing had changed. But in her heart, she knew it had been real. Michael lived! Now their futile attacks had purpose.

"Michael's alive," she told Toga as she kneeled down beside him.

Toga's expression remained calm.

"He wants us to keep diverting the Entity's attention." Carol blurted, laughing wildly with relief. The sound of the drums and chants masked her voice.

"I only have three arrows left. I don't seem to have the power to create more. We need to find another way."

She wanted Michael to live. She wanted all the insanity to stop. There was no time to discuss a plan! The blood on her blade drove her to a level of madness she had never known. The pounding drums – the swaying chanters aggravated her. Their attempts to stop the Entity seemed so futile! Strength flowed into her body from the dark fury in her heart. She stood. Before Toga could stop her, she ran toward the chanters, yelling at the top of her lungs, swinging the sword over her head like a demon from Hell. Carol plunged her sword into the closest body. The blood fueled her frenzy. She wanted them all dead! Turning she saw another chanter and although he stared at her in horror and raised his arms to stop her, she viciously sliced through his body. The drums stopped. The chanting stopped. The dancing stopped. She didn't want them to stop, she wanted them to die. Screaming, she ran towards her next victim. Death, that's all she knew. Death and wanting to give Michael the time he needed to come back to her. She saw the Entity step forward, rage blazing in his eyes as he raised his arm to attack her.

"Carol! I am with you." Michael spoke in her mind.

Strength flowed into her and her mind began to reassert itself. She leapt to one side dodging the beam of power launched in her direction. She rolled to a standing position behind a boulder. The ground began to vibrate. The sound of rushing water dominated the world. A geyser erupted into a roaring column of boiling water that shot straight into the steamy sky. The Entity stepped back in surprise. As her eyes refocused, she turned and stared at Toga. He stared at the dais. Carol followed his gaze.

Michael opened his eyes. The chains fell from his body. He struggled to stand.

Carol commanded the Fates. Give him the strength to fight!

Michael stepped towards the Entity. Some of the chanters quailed at this sudden show of power from their victim. The rest turned to their master for instruction, but he turned his back to them.

Carol yelled, "He will not help you! He does not care for you! Help us stop him. Join us!"

The Entity bellowed his rage. "You shall not abandon me!" He raised his arms and a ball of red fire appeared. He sent it streaking toward his throng of followers. The chanters scattered. Those who were not killed outright fled to the gate but the Entity would not release them. Laughing, he made a slight gesture making the bubbling hot mud rise from its boiling bed, sending it towards those at the gate. The screams of the dying filled the air and the stench of burnt flesh was added to that of the sulfur.

Carol fell to her knees. All the fury to kill gone. Tears ran down her face as she reached towards the nearest wounded chanter. She died before Carol could help her.

The Entity laughed. "No one will stop me!"

Carol saw Michael extend his hand and a blue beam emanated from his palm. The Entity turned and his body radiated a white light that deflected the blue light away from him. Whirling, his hood fell from his head and Carol caught a brief glance of pale skin and colorless eyes before the

Entity jumped from the dais and ran into the flat land beyond. Michael ran after him. Toga yelled for Carol to follow him and together they hurried after Michael.

Before Carol took two steps a huge hand grabbed her by the neck and yanked her off her feet. Toga whirled around at her cry of alarm as the last remaining guard's ax rose to strike. Carol struggled, she had dropped her sword when he grabbed her. An arrow appeared in the guard's chest and the weight of his own ax tipped him over backwards, dragging Carol with him. She struggled out of his grasp.

"That makes us one for one." She smiled her thanks.

Toga acknowledged with a nod and grasped her hand to help her stand.

Carol and Toga reached the dais. Toga put his back to its side and peered beyond. He motioned for her to follow as he rushed in the direction the Entity ran. Rounding an outcrop of rock, they found themselves in an area honeycombed with lava formations from long past eruptions, and mountains that thrust upward from a long ago quake. The stones stood as sentinels in a semicircle around the mud flats. The ground shook again and another geyser erupted to their right. They dived for cover from the boiling water. This one lasted longer. When they stood to look, Michael and the Entity were fighting hand to hand at the edge of a nearby outcrop.

Toga raised his bow but could not get a clear shot. The two struggling bodies parted. The Entity raised his arms to attack Michael, who staggered a bit but stood to meet the onslaught. Toga quickly brought his bow to bear but as he released the arrow another quake shook the ground and his shaft flew wild. Carol and Toga were thrown violently to the ground. Rocks pelted them. Some of the ground collapsed and many of the mud holes merged. Their boiling contents angrily surging together.

Beams of power snaked from the Entity's palms to blast Michael, who fell to his knees. As Michael struggled to regain his footing. The Entity grabbed him by the arms and began dragging him to the edge of the outcrop which now overlooked the steaming mud. Michael struggled but could not break the hold.

Toga regained his footing and quickly rearmed his bow with his last arrow. Carol sensed that he had made a decision to shoot Michael if necessary in order to kill the Entity. She could not allow this. She had to do something fast. She could not bear losing Michael now.

An intense aftershock hit, making it impossible for Toga to shoot. It took all Carol had to stand, but running, stumbling, crawling; she clawed her way towards the fighting bodies in spite of the heaving rock under her feet. The noise of grinding stone deafened her. Small geysers erupted all around her. Her determination to save Michael burned in her. Using every ounce of energy she possessed, Carol reached the Entity. With the strength of all her anger and frustration, she shoved him. He let go of Michael and looked at her surprised. Carol, too drained to move, watched the Entity's arm rise. A hand grabbed her arm and yanked her off her feet as the energy beam shattered the stone where she had stood. Carol fell, realizing Michael had saved her. Rocks rained down from the mountains as another quake reached a higher pitch. Huge cracks spilt the steaming land.

The Entity raised his arms yet again for the final blow. An arrow appeared between his eyes. His face slackened. He just stared at Carol and Michael with eyes that could not see. The edge of the outcrop collapsed. As the Entity's body fell with the rock, the quake stopped. A cold wind roared through the ravaged land. Rubble continued to fall as Nature reasserted itself.

Carol and Michael ran from the remaining section of outcrop as it too began to crumble. Toga rushed over and together they helped each other hurry back to the gate. All became silent. Balance had been restored.

Reaching the gate they paused to catch a breath. The battle had taken a tremendous toll. No sign of guards or chanters remained. Michael flopped against a boulder and Carol kneeled wearily in front of him while Toga leaned on the gate next to Michael.

Michael's voice sounded rough and weary. "We make one hell of a team."

Carol stood and threw her arms around Michael's neck. Then she hugged Toga. He stiffened, but she didn't care.

"We won!" she shouted. "We stopped him!" She laughed, exhausted but ecstatic.

Michael and Toga joined hands then reached for Carol's.

Instantly they were lying inside the magic circle in the warm security of the library. They stood and grinned at each other.

TWENTY-NINE

SARAH leaped to her feet the moment life returned to the three bodies on the floor. Rushing to them, she sputtered. "Are we safe? What happened? You only left a moment ago! Are you all okay?"

Michael gathered Carol into his arms and kissed her. She returned his deep kiss, responding to how vital he seemed to her now. It felt wonderful to be in his arms.

"Will somebody talk to me!" Sarah yelled.

Michael released Carol and she hugged her friend. "Give us a moment. We'll tell you everything."

Sarah frowned. She moved to Toga's side and took his hand. He reached for her and held her close for a moment.

Michael stepped beside Carol and she willingly went back into his arms. "You!" he laughed, "were the biggest surprise of all."

Carol nuzzled into his shoulder. They were back. They were alive. Her love for Michael flowed through her bringing a contentment she had never known. She didn't want to leave his arms ever again. She didn't want to think. She didn't want to remember the horror.

Michael's voice was kind. "That was a fool hardy stunt, pushing the Entity like that."

"I couldn't lose you."

He caressed her cheek. "Now you know how I feel about you."

Michael released her and took her hand leading her to his desk. "I know this is the last thing anyone wants to do, but we need to discuss what just happened."

Sarah nodded and sat down. Carol's mind fled to her murderous rage and the killing of the chanters. How could she live with herself?

She must have looked horrified, because Michael helped her sit down then kneeled before her.

"I know what you are thinking. Don't punish yourself."

She interrupted him, "But I slaughtered two people! Two un-armed…" She burst into tears.

Sarah was horrified. "What? Carol, that's not possible!"

"No it isn't," Michael added. "Carol, listen to me. Remember our time on the plane? Places, people, things are created by the mind of the person there. Your spirit experiences the other dimension not your body."

Carol still felt miserable. "But you don't understand. I was furious; out of control. I just killed them without mercy. I would have killed them all if you hadn't come to."

"I understand. I can help you through this. You need to know that all you did was send those chanters back to their bodies. You did not actually kill them."

"What?" The information slowly sank in but it did not release her from the realization that she had every intention of truly killing them.

"You have discovered something about yourself that is not in line with who you thought you were." Michael reached for her hand. "It can make you stronger." He offered.

"Stronger! Why…Oh God! We're not done yet!"

"No." He released her hand. "We must find the Guardian's physical body here on earth and see that he is stopped from ever being in the astral dimension again."

Sarah started. "You mean we have to do all this again?"

"This battle was always twofold. We had to get as much knowledge and experience as possible then weaken his hold on the plane." Michael saw Sarah's shocked face. "Yes, we have another battle to fight here on Earth that will stop him forever."

"How do we find him?" Sarah asked quietly, then added, "Was he Darren?"

Michael sat at his desk. "I caught a certain vibration from him in spite of all his protection. That should give us a clue." Then, he an-swered her second question. "No, the Entity is not Darren."

"Then he was helping the Entity." Carol stated flatly.

Toga leaned forward. "He might be a lead, if we can find him."

Sarah frowned. "You're sure Darren's part of all this?"

Toga nodded.

Carol lowered her eyes. "It's so obvious now. The coincidence of meeting him twice in two days, the ease of finding and buying the candlestick—"

Michael stopped her. "We need to find him. We don't know what part he plays in all this. I'm afraid we don't have much time to celebrate our victory."

Sarah stood. "I'm ready. Let's track him down."

The doctor smiled wearily. "If you still have some energy, please feel free. We need to talk to Mr. Darren Campbell."

Sarah nodded. "Got a little left in me."

Carol suddenly remembered. "His card is in my purse."

Sarah left to get Darren's card.

Michael stood and reached for Carol's hand. A sensation spread through her body. It brought peace. "We need to talk in private before we make any more plans about the Entity."

Carol couldn't read Michael's face. She followed him to the library table where the candlestick shone at the bottom of the bowl.

"You must remove the candlestick," he said handing her the towel that still lay on the table.

Carol carefully removed the silver antique and dried it.

"Now that it's been purified, it can be used for the purpose it was intended."

Carol gave him a quizzical look. "This candlestick is more than Darren's device?"

"Follow me." He headed towards the solarium.

She glanced at the candlestick as she followed him. It still had a brilliant shine in spite of its time in the herbal brew. She almost dropped it when the snakes on the bottom started to slowly move. She whipped the towel over the piece and hurried after Michael careful to hold the candlestick by the top away from the snakes. "They're not real. They're not real," she mumbled.

Michael motioned for her to have a seat at the breakfast table next to the fountain. The full moon was rising over the hills in back of the house, its light giving the solarium a soft other worldly glow.

He sat across from her. "Please place the candlestick on the table." His eyes held his love for her. "The time has come to explain what is happening to you."

"Will this be complicated like the other dimension?"

"I hope it will be enlightening. I promise to make this as easy as possible." He smiled.

She glanced out the window. The moonlight caressed her with its radiance. She felt its power seep into her weary bones. She was not sure if she wanted to hear what Michael was about to tell her. "Will it help?"

He nodded. "You seem able to accept that the Entity is the reincarnation of a magical ancient being, a Guardian."

"There wasn't much time to think about it, but, yeah, I can accept that." She looked at him with a puzzled expression. "I even understand on a deeper level what you told me about all of this being as natural, as normal as life itself."

Michael bit his lip. He gazed intently, lovingly at her. "Carol you are also a reincarnated ancient soul." His eyes became anxious.

"What? Like the Entity!"

Michael's voice soothed. "Yes. I know this is a shock.

She took a deep breath trying to clear her spinning mind. "What does this all mean? How can I be like him?"

"You are better than him. Think a moment. I know you're beginning to see magic as you call it. You were a very capable fighter against the Entity. Being adept on the other dimension has come so easily to you."

"Why don't I..."

"...know you're reincarnated?" He finished for her.

"I'll start with that."

"Remember what you said under hypnosis in my office?

The memory flooded back. "The Master Spirits telling me I had lived many times before?"

"Yes, but the ability to remember them had been taken away from you." Michael reached for her hand.

Carol took his hand to keep her anxiety down. "What does all this mean?"

"First, are you up for another leap of faith?"

She managed to nod. She held her breath.

"I've been reincarnated many times just as you have. I can remember all my past lives. The only thing that can interfere with this process is suffering a violent death at the hands of another like yourself."

"Is that what happened to me?"

"Yes. You were murdered."

"How do you know all this?" Fear chilled her.

"You died in my arms."

"Oh God!" She trembled, visualizing how horrible it must have been for him. It did not feel like he was talking about her exactly, although deep inside she knew he was. "But if I can't remember anything. I don't see how this helps anything."

"As you died, I placed what I could of your past life memories in a device created for this purpose." He tried to smile. "The device is that candlestick."

Carol's heart began to beat hard. She stared at the candlestick. "I'm confused. If you could do that why didn't you keep the candlestick? Why didn't you protect me?"

"I found you dying too late to save you. Then the candlestick was stolen from me."

Carol's frowned. "Why a candlestick?"

"It was to keep the device a secret. Hidden so no one knew what it really was. The candlestick was your idea."

"What?"

Michael slowly closed his eyes. "We have been together since the beginning of time, always rejoining after reincarnation to start another life together. I have been waiting for you for a very long time."

Carol just stared at him in shock. She lowered her head. So this was why she felt for him so deeply. Tears filled her eyes.

He opened his eyes, his voice lowered. "I've searched the world and never found the device until the day I walked into your bungalow and saw it sitting on your mantle." His voice broke. "You have no idea how hard it was for me to remain calm as I picked it up and felt your essence caress my hand. I had to take it."

He stood and came around the table. She felt him wanting her to reach out to him. Fear shadowed his expression. Was it of rejection? She stood, opened her hand, and touched his chest. Her breath caught in her throat. A surge of longing so strong came from Michael, she gasped. There was a connection. There was truth. There was trust. She felt on the brink of being complete. The emptiness inside her begged for it.

Tears flowed down Carol's cheeks. "Make me whole again," she whispered.

Michael held her close. "I'm so lost without you." He kissed her.

Carol returned his kiss as fiercely as it was given.

He let go of her. "Come."

THIRTY

MICHAEL took her hand and led her to a door at the back of the solarium. Carol clutched the candlestick firmly in her other hand as they stepped outside. The full moon revealed a little garden of roses and ivy that butted up against the hillside behind the house. The air was charged with power that tingled over her skin.

Michael walked straight up to the ivy-covered hillside and reached through the greenery. A small wooden door opened and, ducking a bit, Michael walked through it, motioning for her to follow. Just inside, he pulled down an oil lamp and matches from a niche in the wall. Lighting the lamp he held it high.

Carol could see a tunnel disappearing off into the hillside, the ceiling tall enough for Michael to stand upright. She followed him. It was so quiet, so calm. A sense that the very hill was alive and aware of them, came to her. Awe filled her heart.

The sound of dripping water teased her curiosity as they made a turn in the tunnel. She gasped at its beauty when Michael's lamp lit the grotto around the bend. The walls were pure crystalline quartz. The floor cradled a small pond that received water from the underground spring that flowed from the ceiling down one wall. Moss covered the crystal beneath its gentle flow. The grotto became lighter than the lamp alone could illuminate. Looking up she saw a hole in the top of the grotto about four feet across. The moon had reached the sky just above the opening and its light filtered down, dust motes floating in the pale light. An altar constructed of pure silver stood next to the pond. The moonlight glinted off the surface, the cold light dancing as if alive.

Michael took her by the hand and led her to the other side of the grotto. Setting the lamp down on the altar, he reached for the candlestick. Trembling with anticipation, she gave it to him. He raised it into the air as though showing the candlestick to the spring flowing down the wall. Carol heard something scrape and a patch of the moss fell from the wall. A niche appeared to the left of the spring. Something glinted in the moonlight from within. Michael walked to the opening and pulled another candlestick from its depths, a twin to the one in his other hand. Carol held her breath. An urge so strong it took over all reason, a frenzy to be complete obsessed her.

Michael turned to her, his voice gentle. "Take off your clothes."

Michael and Carol both removed all their clothing, facing each other without shame. Her eyes trailed across Michael's body. He looked so beautiful to her. His body was slim but hardened muscles molded his body into masculine perfection.

He placed his right hand on his heart. "Too long have we been apart." He lifted her into his arms and lay her down gently on the silver altar. "Too long have you waited to become whole." His voice echoed off the walls.

The cool clear waterfall began to sparkle as though diamonds flowed within. The entire grotto glowed with an inner light that brought energy and strength to the couple. Michael took both candlesticks and held them over Carol's body. "That which has been separate will become whole. That which was taken shall be restored." The power of his voice was raw. Pure male energy radiated as he commanded the forces to do his bidding.

His power enthralled her.

He brought the two candlesticks together abutting their bases. With a half twist, there came the sound of a click. It became one piece. It began to hum. It pulsed with white light as the throbbing hum became louder. Wind rushed in from the opening above, flowing through the grotto. The pond began to churn.

Warmth spread through her entire body. The throbbing from the candlesticks now matched her heartbeat. The wind lifted her and held her aloft as though she weighed no more than a flower petal. Blood red light erupted from the candlesticks and entered her body flooding into her womb.

Life began. Visions of places and people swirled through her mind, one moment a Lady in a King's court, then a servant scrubbing her life away in the bowels of a fine mansion, and yet more came. Rich, poor, slave, and master – flashed into her memory. Yellow, white, red, brown and black faces whirled, all of them her. She relived the horror of her last death, her murder in a vision of darkness; of wet streets – attacked from behind – viciously stabbed. Each cut of the blade excruciatingly painful until the final slice across her throat. In terror she watched her own blood flow away, her mortal life with it. She didn't even know who had wielded the blade. In all this, one thing remained constant. She had never been alone. She saw him. Michael. Their souls mated for eternity, they would never be apart.

A different awareness entered. Subtle and loving, Carol felt the Canyon's influence. Finally an understanding of what she had felt from the nature around her since she arrived in the Canyon. An ancient power and wisdom beyond conscious meaning, a living power beyond mere words. Instinct allowed her to understand without question that something powerful had been brewing here since the beginning of time. A power neither evil nor good; it simply was. Wisdom so deep to be alive, weaving its spell into her very being.

Old magic.

Earth magic.

Pure magic.

She took a deep breath, the breath of a newborn. The wind gently laid her back onto the bench and she gazed into the eyes of her beloved. He lowered himself onto her and she took him into herself. He tenderly held her, as his passion possessed her body and soul. Golden light radiated from the mating pair as they luxuriated in the sensations of love beyond time, moaning in the sheer joy of being joined together once again. As the crescendo of this rejoining grew to climax, golden light flooded from them becoming a beacon out the top of the grotto all the way to the stars.

The ritual was complete.

Gently rising from her, Michael reached out for Carol to help her stand. They embraced, celebrating their reunion, their love. He gently lifted her into his arms and carried her out of the grotto, back into the house and up to his bedroom.

Time began again.

THIRTY-ONE

STRETCHING her body in the silk sheets of Michael's bed, Carol opened her eyes feeling calm and content in those first few moments of limbo between sleep and wakefulness. No longer just Carol, a host of other selves joined her. She remained the major personality, but she would never be alone. She remembered loneliness. She knew it well from her current incarnation. Carol preferred the company of her other lives and the vast expanse of experience, wisdom, and skills that supported her. How different things seemed. The life she had led until now was only a brief memory amongst many. How silly it was now, how inconceivable, to have feared the other dimension. Her concept of the Entity and his immense power became the clear threat. She had to admit she still had fear, but not in the same way as before. Her fear was not of the Entity but of not finding a way to stop him. She was angry that he used his power to subjugate others, and she still remembered the agony he had caused her. A surge of hatred rushed through her. She shivered. Could they manage to stop him without harm to anyone she loved?

She did realize complete clarity was not hers as yet. When thoughts came to her she was not always sure where they came from, which of her previous lives had answered the call for knowledge. She would have to learn an entire new way to live.

Sunlight poured through the arched diamond paned windows that dominated one wall of the master bedroom. Carol reached up to caress the sunbeams passing over the dark blue velvet bedcover. A larger hand joined hers and Michael brought her hand down to kiss it softly.

"Good morning." His tone low and soft.

She stroked his cheek. "How do I thank you?"

182

Michael kissed her gently.

She remembered and laughed softly. "How frustrating it must have been for you, unable to tell me until I was ready."

"That doesn't matter anymore."

Carol suddenly felt dizzy as a surge of memories floated to the surface of her mind. Trees, dirt roads, and wooden carts dominated her mind for a microsecond.

Michael stroked her cheek, he had seen what was on her mind. "Remember, you are the first to experience our Rejuvenation Device. I think it's going to take a while for your mind to completely assimilate all your past lives." He kissed her again. "Promise you'll come to me if something comes up that confuses or frightens you. No more running away."

"I promise."

He reached for her and kissed her with heated passion. She knew what he liked and wanted. A ferocious smile curved her lips. She loved having sex with him in his various incarnations. It felt deliciously naughty to have a different body to enjoy every few decades. He rolled her beneath him and in a heartbeat she was breathless. He knew what she liked too. Sliding her arms around him, she arched her back as waves of desire took hold. His kiss made her sigh as he reached behind her and caressed the curve of her back, pulling her tighter to him. She luxuriated in his sex, his scent making her want him more. The power of his need washed over her and she kissed him fervently letting him know her need was as strong as his. Contentment was theirs at least for a brief moment.

Coming downstairs, Michael and Carol joined Toga and Sarah for breakfast in the Solarium. Everything tasted extra delicious this morning. As she sipped her coffee, Carol glanced at her friend. Sarah looked up but quickly lowered her gaze to her plate when their eyes met. Carol noticed that her friend just picked at her food, sitting quiet and subdued, not at all her usual buoyant self.

Carol put her cup down and smiled. "Sarah, I need to tell you what happened…"

"Good! Go ahead. Try! I've lost you. Do you know how that feels?"

Carol was stunned. "I'm still me. I just have memories of past lives, that's all." She added slowly, "You're still my best friend."

Sarah's eyes shone with anger. "But that still makes you different. I'm not sure I can handle all this. I should just leave."

Michael's voice was gentle. "It's your choice, but we would never be so cruel to make you leave. You're part of the team."

"Please. Don't patronize me." Sarah fumed. "Toga told me the basics. I'm not in your league, not even close. I don't want your charity. Makes me feel like a pet!" she spat.

Toga reached for Sarah's hand. "You are needed. I need you"

Sarah began to cry. "This is all too much. I need to think."

"Sarah," Carol pleaded. "I never want to lose you. We've been best friends since high school." Tears filled her eyes. "Please stay. I can't do this without you. I thought you'd be jazzed about being a part of this. We need your help."

Sarah wiped her tears away. "Have you heard anything I said? You may still be Carol, but you are so much more now. You are different."

"You're right, I am whole again. I can't make you stay. I don't want to make your life miserable just because I want you to be my friend. I can't be that selfish." Carol stood and walked to the fountain. She felt guilty for thinking that Sarah would just accept all this and not be affected by it. It would break her heart to loose Sarah.

"Help me then. Toga said you'd have to give me the details. Go ahead."

Carol turned, relieved that Sarah wanted to hear more. There was so much to explain. But she needed to be careful not to upset her friend even more. She thought of something Sarah might find fascinating. "You're going to love this. I know you've heard the theory that a race from another planet came to Earth eons ago and helped humankind develop?"

Sarah groaned. "Yeah, and they created all the pyramids and stuff no one can explain. Don't give the human race any credit at all."

"They did come."

Sarah crossed her arms. "I'm not a fool. That's just the stuff they put on TV."

Michael stepped in. "I see your point. Forget TV, they did come but not quite the way the theorist believe." He paused to let her think. "These aliens chose a few of the promising races of prehistoric bipeds for research. They developed tribes, made them DNA compatible to themselves. This made them most likely to survive. Out of that research and the DNA manipulation came the first true homo sapiens."

"You're not kidding, are you?" Sarah glared at him.

Carol jumped in unable to control her need to make Sarah understand. "It's the truth. Please, there's more."

Sarah hesitated then nodded.

Michael continued. "The alien race never intended to stay on Earth but they wanted to leave behind a legacy that would continue to help the new humans develop."

Carol walked back to the table. Anxious to help Sarah. "They chose the most promising of these new humans to develop what we now call the Guardians. The aliens changed the DNA of these Guardians even more. Gave them the ability to remember their past lives when they reincarnated as well as other enhancements."

Sarah uncrossed her arms and looked at Carol. "So that's what you call yourselves? Guardians. You, Michael and Toga?"

"Yes, I didn't know until Michael returned my past lives last night."

Sarah's eyes widened. "This is incredible." She stood and paced to the fountain and back. She was actually breathing hard.

"You okay?" Carol worried.

"Ah, sorta. It sounds like a science fiction story. Still don't see my part in the plot."

Toga stood and held out his hand to Sarah. She sat back down, her face flush. He sat next to her and reached for her hand. "Guardians are the servants of Humankind. The aliens gave us knowledge and skills to keep us viable teachers for all the future generations. We have always worked with humans. We are human too."

Sarah started to cry again. "I'm beginning to understand. I'd stopped thinking of you as human. Felt so alone and useless."

Toga held her while she cried herself out.

Carol felt uncomfortable at Sarah's distress. She looked at Michael and projected her thoughts. Perhaps we should leave until Sarah is better?

"I don't think that would help. She needs us right now. There is more to tell her and she deserves to hear it. Michael smiled.

"Sarah," Carol began. "We have more to tell. Do you want to hear it?" Carol turned to Toga.

Sarah sat back, a grave look on her face. "Sure." She wiped away her tears.

Toga spoke. "The Guardians developed Councils of their own. We knew we needed to create rules to govern our actions. We were here to help not force humans to develop."

Sarah took a shuddering breath. "Humans haven't figured out how to run a government yet, if you ask my opinion."

Carol smiled. "We try. We base our doctrine on all spiritual as well as scientific concepts and theories."

Michael took over. "We have only three basic rules. First, form an alliance without distinction of race, creed, sex, caste or color to help the human race develop and prosper."

Sarah turned to Toga as he added. "Second, encourage study of the various religions, philosophies and sciences to discover how to incorporate them effectively into the evolution of mankind. And third, explore the laws of nature to develop and enhance the powers humans already have but do not know they possess."

Sarah's brow furrowed. "Just three. Does it work?"

Michael answered cautiously. "Yes. But the passage of time changes the interpretations of these three doctrines. We are still human in spite of all our genetic enhancement, knowledge and experience. The majority temper their judgment by adopting a no harm to others policy."

Carol added. "It's not easy. We must remember we are not to judge too quickly, if at all. There is a balance to maintain. Good and evil are terms whose definitions change over time, but to deliberately seek harm to others because you want power is strictly forbidden."

Sarah looked at each of them. "Okay. One more question. How do you "help" us puny humans? Hit us in the forehead, say 'ooga booga' and give us ideas?"

Carol couldn't help laughing. This sounded more like the Sarah she knew and loved. "Oh I wish it was that simple. No, we influence people who seem to be on the verge of greater ideas or discovering truer knowledge of the Universe. Sometimes we take a leading role, but we never let humans know about the Guardians. See it really is humans building pyramids and inventing the wheel, not aliens from outer space controlling everything.

Carol saw a hint of mischief in Sarah's eyes. "So was Einstein a Guardian or a human?"

Toga leaned back. "Human but Copernicus was a Guardian. We don't have an easy job. Although men who showed the way to the enlightenment of humankind are revered later, they often suffer for their ideas during their lifetimes or are murdered for them."

Sarah smiled. "I can see why reincarnation would be useful. But why not just make you immortal?"

Michael's brows met. "The aliens knew that immortality eventually brings loss of motivation. A fresh start each reincarnation keeps our minds active and motivated, freshened each time through different eyes, different perspectives."

Carol hesitated, hoping what she was about to say might upset Sarah. "You need to know about the Entity."

Sarah bit her lip. "Go ahead."

"He's a Guardian."

"A Guardian that does harm to others?"

Carol nodded. "Michael and I have always opposed those who use their power simply for their own gain."

Sarah had one more challenge. "Okay, then why is the Entity going against Guardian Law?"

"We don't understand his motives yet." Carol frowned.

Sarah shook her head in frustration. "Just how do you think I can help?"

Carol felt relieved. Maybe Sarah would stay. "Your computer skills are beyond any of us and I have always appreciated your opinions."

Sarah sighed. "I hear you. But I don't feel like much of a computer whiz at the moment. Toga and I searched every way we could think of to locate Darren on the Internet. So far, no go. The information on his business card is bogus."

Clearly frustrated, Michael ran his hand through his hair. "There is our local Council of the Guardians, but we don't know if any of them are in league with this rogue Guardian yet. And I have my own reasons not to trust them."

Toga turned to Sarah. "We take a great risk seeking any help. The rogue Guardian is powerful even in a weakened state. He could easily intercept any inquiry. We're forced to find out who's on our side by trial and error."

"We need to find the rogue Guardian and discover his motives, so we can stop him." Michael scowled.

"Well since it's up to us." Sarah looked from one to the other. "When do we get started?"

Carol relaxed. She knew her friend. Sarah would stay. She always appreciated Sarah's clear cut philosophy. "Let me grab another cup of coffee, and we'll get back to figuring this out."

In the library, Michael choose to sit at the library table. "We are a team now," he announced.

Sarah smiled and sat between Carol and Toga.

Michael started. "We know that the rogue Guardian is trying to gain power over the astral dimension possibly the Earth itself. We know he has followers. We have to consider he may have other Guardians, perhaps even Counsel Members, on his side. And from mental flashes I got during the confrontation, I believe he is somewhere in the area..."

Carol interrupted, "Do you think he knows I'm a Guardian?"

"We can't rule out the possibility," Toga answered. "I think he chose you for a purpose. I've never put any faith in coincidence."

Carol persisted. "But it's possible he wouldn't be aware that I'm regaining my former reincarnations. Perhaps I could be bait again."

Michael frowned.

"Carol, no." Sarah's voice was still rough from her tears at breakfast.

Carol rushed on. "The last time I spoke with Darren he said he was going to look into who you are and get back to me." She saw Michael's brow furrow. "Well, I didn't really know what you were all about then. I had to see if you were real." Carol grimaced. "Damn! Why didn't I think of this earlier? He called me on my cell!"

Sarah gave her a sarcastic look. "I just spent hours trying to find Darren and you had his number in your cell all this time?"

"There's been a lot happening, you know."

"That's an understatement." Sarah crossed her arms.

Michael spoke, "Being bait is out of the question. We don't know exactly what part Darren plays in all this."

"But isn't it worth the chance?" Carol pleaded. "I'll beg him to come over to my bungalow because I need his company. I could ask him what he's found out about you."

Sarah brightened. "Yeah, that just might work." Then she frowned. "But what if he knows you were in the astral dimension, he may want to trap you."

Michael interrupted, "No. I don't like taking such a big risk."

Carol looked at him seriously. "We could read what's on his mind. Even if we only get a few moments before he realizes what's happening. I feel it can only help us find his master."

Toga nodded. "You'll need help maintaining a shield around your mind. I can connect with you, help the shielding and still stay here to protect the circle in case they attack."

Michael capitulated. "I don't like this but I appear to be out voted. I want to be near in case it all goes wrong. I'll handle the shielding because I'll be connected to you every moment."

Carol hit the number Darren had called her from.

"Hello," Darren answered flatly.

Carol took a breath, both in surprise he had answered and to put on her act. "Darren, this is Carol." She sounded glad to hear his voice.

"Carol! I've been trying to reach you ever since I got back from San Francisco."

189

She made her voice sound weary. "So much is going on, I haven't even looked at my phone. Went back to the doctor. He's kept me on a crazy busy schedule of therapy, I really need a break."

"I've been worried. I just found something you need to hear—"

She interrupted. "Good. I'm taking that break. I'm coming home just for tonight. Can you come over?"

"Of course, but I think you should come home now."

"What did you find out? Is it something about Dr. Cameron?"

"Yes. Can you come home now? I'll meet you there."

Carol glanced at Michael as she spoke to Darren. "Sure, I could be home in about an hour. I haven't even packed yet." She paused a moment to add drama. "I really need you right now."

Darren's voice softened. "I'll be there."

As she closed the phone, she smiled at Michael. "I think we have a good chance to learn something."

Michael looked worried. "I'm still not convinced. Sounds like a trap to me."

Carol shrugged. "Probably, but he's the only lead we have. Even if it's a trap, I have to play my part."

Toga added, "I know a way to help strengthen your shields even more. I will prepare it for you." He turned to Sarah. "I'll show you how I make it." He held out his hand. "I'll add some herbs to brighten your thinking too." They headed to the kitchen.

Carol knew what Toga would prepare. The mixture of herbs and oils had proven to greatly heighten mental acuity for centuries. She remembered a time when making this health drink had been perceived as evil, as if it were a potion concocted in the dead of night under a full moon with Satan whispering the secret formula in your ear.

"Carol, I understand you have to play your part, but I just found you again. I don't know if I can…" Michael lowered his head.

She hurried to him. "You'll be in my thoughts and can help me. Yes, he still thinks he's my boyfriend, but I was nothing more than a job to him. I never want to hurt you."

He kissed her. "I trust you. It's Darren I don't."

Sarah came back proudly holding two large earthenware mugs full to the brim with a greenish brown liquid. Putting the cups down on the library table, she proclaimed, "This stuff's awesome! Toga gave me some, said it would help me concentrate. Wish I'd had this in college!"

THIRTY-TWO

AN HOUR later, Carol parked her VW and looked towards her bungalow. She thought over the plan. Michael had reminded her that Darren thought the candlestick was still on her mantle. She glanced over at it resting in her overnighter on her passenger seat. Michael followed five minutes behind her and would stay close. They had formed their mental link before starting down the canyon. Grabbing her bag, she hurried down the brick pathway to her front door. Darren waited for her by the fountain, looking frazzled and worried. He reached out and held her tight, kissing her full and hard.

"I was afraid I'd never see you again," he blurted. "Hurry, we must get out of sight."

Carol had felt the tingle of connection Darren attempted as he kissed her. It was the same technique Michael used when he took her to the astral plane. Carol also got an impression of her own from Darren at that moment. She saw the shadow of wings on his shoulders. Black wings. Anger surged through her but before the emotion could compromise her guise, she felt a calmness descend that she knew came from Michael. Composing herself, she tried not to think about how Darren, as Bocan, had hurt and captured Michael just hours ago.

Damn, Darren was a Guardian too. She was walking into a trap. Smiling at him, she steeled her emotions. Taking a deep breath to slow her racing heart, she knew she had to keep up her act as long as possible.

Carol unlocked her door and Darren quickly ushered her inside. It felt good returning to her place. It helped calm her even more. She wondered if George had missed her. Walking inside she put down her purse. "I'm nervous. Could you check around? Make sure no one is here?"

"Sure." Darren went towards the bedroom.

Carol quickly returned the candlestick to the mantle.

After checking the kitchen Darren came back. When Darren saw the candlestick he breathed a sigh of relief. "Glad that's still here."

Carol pretended alarm. "Why? What did you find out?"

"I did more digging like you asked and I found out Dr. Cameron belongs to some weird cult that practices satanic rites. Has for years. That candlestick could have some evil use since it belonged to an evil man."

She managed a straight face before saying in a panicked voice. "What! He's been putting me under hypnosis for my nightmares. He could be suggesting all sorts of things."

"Don't go back to him." Darren pleaded. "Come home with me. Or at least go stay with Sarah."

Carol started. "Sarah! She's still at Dr. Cameron's house. She went with me."

"Then come home with me."

"No, I can't leave her there if what you say is true!"

Darren frowned. "How do we get her out of there?"

"I think I know a way." Carol went to her purse. "Cameron gave me a key to his garage when I left." She paused, thinking. "Let me call Sarah's cell phone. I'll ask her to make some excuse to be alone then slip down to the garage. She can call us when she starts down, and then wait for us just inside the garage door."

Darren looked skeptical. "Sounds too simple."

Carol pleaded, "It is simple. That's the beauty of it."

"I don't know…"

"The only other thing I know is to call the police. That could either get Sarah killed or be so messy we'll be in court for months." She thanked Toga's elixir for allowing her to think so clearly. Darren would not want the police involved.

"Okay. You're right. I don't like it, but I see your point."

"Thanks." She gave him a quick kiss. "You've been so good to me through all this," she purred.

He held her and gave her a passionate kiss back. He touched her cheek and a genuine look of love softened his face as he released her. His touch allowed her to know without doubt that his love for her was real. Carol was taken aback. Her anger surfaced again. She didn't know what to do. There wasn't time to consider this twist. He was a Guardian and in league with the rogue Guardian. The thought made it easier to come back to the task at hand. Quickly she refocused her concentration on the con game she was playing.

"Let me call Sarah and arrange things."

She went to pull her cell from her purse as Darren sat on the couch, his face worried. It rang several times and Carol became fearful she would have to leave a message and potentially blow this chance to get Darren up to Cameron's house. Her friend answered.

"Sarah, its Carol."

"Are you okay? Did something go wrong?"

Carol's voice became serious. "Listen to me very carefully. We need to get you away from Dr. Cameron."

Sarah's answer was unsure. "Is this part of the plan?"

"Yes. I'll explain later, just trust me. We need you to find an excuse to be alone."

"This is way cool. Then what?"

"Sneak down to the garage door. Call us when you get there. I've got the key. Darren and I will be there to pick you up. But be careful!"

"I suppose you want me to tell Toga everything?"

"Of course. Don't worry. We'll be there soon after your call."

Carol closed her cell and turned to Darren. "It could be awhile until she calls. Want some coffee?"

Darren looked up. "Good idea." He frowned. "I hope you know what you're doing."

"I do."

Walking into the kitchen, she smiled when she saw George's shadow standing beside the fridge.

"Miss me? Missed you," she whispered so Darren wouldn't hear.

His shadow remained.

"Sorry I was gone so long. Really important things going on."

194

She filled the pot with water, added the grounds to the coffee maker and pushed the button. She was shaking. She wanted this game playing to be over. She hadn't expected Darren to really be in love with her. How could that be? Had she misread the feeling she had felt from him. She knew she hadn't. She reminded herself that he started their relationship under false pretenses and he'd done horrible things to Michael. He'd tried to kill her and Toga. She reached for the coffee mugs.

Anxiety hit hard. He must know she had been in the astral dimension. This was obviously a trap, but why would he take such a chance that she wouldn't recognize him as Bocan? Perhaps he doesn't know she was a Guardian? Impossible! Her alarm grew. Carol needed to find out what she could and fast. Hopefully they could stop the Entity quickly and be done with all this miserable intrigue and fear. She could watch James Bond movies, but she didn't want to be like him.

Turning she smiled at George who still stood by the fridge. "So glad you're here. Wish you could help."

George's shadow faded away.

Calming herself she brought the mugs of coffee into the living room and handed one to Darren.

"I really missed you," he said quietly.

"Mmm, ditto." She sat beside him and cuddled closer. "Thank you for coming over. Again, you have come to the rescue. My knight in shining armor. I really need you tonight."

"Do you want me to start a fire? I mean the kind that goes in the fireplace. We can start the other kind of fire later." He raised his eyebrow with comical lechery.

"I'd love a fire, but I don't think there's enough time…until later." She gave him an equally lecherous grin.

Knowing that her mind remained well shielded she took the chance to experiment. She gently probed Darren's mind just for a brief moment. Carol wanted to find out what kind of trap he was preparing. All she discovered was that he'd not contacted anyone either mentally or otherwise in the last 18 hours. Perhaps this would all work out. If luck remained on their side, the rogue Guardian was still too weak to be an immediate threat.

Waiting for Sarah to call proved too nerve wracking to do anything more than sit and wait. Darren sat on the edge of her sofa. When her cell rang, they both jumped. Carol glanced at the clock. The call had come much sooner than anticipated. Michael must have asked them to speed things up.

Carol tensed as she answered her cell. "Sarah, are you ready?"

Toga's voice responded on the other end. "Yes, we're ready. Michael will follow you. Get Darren out of the car when you arrive and we'll do the rest."

"We're on our way." She turned to Darren as she ended the call. "Let's take my VW. You can help Sarah get into the car."

Leave your keys and I'll get the candlestick, Michael said in Carol's mind.

She grabbed her purse and keys. She threw the garage key to Darren who caught it gracefully. Carol hurried to the door, hoping quick action would not give Darren time to think. He followed her out the door and started toward her car. She dropped her house key on the doormat.

They were speeding up the canyon before he spoke. "Where are we going after we have Sarah?"

"First we'll head to Sarah's house then figure out what to do next. Cameron doesn't know where she lives." Carol glanced in her rear view mirror and caught a glimpse of Michael's car just before she rounded a curve. "Not much farther now."

Sunset began to streak the sky with oranges and pinks as she again ventured a peek into Darren's mind. There seemed nothing but the task at hand. He could be blocking her mind probe, she thought, remembering Michael's explanation on how to keep others from reading your mind. Carol clenched her teeth. Michael's garage door became visible just as she executed the next curve. Slowing down the car, she parked as close as she could to the door, leaving the engine running.

"Darren, this is Cameron's garage door," she whispered. "Go ahead and jump out. Knock lightly on the door. Sarah will be there."

He did as she asked, leaving the car door open and the seat back forward to make it easier to jump back in. Moving silently, Darren approached the garage door and gave a light tap. Carol heard him whisper

Sarah's name before he unlocked the door. But it wasn't Sarah who stepped out. Toga delivered a well-aimed blow to Darren's jaw. Darren dropped at Toga's feet. Michael ran up from his parked car and helped his friend carry Darren's unconscious body into the garage before anyone saw them. Carol maneuvered her car in after them.

Carol was shaking as she got out of her car. Following Toga, Michael, and Darren's body into the house, she tried to calm herself.

Sarah held the door open for them. "Wow, just like in the movies! Were there any problems?"

"None. It was really simple." Carol looked at Sarah with concern. "He's just trying to fool us though. Turns out he's Bocan. That winged bat creature we told you about. He's definitely on the side of the Entity."

Sarah gave her a cagey smile. "Batman or not, he's a man. You already had him wound around your little finger when you played damsel in distress over the phone."

Carol hoped Sarah was right. Together they followed Michael and Toga as they carried their captive towards the solarium. The grotto would be perfect. Darren wouldn't know where he was when he woke up.

Sarah stood at Carol's side. "Toga's been casting extra protection spells around that place since you guys left. That should hold Mr. Darren Campbell." She gave a satisfied nod.

Carol could tell that Sarah still felt bad about Darren being the bad guy. The brave front was to keep Carol from worrying. Carol ran ahead to open the door to the back garden for Michael and Toga. She and Sarah stayed in the garden outside the grotto while the men opened the entrance in the ivy wall and took Darren inside.

Carol mentally crossed her fingers hoping it could really be this easy. "Well, if we can get any information out of him, we're headed into some very interesting times." She chuckled. "I think that's an old Chinese curse isn't it? May you live in interesting times?"

Sarah frowned. "It's a curse all right. Look where we are compared to a week ago!"

Carol remembered something. Leaving Sarah, she rushed to Michael and Toga finding them in the grotto next to Darren's still form.

"Wait." She ran up to them. "Just remembered. Darren knows about this place. Mentioned tunnels when he told me the story about the candlestick."

THIRTY-THREE

MICHAEL stared at her a moment, concern clouding his eyes. "That's disturbing. I didn't think anything about the demon door on my house. Anyone can see that. But to know about this place…"

Carol added, "Said there were two skeletons here."

Michael became alarmed. "There are." When he saw Carol's startled expression he added. "They belong to us. You and me."

Her expression did not change.

"From our last life. Because you weren't allowed to reincarnate as a Guardian, I buried your body here in some wild desperate hope it would help me find you again."

What else didn't she know? Right now even the rogue Guardian and Darren appeared to know more about her than she did. Carol couldn't help wishing that her assimilation process could go faster. Time was her real enemy.

They all turned at the sound of Sarah entering the cavern. Her eyes wandered in awe over the crystal walls and the pool. "This is amazing," she whispered. "Is everything okay?"

Carol went to her friend and hugged her. "Sorry I just left you out there. We're deciding what to do with Darren."

Toga confirmed Carol's fears. "We need to hurry. They seem to know a lot more about us than we do about them."

Michael looked down when Darren moaned. "We have to find out something from him."

"Should we let him wake up here?" Carol worried.

"It doesn't really make a difference. Since he knows about this cave, he'll probably guess where he is."

Sarah looked at Darren. "Can't you just read his mind while he's unconscious?"

"Unconscious, his mind is nothing but a twisted jumble. Finding correct information would be near impossible." Toga explained.

Carol had a flash of inspiration. "Why don't I continue to play your victim?"

Michael frowned. "I know where your heading and I don't like it."

"Darren will think I was captured too. If he relaxes his guard, I might even get some information."

Toga stepped forward. "Michael, she's right. We have to use anything we have to our advantage."

"We should keep Sarah separate." Michael realized. He turned to Sarah. "He'd read your mind and the game would be over."

"I understand." Sarah gave Carol a stern look. "You be careful." As she left, she cast a smile at Toga.

Darren groaned.

Carol looked down, "Either knock him out again or tie us up." She turned to Michael. "My mind shield still working?"

"Yes." Michael's mouth became a tight line of tension as he stepped forward and began tying Carol's wrists behind her back. He leaned forward and whispered, "Please be careful. I'm still mentally connected to you if you need me." He kissed the back of her neck.

Toga finished tying Darren's hands behind his back. Both men hurried out of the grotto.

Darren rolled over, his eyes opening. "What did you hit me with?" he asked Carol groggily.

Carol dropped to her knees, crying. "It's all my fault. They knew we were coming. Toga hit you the moment the garage door opened. They tied us up and threw us in here. They took Sarah somewhere."

Darren struggled to a sitting position. "Are you okay? They didn't hurt you?"

"No, but I feel just awful. What are we going to do now?"

Darren looked around the grotto. "Okay, you can drop the act. Tell me what's really going on."

"What do you mean?"

"I assume this place is protected? No one can read our thoughts?"

Carol knew the game was over. "Yes, it's protected. When did you know?"

"I wasn't sure until I opened the garage door and someone smacked some sense back into my head." He gave a little laugh. "You're good. Had me fooled all along."

Before Carol could respond, Michael and Toga entered the grotto.

"Ah, the cavalry has arrived." Darren frowned.

Toga untied Carol as Michael demanded, "We need to know where your leader is."

"Of course you do." Darren shifted his body and grimaced. "I don't suppose I could talk you into untying me first?"

"Why would I do that? You're in league with an evil Guardian!"

"I see your point." He looked at Carol as he continued. "What you don't see is that I'm really on your side."

"You've been taking me for a fool since we met," Carol spat. "I only discovered you were Bocan tonight. How could you possibly be on our side?"

Darren's face reddened. "You can read my mind." His gaze turned to Michael and Toga. "I won't block anything. You'll know if I do."

Michael nodded. "We'll take you up on your offer, Mr. Campbell.

As Darren shifted himself to a more comfortable position, he closed his eyes. "I'm ready."

Carol felt the mental connection start. Her mind was pulled along too and she found herself in a darkened stonewalled room in Darren's memory. She looked at the five white robed and hooded men sitting in high backed chairs at a long dark wooden table. One chair remained empty at the far end. They were the Guardians' Council. Before them Darren stood in a pool of light, his head bowed. He only wore simple black robes, his hood down.

The first Councilman spoke, "You have proven yourself worthy of our trust. Will you consent to do our bidding?"

Darren did not raise his head. "I will, Lord Councilor."

"*We are but five Councilors now that our sixth member has betrayed us. He has turned his back on the laws that govern our actions. He only wishes to use his powers for his own purpose, no matter the cost to others.*"

Another Councilman said in a low tone, "*He intends to influence all other Guardians into following him. He wants all the power he can manage. He already has knowledge and skill beyond most of us.*"

"*He is persuasive. Claims the Ancients are returning soon and we need to be ready,*" said the Lord Councilor.

Darren raised his head. A puzzled look darkened his features. "*Is he so powerful?*"

The entire Council nodded. The Councilman spoke again. "*When he broke from the Council, he ritualistically murdered another Guardian without pity or remorse.*"

"*What is it you wish me to do?*"

"*First, gain the trust of our renegade Councilman. Try to learn everything you can and report back to us.*"

"*I will.*"

"*Second, see if you can find the Guardian he murdered. She has reincarnated without all her past souls but there may be a way to restore them.*"

"*I will.*"

"*We know we ask much of you. But we would not place this task in your hands if we did not feel you were capable.*"

Darren put his hands behind his back. "*I understand.*"

"*Please go to the shielded chamber and await us there.*" We will open our minds to you and provide accurate information and images to help you with your task.*"

Darren turned and walked out of the council chamber.

Carol suddenly found herself back in the grotto staring at Darren. He was telling the truth! Could she be the murdered Guardian the council had sent Darren to find? She had to be. Carol took a step towards Darren but before she could speak, a pressure in her head made her stop. Images whirled into her mind.

She again stood before the Guardians' Council. This time six hooded men sat before her. Carol had long blond hair tied back from her face, and gray eyes that looked at the Council with excitement. She recognized her last incarnation, Christa. She turned and looked at the man standing beside her. He had auburn hair that brushed his collar and his eyes were large and liquid brown. She knew him immediately as Michael's last incarnation, Erik.

The Lord Councilor smiled at them. "We understand that you have developed a way to collect and restore past souls to Guardians who have lost the ability to reincarnate fully."

Erik answered with a proud smile. "Yes, we have, sir."

"Our numbers have remained almost the same over the centuries while the world's population grows." Christa explained. "We feel it will be of great value in keeping Guardians strong and able to continue helping humankind." She stepped forward in her excitement. "And we are working on adding lost past lives to a different Guardian or even a mortal in order to keep our knowledge and experiences viable for the future."

Another Councilman spoke quietly from the depths of his hood, his tone cold. "You do not feel this is an abomination of nature? Perhaps we are not meant to be here forever."

Erik frowned. "No, we think with proper guidelines for its usage, it will aid nature not defy it. You did not think of calling penicillin an abomination of nature because we decided to use it to cure disease."

The Councilman nodded. "But to consider giving mortals the past lives of a Guardian, would this not be impossible? They would need to be modified as we were."

Christa felt a chill she could not understand. She looked at Erik but he did not seem to notice.

"We feel our current knowledge of DNA will make modification possible now," Erik answered.

"This is a powerful discovery." The Lord Councilor responded. "I think we should consider all the facts scientifically and decide the best way to utilize this discovery."

The other Councilmen nodded. Christa noticed that the sixth Councilman did not move. She knew without seeing the face hidden in the shadow of his hood that he watched them.

Carol came back when she felt her body being lifted to a seated position. She looked up into Michael's eyes and started to cry.

"What just happened?" Darren demanded.

Michael looked at Carol with concern. "I think she just had a past memory."

"So you gave her back her past lives?" Darren frowned. "Of course you did."

Carol watched Toga untie Darren and help him to his feet. Michael held Carol as she regained her composure. She desperately wanted to ask questions but her emotions ran too high to easily control. She began to realize what really happened.

She clung to Michael as she struggled to pull herself together. "I...," her voice sounded strange, "We...Christa and Erik were standing before the Council, all six of them." She struggled to sit up. Michael helped her.

"So the evil Guardian was still there?" Darren asked.

Carol nodded. "We were bringing our new discovery to the Council for consideration. The past lives storage unit."

Darren stepped forward. "When I met the Council in the shielded room for final instructions they told me about this device, disguised as two candlesticks, one for storage and one to operate the rejuvenation."

Carol continued, "The day after we met with the Council we were attacked. I never knew who it was." She shuddered. "That's when I was murdered. Tell me, was it the sixth Guardian?"

"It was," Darren spoke softly. "The Council told me. They asked me to secure the candlesticks before the rogue Guardian could find them. I only managed to find one, but that was enough to put a stop to using them."

Michael glared at Darren. "So you were the thief that made it impossible for me to return Christa's past lives to her!"

"Please, we had to keep the device from being used by the rogue Guardian." Darren took a step back as Michael stood.

"That's why the Guardian Council refused to help me find it! I've never forgiven them for that!"

"Stop it!" Carol demanded.

She saw Toga relax. Carol glanced at him, nodding her understanding that he would have stopped any fight if she hadn't.

"We don't have time for this. Please. Let's figure all this out. Quietly."

Michael sank down on the bench against the wall, lowering his head. When he straightened he rubbed his face with one hand as if to erase all the emotion he felt. Carol knew his pain as her mind flooded with the years of frustration and loneliness Michael had suffered trying to reunite with her. It was overpowering.

With tears in her eyes, she sat beside him. "We are together again. We must stop this evil Guardian from ever doing this to anyone else. You've been through enough."

Michael turned to Darren. "Tell us what you know."

"The rogue Guardian is convinced that the Ancient's are returning and soon. He's manic about being prepared for their return."

Toga interrupted. "We've had certain Guardians push their personal agendas since the beginning of time. The Council has always managed to stop them before."

"He wants to use our rejuvenation device, doesn't he?" Carol stood. "Is that why he was pulling me onto the astral plane? Did he think I had the knowledge he needed?"

Darren's brow furrowed. "In a way. He is convinced the Ancients will judge all the Guardians as insufficient. That we have not lived up to their expectations. In order to make up for our failure and to please the Ancients, he wants to develop your Rejuvenation Device. Be able to show the Ancients how far we have evolved, how well we have found ways to remain the Guardians they wanted us to be."

"So, he knew who I was even when I didn't?" A chill ran down Carol's spine.

"Yes. He has powers I've never seen before and he has followers."

"How bad is it?" Toga asked.

"He is very persuasive and has many on his side already, even some Councilmen from other districts. I know that he hides an agenda of his own. He will present the device as his own creation in hopes of gaining the Ancient's trust. Become head honcho over the rest of us Guardians. He wants to force all of Earth's population into being worthy of joining other enlightened species throughout the Universe. He really believes this was the Ancients purpose."

Toga stood. "No one knows what purpose the Ancients had in mind. No one!"

"Let me guess." Michael frowned. "He thinks he can use the device to manipulate what souls are given to which Guardian, his way of improving our status for the good of all."

"Probably. Fits his mania."

"This is more than I realized." Michael said.

Darren looked down. "He knew Carol wasn't a Guardian anymore, because he'd murdered her. But he hoped he could find you by torturing her in the astral dimension. And you fell right into his hands."

Michael looked miserable.

Darren's words were clipped. "I tried to keep you and Carol apart but..."

"Then why did you let me find the candlestick?" Carol asked slowly.

"I didn't." Darren's eyes pleaded for Carol's understanding. "The Guardian Council tried to use the candlestick as bait for the Rogue. Their plan failed. It was the Rogue who then used it as bait for you."

Carol stepped towards Darren. He had been trying to keep her safe, trying to keep the world safe. He had made up the story about the candlesticks so she would panic and run away from Michael. He had recognized her in the astral dimension and merely slowed her down hoping to keep her out of harm's way.

Darren sighed. "There's one more thing you need to know. There are clear indications that the Ancients are truly returning. Many think soon."

Carol looked at Michael. He was shocked. So much at stake, so much without positive proof, yet powerful Guardians were acting as though it was absolute. Madness! It was daunting. How could they possibly stop this?

"How do we keep him from getting the rejuvenation device?" she asked Darren, her voice shaky.

"I will help where I can. Defeating him in the other dimension has weakened him, but not for long. He will not underestimate you again. He doesn't know I've told you who I really am." He rubbed his jaw where Toga had struck him. "I can still be a double agent."

Before anyone could respond, alarms shrieked through the grotto. Toga started running towards the house. Michael put a hand up to stop Darren from charging after Toga. "Stay here. We can't afford you losing your cover," he shouted over the screeching alarm.

Carol and Michael ran after Toga. As they entered the solarium they could see smoke. A bloodcurdling scream came from the library.

THIRTY-FOUR

FIRE RAGED through the shelves of books. Not just some corner where it might have started, but the entire room. Flaming books fell from the second story balcony to add to the conflagration below. Sarah lay crumpled on the floor in front of Michael's desk. Carol fought her way towards her friend, smoke stinging her lungs. The house alarm shrieked and the roar of the fire brought terror to Carol's heart. This was no illusion. It was real and it meant to destroy everything.

Carol turned Sarah's body over and tried to lift her. She shuddered as she remembered her nightmare with Sarah's fiery death. She felt other arms lend their strength to her efforts to get her friend out of the library. Toga lifted her with ease. He nodded to Carol and headed to the door. Michael appeared out of the smoke and helped Carol back to her feet. Coughing, she rubbed the sting from her eyes.

"How do we stop this?" Carol yelled over the roar. When she turned to look at Michael, his face ashen and his eyes staring in horror, she panicked. "Michael! Please. We have to stop this!"

Without looking at her, he stepped forward and raised his arms. He moved like a conductor before an orchestra. The flames swayed and obeyed his unspoken commands, swirling around the room, around him, then up and out the now destroyed stain glass windows the dome once proudly held. Nothing but blackened desolation remained of the once glorious library. Michael lowered his arms, his eyes empty and hollow all emotion rung out of them.

Carol knew his despair. Centuries of careful collecting reduced to ashes in an instant, all the knowledge and philosophies of generations wiped from the Earth in moments. The help it could have provided in the war against the Rogue gone or useless.

Carol realized the fire alarm had ceased. She held out her arms to Michael.

He embraced her, resting his head against hers. Toga came towards them, Darren at his side.

Michael glared at Darren. "I told you to stay put."

"Toga said the attackers were gone. I thought I'd help."

Carol turned to Toga. "Sarah. Is she okay?"

"They tried to read her mind. They were not gentle."

Darren spoke quickly, "Where is she. I can help her."

They hurried after Toga. Sarah rested on the couch in the living room, her eyes glazed in shock. How much damage had her friend suffered? "Please do what you can to help her," she begged Darren.

He lowered himself to his knees and put his hand on Sarah's temple. He closed his eyes and concentrated. Darren frowned. "Being in a hurry, they were crude. But I don't think there is any permanent damage. Let's see if a restorative drink will bring her round."

Toga started toward the library. "I'll see if any of my herbs survived the fire. I know which ones you need."

"Thank you." Carol put her hand on Darren's shoulder.

Michael cleared his throat. "If I can help..."

Darren looked up. "Thanks. But I can handle this."

Michael seemed lost, uncomfortable. Carol dipped into his mind. His anger slammed her. He cursed himself for allowing the destruction of the library. He was an academic, a scientist before anything else. The library and its knowledge had been his world. He should have known they would attack. It had protection, but he should have added more. Why had he been so stupid! And he hated how Darren had taken over and put himself in charge.

Carol needed him. He was still her lifeline, her helpmate. She tried to bring him back. "Michael," she said gently, "Did the evil Guardian do this or did he send others?"

Michael rubbed his neck and took a breath. "I don't think he would come in person. I don't see how he could be strong enough yet."

Darren looked up from Sarah. "You're right. I don't think he'd have ordered the destruction of the library, but he wouldn't have objected to what they did to Sarah."

Toga entered the room, a large glass of clear liquid in his hand. Darren rose and allowed him to administer the treatment they all hoped would bring Sarah back. She did not react as the glass touched her lips, but as the first sip trickled down her chin, she seemed to understand that she should drink. Slowly at first, Sarah took a bit of the liquid into her mouth and swallowed it. A small spark of life came to her eyes as Toga raised her to a sitting position, making it easier for her to drink the remaining tonic.

With the last sip, Sarah smiled weakly. "That's got to be the nastiest shit I've ever tasted." She looked tenderly at Toga.

Carol sat down next to her friend. "Welcome back."

"What the hell happened?"

"You had a run in with some of the rogue Guardian's friends," Michael answered. "They tried to read your mind."

Still not fully conscious, Sarah chuckled. "There's not much in there."

"You couldn't block them, they probably found out everything you know about us." Darren spoke gently.

Sarah panicked, becoming more alert. "Who were they? Did they come from the other dimension to attack me? I don't understand."

Michael answered her, "Not from the astral dimension. From here."

Darren added, "My guess is they acted alone in hopes of impressing their leader. He's not able to keep his followers under strict control at the moment. But he'll be back too soon for comfort."

"At least you weren't in the grotto when we discussed options." Carol tried to sound hopeful, but when Sarah frowned, Carol hugged her friend. "They don't know everything."

Sarah lowered her head as Carol released her. She turned her face away and slid back into the couch cushions. She asked in a muffled voice. "What hope do we have now?"

Toga's voice was confident. "There's always hope."

Carol agreed. "As soon as you feel better you can help us assess the damage."

"What didn't they get from Sarah?" Darren asked.

"Well, they don't know you're a double agent, only that you were a prisoner here. That's something in our favor," Michael answered.

Sarah turned. "You're not evil after all?"

"Nope."

"Good." Sarah turned her face back away.

Carol knew her friend. Sarah worried about being the one the evil Guardian had gotten the information from. "It's not your fault, you know."

Sarah turned back. "I know. But I don't have to like it."

Carol continued her assessment. "They will know I have all my former lives back."

"Okay, there's one thing in our favor and one against," Toga said.

"The Council will need to know what happened here. I need to report in," Darren stated. "I'll ask for help but they are fighting this on many fronts."

"Tell them if you must. I don't expect any help." Michael frowned.

Darren reasoned. "We definitely need to hide the device."

Toga looked up from Sarah. "The best way I know is to hide the candlesticks between dimensions, but we don't have the means to do it here."

"Great idea." Darren smiled. "That's certainly something the Council could help us with. But we need to find a hiding place for it 'til then."

"And we need to hurry," Carol added. "I dread this but we need to check the library and see what's left."

"I can help with that. I'm feeling much better," Sarah offered, her face still very pale.

Darren turned to Michael. "If you don't need me for this, I'll head to the Council. Don't tell me where you've hidden the device in case I become compromised."

Carol put her arm through Michael's and dipped into his mind again. He felt more in control now. He realized he had to stop his descent into despair. It made him weak and incapable of taking control of the situation. Thankful that Carol, Toga and Sarah were alive, he would find a way to go on. But it would be awhile before he could truly accept the loss of his library. He still did not care for Darren, but realized he could be an asset. He would be cautious; he was suspicious of the Council and Darren's ties to it.

"Thank you," Michael managed.

Darren only nodded then left.

Carol clutched her head. The room swirled around her. She heard Michael call her name. All turned black.

THIRTY-FIVE

CAROL STOOD ALONE on a narrow dirt road that wound down a mountainside. Most living creatures had scurried into the shelter of the tall pines and wide oaks, out of the harsh sun. She watched a small dust devil wind its way towards her sending clouds of hot dirt into the stifling air. A trickle of sweat ran down the back of her neck and she absentmindedly wiped it off. The cool feeling of the evaporating liquid gave her a moment's respite from the muggy noontime heat. Turning, she saw that her mule had meandered to the roadside trying the grass that grew on the shady side. Reaching for the rope that led to its halter, Carol remembered her name was Alice May and she had seed in the mule's panniers to sell in the valley below. Alice May knew she needed to hurry. Her Papa would tan her hide if she didn't get back by sundown with the money the seed would bring.

Alice smiled. She had plans of her own too. Papa wouldn't miss the penny she planned to spend at the Bear Creek Dry Goods Store for a few pieces of candy. It would all be et before she got back home. She also planned to ride the mule part way to make up the time it took her to choose just the right pieces to satisfy her sweet tooth. And she knew she wouldn't fail as long as she stuck to her plan. All she had to do was keep faith that she could accomplish her goal.

Carol felt a hand on her arm and she turned to see Michael, a look of concern on his face. "You okay?"

Alice May faded and Carol nodded. She felt Michael's relief.

"Alice May was one hell of a woman," he said. "I could see where you were."

Carol straightened. "Let's get back to figuring out what we should do." She still felt Alice May's courage and determination flowing through her spirit.

"What just happened?" Sarah asked.

"I'm still assimilating past lives."

"Looks painful."

"No, I'm just somebody else for a bit." She was glad Alice May had come back to her. It was that kind of determination she needed right now.

Toga stood. "We need to hurry."

Sarah put her feet on the floor and held out her hand to Toga. "Just help me up and I'll see what I can do."

"I will, but you're still under my orders to rest."

Carol noticed less destruction than she had originally thought but still too much to be happy about. There were sections of the library where protection spells had managed to prevent the fire's devastation. The computer remained untouched. It held loads of information that the library had in book form but not all. Michael approached his un-scathed desk and slowly started sorting books and papers. Carol knew he still dealt with the blow to their defenses as well as his entire world. She walked over to the dais where the protection circle remained undisturbed, another blessing to be grateful for.

She turned to Michael. "Circle looks good. Toga should check it, though. We can have protection if we need to go after the rogue Guardian in the astral dimension again."

"Good," he said in a flat tone.

"Say, can we use the circle to keep the rejuvenator safe?"

Michael looked up, his eyes brightened. "That might just work." He called to Toga, "Let's see if we can use the protection circle to keep the rejuvenator safe for a while."

Toga left Sarah and walked towards the circle where he knelt down to examine it more thoroughly.

"I'm worried," Carol sighed, "when I'm assimilating past memories, I'm useless. What if I cause us to lose a fight or someone could die because I'm off in 'la-la' land!"

"I wish I knew a way to speed your assimilation." Michael said. "You're the first to try the device. No data on how to predict how you'll react."

"I just hope Darren or the Council deal with things from here and we don't have to."

Michael voiced his contempt, "Who knows what the Council will decide to do. We're probably on our own again!"

Carol knew he was right. Darren had made it clear that the rogue Guardian was after them and their device. He would not stop until he had it. It was vital to his plan for domination. Darren had also said the Counsel was fighting on many fronts. The Rogue would make sure they would be too busy to help them. Somehow, hindered by assimilations or not, she would have to try. No, she amended; win against this evil.

Toga reported, "The circle is still very strong. I think if we make them invisible, it could serve for a little while."

"Invisible? Can you do that?" Carol asked.

"It's only putting objects slightly out of time phase, easy really," Michael answered.

"Oh." Carol straightened. "Just got that information from somewhere in my mind. Sometimes I get full assimilations, sometimes just bits and pieces."

Toga smiled at Carol. He continued his assessment. "As far as the damage to the library, several protected areas remain unharmed but there is considerable damage elsewhere. This was no ordinary fire. It broke through our shielding too easily."

"The computer is functioning as though nothing happened." Sarah still looked pale. "I thought there would be smoke damage at least, but it's all good. Wish I'd known some protection spells when I installed my system."

As Toga left to retrieve the candlesticks from the niche in the grotto, Michael asked, "Would you bring a black sphere from the cabinet near the computer to me?"

As Carol pulled the device off the shelf, it started to hum. She took the black ball with silver inlaid symbols on it over to Michael who stood in the protection circle murmuring words over a narrow wooden box.

He looked up as Carol approached him. "The box has the strongest protection I can provide."

Toga walked in holding the candlesticks and handed them to Michael who placed them inside the box.

"Toga, would you add more protection?"

His friend smiled. "Guess from here on out, we should double protect everything. We're in for a wild ride." He rubbed his hands together and knelt adding his protection to the box.

As Toga finished, Carol handed the black spherical device to Michael. He placed the humming ball on top of the box then pushed a small button on its side. Black ball and the box holding both candlesticks disappeared.

Carol kissed Michael on the cheek. "You make it all look so easy."

Michael looked around. "I want to put stronger protections on this library. We should all move in here for the duration. We need to hurry. The Rogue's followers are attacking whether he orders it or not."

Carol nodded. "Good idea. Do you have powerful enough protection?"

"No way to know." Michael rubbed his neck frustrated. "He's one of the strongest Guardians I have ever encountered. He has the advantage of being on the Council for decades and privy to information only known to them."

"So, we're not safe at all!" Sarah stood and started towards Michael. "What…"

Absolute darkness engulfed them. Carol steadied herself against a shelf. Sarah cried out as something whished overhead. Hellish screams descended from it.

"Carol," Michael yelled and she felt his hand on her arm. She allowed him to steer her towards the protection circle.

"Toga, where are you!" Sarah cried.

From the shuffling sounds behind them, Carol knew Toga pushed Sarah in the same direction. Michael started an incantation as they stumbled over the debris to salvation. A white glow fell around them and she could see. Another hellish scream made Carol look up. Beautiful but terrifying in their cold perfection, colorless eyes glared with malice from exquisite female faces. Their perfect bodies seemed molded from glass yet they moved with graceful icy precision, gliding above them without wings.

One dived, striking Toga who fell without a sound.

Sarah's face reflected her horror as she dropped and covered him with her body to stop further harm. "Go away!" she shrieked at the glassy horrors.

Another swooped towards Michael but he ducked, dragging Carol to the ground with him. She hit hard. Turning she saw Michael roll over to face the frigid horror, making a dismissive motion with his hand. The descending demon fled. Carol jumped up. They were only a few feet from the circle. She threw her body forward and into the circle. As Michael scrambled to his feet, a demon struck from behind and his limp body crumpled to the floor. The demons vanished and the light returned.

Carol stared at Sarah's horror-stricken face. She still guarded Toga's body. Carol brushed away the tears that coursed down her cheeks. She looked down at Michael. He breathed, but slowly. Carol knew what had happened. The glassy demons had taken Michael's spirit to the astral dimension.

"Is Toga breathing?" she asked.

"Yes, slowly."

"Help me get Toga and Michael into the circle."

Sarah nodded and stood, reaching down to grab both of Toga's arms. Carol did the same with Michael. Together they managed to pull both bodies into the protection of the circle.

Carol collapsed next to Michael giving way to deep despair. What were they going to do now? How could she possibly face the rogue Guardian alone? But she had no choice. She knew she needed help even though her assimilated past lives were there to help. She did not possess enough knowledge yet.

Carol took a deep breath and sobered herself. "Sarah. You okay?" she managed.

"Yeah," came the slow distracted answer. She stared at Toga's body never looking up. "We never seem to get a break do we?"

Carol checked her pocket and, with relief, pulled out her cell phone. "Darren! It's our only choice." Her voice sounded shrill. She attempted to calm her rising panic. Her call immediately went to his voice mail. Damn it! "Ah, Darren. Guess who? The doctor and his friend just left and we thought you'd like to come over to watch an old movie. We're showing "Help", you know, The Beatles?"

Sarah raised her head. "That was weird. Do you think he'll understand?"

Before Carol could respond, the blackness of another assimilation fell.

She stood in the dim hall of a medieval castle. The stone walls held tapestries that slowly moved with the drafts that whispered relentlessly through the castle.

"Lady Catherine, a messenger has arrived." Her steward announced.

Turning, she saw a small man in filthy livery approach and bow to her. "My Lady." He handed her a piece of sealed parchment.

She recognized the seal of the Templar Knights and her hand quivered as she opened the parchment. She read the coded words although she already guessed what they would say. The Templar's were the regional Guardians Council and they knew the Church was out for their blood. Hope for negotiation was over. It had never really been possible. Only lies and deception came from the King and Church these days.

Lady Catherine paid the messenger saying she had no response. As he left the hall, she nodded to her steward who turned and headed to alert the rest of the household. It was time to leave.

They lived in dangerous times. Although the Knights Templar had been held in high esteem for many decades, the Church and King Philip IV of France were jealous of their power. The Templar Knights, being Guardians, had helped many achieve their goals: goals that would help humankind in the future. They were considered by most as being more helpful than the Church. But the Church grasped for all the power it could get under the rule of Pope Clement V. As a Guardian herself, she had seen this type of greed many times before. She had a plan. The entire household would escape to the east into the great mountains where she would join her husband. All the plans had been in place for months.

Glancing out a window, she reflected on how many times she had faced what seemed to be insurmountable odds. Here she was again. No one but she and her husband knew of the secret passage that led deep into the woods behind the castle. Once more she would trust that right would prevail and the balance would be restored. Once more on her own she could and would defy another evil and no one in her household would be harmed. They would escape and continue the work of helping humans learn to better themselves. Another age of enlightenment would come in time.

Feeling a hand grasp her shoulder, she looked back in terror. Carol sat in the protection circle still holding Michael's hand but looking into the dark worried eyes of Darren. Sarah stood next to him, her face streaked with tears.

"I got your message."

Carol swallowed hard trying to pull herself together after experiencing Catherine.

Darren helped her stand. "So, there's been another attack. I assume they took both Michael and Toga's spirits to the astral dimension?"

Sarah gasped, "How do we get them back? Can you help us?"

"Yes." He held Carol, comforting her until she completely returned to the here and now.

Carol regained herself quickly. "Seems I've been in a similar situation before. I figure the Rogue will hold Michael and Toga hostage in return for the device." She felt Darren nod in agreement. "And I suspect he'll not honor his side of the bargain. There's too much at stake for him to risk losing the knowledge Toga and Michael have."

Darren released Carol. "The Council gave me orders to help you."

"What a relief," Sarah declared.

"They'll provide the dimensional shift to keep the device safe. Told them Michael wouldn't accept their offer. You need to know that the Council decided to take it from him and hide it to restore peace."

"Fools! Damn the device! I'd rather destroy it than let anyone have it! Will you help us or the Council?" Carol demanded.

Darren's eyes revealed his turmoil. "I'm oath bound to the Council. They've ordered me to help you but if I let you destroy the device, we're all at the Council's mercy for opposing them."

"Hiding the device doesn't make the world safe."

Sarah agreed. "If we can't keep it out of other hands, it should be destroyed."

Darren frowned. "I see how hiding it won't solve the problem but is destroying it the answer? Can I destroy something that could bring hope to so many?"

It was a terrible choice. "I helped create it. I can destroy it. I just need to know if you are going to stop me." Carol could feel his love for her and the anguish it caused him.

Darren looked down. "I can't stop you. I'm willing to face the Council for my actions."

Carol still loved Darren but not in the same way she loved Michael. When she met Darren, she had not known who she really was and their love affair had been wonderful and intense.

Darren stepped close. "I still love you." He swallowed hard. "I've not met my life mate yet. If it feels half as strong as what I feel for you, your love for Michael is to be honored above all else."

"Thank you." She did not want him to think she was taking advantage of his feelings for her. She spoke softly, "I still love you too. Having my past lives back doesn't change that." She took his hand. "I truly appreciate your help, even though I have Michael back."

Darren stepped away. Carol noticed Sarah standing with her head down, uncomfortable with the scene playing out before her.

Darren bit his lip. "You also need to know that things are worse than I thought. The Rogue has many Guardians on his side and the Council has their hands full keeping order. But sooner than later the Council will be coming to take the device."

Sarah interrupted. "What else is going to happen? Not only are we fighting the Rogue, we're fighting the Council too! I hate damned if you do, damned if you don't scenarios! Why don't we just add some evil trolls from World of Warcraft while we're at it!" she yelled. Taking a deep breath she looked at Carol then began to laugh.

Carol laughed too. Looking at Sarah, she raised her fist into the air and cried, "All or nothing!"

With a defiant look, Sarah raised her fist as well, "All for one and one for all!"

Darren shook his head. "Crazy. Both of you. Carol turned to him, her face bright with emotion. "We've got to act fast. I'm certain they wanted me too. I barely made it into the circle in time. The Rogue will need both Michael and me to show him how to use the device. He has to let Michael come back here."

Darren spoke hurriedly, "Here's an idea. I didn't leave the Rogue's service on good terms. He hasn't called me back since Toga shot me down. If I were a devoted servant, I'd be looking for ways to return to his good graces."

"I see where you're going. If you take me to the Rogue, you could say you were doing it to return to him." Carol was intrigued.

Darren nodded. "He's conceited enough to buy it; but intelligent enough to see a trap. We must be convincing."

"When I assimilate past lives I'm useless. I could ruin any chance we have."

"We'll be honest. Use your assimilations to our advantage. He will be interested in how the device affects you."

"No!" Sarah interjected. "There must be another way," she begged, looking at Toga's body. "We could lose everyone and everything."

Holding out her arms, Carol invited her friend into her heart. "All or nothing, remember? We can't abandon Michael and Toga." She gently wiped the tears from Sarah's cheeks.

With utter misery, Sarah backed away. "Everyone I love will be out of reach. I'll be lost. You have to come back. You all have to come back." She lowered her head and took a shuddering breath. "I'm…sorry. I know you have to go."

Carol could see her friend's vision, sitting alone in the protection circle surrounded by the lifeless bodies of those she cared about and loved, driven mad by being totally helpless to bring them back to their bodies. "You will have to be the bravest of us all."

Sarah only nodded without taking her eyes off Toga's body.

Carol spoke softly. "Darren, the Rogue has to be in his corporeal form to accept the device. Both Michael and Toga put protection spells on it. He'll need Toga too."

Sarah stepped forward with a determined look. "If the Guardian Council comes while you're gone, I'll try to keep them here."

Darren smiled at her. "The Council knows where Cameron lives so they'll come here first. Stay inside the circle. They won't be able to read your mind. Tell them we went to get the device and are bringing it back to them."

Carol worried. "Timing will be crucial."

"Since we have to arrange to meet here after we've all left the astral dimension, we'll have some time before the Rogue arrives in person to claim the device."

"The Council is our only unknown factor then." Carol asked.

Darren nodded.

Carol calmed herself. "Wish we had a better plan but there's no time to think of one. I'm sick of being the Rogue's victim."

Sarah shrugged. "I'm not much help but at least I still have the instructions Toga left me the last time you left. I can protect the circle."

"That's going above and beyond if you ask me." Darren kissed her forehead.

Sarah smiled weakly. "Just don't go getting killed on my watch, okay?"

Darren and Carol stepped to the crystal and lay down. She smiled at Sarah who sat next to Toga's body, and reached for Darren's hand. The library disappeared.

THIRTY-SIX

THE ANCIENT FOREST *seemed to whisper foul curses as the branches creaked though no breeze penetrated its dank depths. Carol felt Darren's hand on her arm and turned, momentarily surprised to see Bocan, holding her. His blank compassionless eyes stared through her. She smiled but he only laughed cruelly. Ropes appeared and he roughly pushed her back around, binding her hands behind her. Closing her mind to prevent anyone from knowing her thoughts, she did not struggle, trusting Darren only played his part. Picking her up in his arms, he rose into the air, his huge black wings supporting both of them easily. With astounding speed he headed towards the center of the forest as though he knew exactly where to find the Rogue. As he began to descend, Carol could see a prehistoric stone labyrinth winding its way through the thick forest floor. Bocan descended into its depths. Carol's senses became overwhelmed by the smell of wet rotted leaves and bird excrement.*

Deformed creatures oozed from the labyrinth walls, their harsh voices jabbering excitedly as they slithered towards them. One of them rose to its full height upon approaching Bocan. "He wishes to see thee." Its red eyes narrowed as it tilted its head. It attempted a grotesque smile, thin lips parting to reveal needle sharp teeth. It hissed, "Follow me."

Bocan put Carol down and pushed her in the direction the creature indicated. She stumbled forward from his shove, falling to one knee. She cringed when the red-eyed creature rushed to her as though she was fallen prey to be devoured. Bocan grabbed her and pulled her roughly to her feet before the foul beast could descend upon her.

"She's not for you!" he roared.

Cringing and bowing, the creature backed away, motioning with its long thin gray-skinned arm where they were to go. Carol noticed its red

223

eyes narrow as they passed him. She heard its thoughts. When they have finished with them, he will let us have what is left. He has promised. It smiled cruelly as it followed them into the labyrinth.

Carol gave up trying to remember every twist and turn as they wormed their way through. She totally depended upon Bocan who, disconcertingly, seemed to know where they were going without any help from their smarmy guide. Taking a left turn, they came to an open area, the ground solid stone. The labyrinth walls were higher here with spiral symbols etched so deeply into their surface they appeared to have been there since the beginning of time. A different foulness assaulted her nose. On top of the rotten leaves and bird excrement she now smelled the acrid stench of burning flesh.

Carol's vision narrowed until only blackness reigned. Another assimilation begged to enter.

As she raised her head to face her accusers, the smell of seared flesh stung her nostrils. Her name was Maria and she stood before the Holy Inquisition.

Three men in scarlet robes scowled down at her. "Do you, Maria Sanchez, deny you practice the unnatural art of witchcraft?"

Maria squared her shoulders, still bleeding from the lashing she had just endured. "I practice no unnatural arts."

"The Mayor himself gives witness against thee. He swears you killed his wife and child during the birthing. How can you deny this?"

"I could have saved them both if he had called me sooner." Maria knew she was doomed no matter what she had to say. She might as well speak her mind. A man's word against a woman was taken as gospel. Women held the burden of original sin and could never be trusted to act in a Godly fashion.

"You admit to being present at the birth."

"I was asked to be there by the Mayor himself."

"What spell did you cast to murder mother and child?"

"I cast no spell, your Eminency."

"Yet the Mayor and all his servants heard you chanting."

"They heard me praying."

"*Liar!*"

Maria chanced a look into the gallery and saw that her husband and soul mate, Julio, sat watching her. She hoped he would not be heroic. Her condemnation as a witch would keep him blameless and able to carry on their work. The Guardians would not expose themselves even if it meant saving their own lives. She would be reborn, but that was little comfort right now.

The Holy Tribunal demanded her attention. "Since you have not confessed under torture and stand here in defiance of the laws of God, we have no choice but to condemn you as a witch and sentence you to death by burning to purify your soul!"

Grabbed roughly by her hair, Carol came back, still standing in the middle of the labyrinth; the courage of Maria still running through her. She was prepared to die if necessary to stop the Rogue and the Council to save her loved ones. She also knew that nothing she could say would persuade either the Rogue or the Council to veer from their plans. Bocan released her and she struggled to keep on her feet. Before her, thick black smoke wavered in near-human shape.

A mocking voice came from within the smoke as fire flared inside it in rhythm to its speech. "I am flattered that you have brought me the bitch I've been seeking, but she appears to be damaged goods."

"She is assimilating. Dr. Cameron has given her all her past lives. I thought you would be interested in the effects of the device."

"I am. It is good you wish to return to my service."

Bocan bowed to the smoke and flame.

"Or, perhaps you return only to entrap me." The flame flared as the sound of mirthless laughter assaulted the air.

Bocan straightened. "I do not possess the power to attempt such foolishness."

The smoke and flame remained silent.

Carol felt the tension. She sensed there were others watching, but she could not see them. Maria's courage and insight still bolstered her as she stepped forward. "Your pet dog has brought you what you want. All you need is the device, am I correct?"

Cold laughter answered, "She knows what you are to me, Bocan."

"Am I correct?" Carol repeated.

"No need to be impatient. You are my guest," he soothed.

Carol glared. "Guests don't arrive with their hands tied."

"Bocan, you have forgotten your manners. Please untie our friend."

Carol wanted to dip into Darren's mind as he untied her, but she knew it was too dangerous.

"See, I only wish to talk with you."

Carol asked carefully not to sound demanding. "Where are Michael and Toga?"

The Rogue turned to Bocan. "She is impertinent. I did not know she possessed such spirit. But then, we are dealing with a new Carol, are we not?"

She squared her shoulders. "The device is well protected. You need all of us to obtain it and learn to use it."

The smoke and flame swirled with anger. "Be silent!"

Carol involuntarily took a step back. The power he possessed frightened her. She couldn't help it.

The smoke became denser and the fire brightened. "Do not tell me what I already know!" the voice roared. "Since you are so impatient, here are my terms. I know the device is in Dr. Cameron's library. We shall meet there. Although I need you and Cameron to show me how to use the device, I do not need Toga. No protection spell can stop me. Toga will die if you do not comply with my wishes."

"I will not agree until I have seen Cameron and Toga."

"Ah, she is suspicious. Even if I show her, how will she know it is not an illusion?"

"I still will not agree until I know they're alive."

"As you wish."

The stone wall next to the smoke and flame rumbled aside. Carol could see Michael and Toga chained to a great iron ring in the floor of their cell. They looked at her. Michael nodded.

"When will you bring them back?" Carol asked.

"Show her how such questions do not deserve an answer."

Black wings spread wide and without hesitation Bocan held out his hand and turned his palm towards Carol. All went dark.

THIRTY-SEVEN

CAROL'S EYES flew open to see Sarah's anxious face watching over her.

"What happened?" Carol mumbled.

"What do you mean, what happened? You tell me!"

"The Rogue is coming. We don't have much time."

Sarah looked around. "What do we do?"

As Carol stood, a thrill ran through her body. It wasn't another past life. It was deeper than that. It was knowledge beyond time. It was the power of the Canyon. And it called to her from the grotto.

"Sarah, can you feel that?"

"Feel what? If you mean panic, yeah, I feel that."

She was given no choice. She had to go. "Stay here in the circle. I need to go to the grotto."

"Why? What do I do if the creep comes?"

Carol ran towards the grotto. "Nothing, or tell him I'll be right back. Never leave the circle, no matter what! I'll know what to do when I get back. Trust me."

The closer Carol got to the grotto the stronger the power penetrated her being. As she hurried down the tunnel, she could hear whispers and feel breezes she instinctively knew came from the Canyon. Stepping into the grotto felt like entering the eye of a hurricane. All was calm but she could sense the immense strength whirling around her. She saw shadow and light moving over the pond's water. A mist poured into the room from the opening above to be captured by the power and swirled around the walls. The whispers became voices and she heard them calling her most ancient names.

Without knowing where the words came from only that she knew what to do, Carol raised her arms and called out. "Beautiful Spirits, fountains of true wisdom who grace this canyon, those who can open the mysteries of being and not being, who know the imperfections and inner darkness of humankind. Though I am less than the sand before your mountains, I have come as you have beckoned. I, Carol Knight, a fragile vessel, stand here and ask what it is you want of me.

Many voices answered in unison, "The Earth faces an untimely end. We do not interfere with humans. Your ways are meaningless to us. But we listen to the Master Spirits as you do."

"Tell me what to do."

"This is our command. Let your enemy see what he seeks but do not give it to him."

"That will mean a fight." There was no time for fear, Carol asked, "Will you help us?"

Anger tinged the answer. "Yes, we will aid you and yours in this fight to come."

Carol felt fear chill her bones. Here was a power so ancient it held no regard for the comings and goings of humans.

"How do I know you won't simply kill us all to stop the destruction of this world?"

"There is one among us who will not allow harm to come to the humans who fight this evil."

Carol's jaw dropped. "Who?"

"It is not important."

Carol knew this would be all she would get from them. "I thank the Spirits of the Canyon for you are my light and my comfort in this world."

She bowed to the Powers and turned to go back to the library. She hoped she had done the right thing. What if she had unleashed more than she bargained for and only made things worse? But the Spirits had not given her a choice.

As Carol hurried back to the house, a cold chill assaulted her senses. The Rogue was there. Sarah! She slowed down. She spread her arms in supplication and whispered, "Blessed Spirits of the Canyon give me strength to do your bidding." In response she was washed in a glowing sense of security and confidence. Lowering her arms, she thanked them.

She was prepared to meet the evil that awaited her when she entered the library. Michael and Toga stood in the midst of four darkly hooded men behind the Rogue. Carol noticed that Darren was one of them. A quick glance to where his body had been confirmed it. Would he still be on their side? Sarah remained in the circle. Michael's glance asked if she was all right. Her slight nod assured him.

The Rogue stood apart from the other hooded figures. He wore the white robes of the Guardian's Council. His hood was down revealing a sharp featured face with pale blue eyes and light blond hair cut so short he appeared to be bald. His cold eyes flickered with annoyance. "Where is the device?" he demanded.

Carol solemnly acknowledging his presence. "We'll remove the protection first." She nodded to Michael and Toga. Together they began to walk towards the circle. When Sarah started to say something, Carol's look silenced her.

"Stop! You bring me the device."

"She does not know the spells we used. I thought you said no protection spell could stop you."

Rage filled the room. The Rogue spoke to his men. "Surround the dais. If they try anything, kill Toga."

The hooded men followed orders, holding Toga outside the protection circle. Sarah started to protest, but Toga silenced her with a shake of his head. Carol walked into the circle. Michael followed her. Sarah's eyes locked on Toga. Michael bent to the hidden device and turned off the time phase device. He put his palm onto the box and began to remove his protection.

Knowing they had little time, Carol projected her thoughts to Michael, 'The counsel is coming. Maybe they'll come in time to stop this."

"What has happened?" Carol's mind heard Michael's question, "You know something more."

"The Council wants the device." Carol felt his anger surge through her. "The Power of the Canyon will help us." Carol sensed his alarm.

"Why? What have you done?"

"They offered help. It was not something I was allowed to refuse."

"If we wait for the Counsel, we only face a larger battle. I think we should fight now and face the Counsel when it arrives. Perhaps we can avoid a second battle."

"But how? Darren says the Counsel is determined to have our device." Carol worried.

"I understand. I see no choice but to face them one at a time. We are too few."

Carol saw Toga's slight nod. She knew, although he could not hear their thoughts, he would be alert and ready for whatever happened.

As Michael released his protection spell, he asked the Rogue, "I see you still wear the robes of your council position. Isn't that in opposition to your new world view?"

Carol looked at the Rogue with seeming interest. She knew Michael was trying to keep things calm until they were in a better position.

"I am a Council member. I have many other council members from all over the world who have joined me. We all feel that a new world order is inevitable. The time foretold has come and it is necessary to reveal the truth since the Ancients who gave us these powers are returning. You should consider joining me. Stop fighting. Together we could do amazing things."

Toga joined the conversation. "If the Ancients are returning, why do you seek our cooperation? Surely it is insignificant in the scope of their return."

"You don't understand." The Rogue's eyes brightened. "I will use the device to prove to them that leaving Earth in our hands has succeeded beyond their expectations." He took a step forward, his face burning with passion. "You, who have the power of the Ancients. You, who possess the means to decide the fate of others. You, who have a mind capable of creating anything you wish. Why not accept these truths and join me. Show the Ancients we are capable of more knowledge, more power!"

He fell silent and calmed himself. He grabbed Toga by the arm. "Enough! Dr. Cameron, come out of the circle while Toga removes his spell."

Michael stepped out and Toga was pushed into the circle. He removed his protection spell and opened the box. Carol held her hand out to Toga. When he gave her a quizzical look, she winked. He gave her the candlesticks. Together, standing in the middle of the protection circle, Carol, Toga, and Sarah faced the Rogue.

Carol raised her arms to show the device, a candlestick in each hand. "I have been commanded by the Earth Spirits of this Canyon to show you but not give them to you."

"What!" roared the Rogue. "Earth Spirits? Why would they be concerned? Who are they to stop me?" He held out his hand.

Carol felt the mental connection. He'd gotten through the protection of the circle! She took a step towards the edge against her will.

Michael whirled out of the grasp of the hooded man who guarded him, and before the two remaining Guardians could react, he ran into the circle and grabbed Carol before she took another step. "Let her go!"

Toga began chanting under his breath.

Carol felt the Rogue's control slip but not enough to disobey his order to fight her way out of Michael's grasp. "No!" she yelled.

Michael grabbed both of Carol's arms but she wrenched one arm free and swung at him, candlestick still in her hand. He ducked, but the candlestick grazed his ear causing it to bleed.

Seeing the blood, Carol wrenched her mind free of the Rogue's control. The all-encompassing rage she had felt in the battle in the astral dimension returned. She screamed at the Rogue, "You will die!"

Carol saw Darren step forward as though to help the Rogue. She dropped the candlesticks to the floor of the circle.

The Rogue whirled to face Darren. "Traitor!" He raised his hand and Darren stood still, his face twisted in the torment that flooded his body.

Carol ran out of the circle. She didn't know if the Spirits guided her or she simply did not want Darren to die.

"Carol!" Michael yelled.

The Rogue's followers ran towards Carol as Michael and Toga rushed from the circle to keep them from catching her. The Rogue pushed Darren aside. He smiled as he watched Carol approach. Dazed by the pain, Darren fell to one knee.

The Rogue raised his hand toward Carol. Laughing, he watched her stop as a glazed expression froze on her face. "This is wonderful! My power has grown. I no longer need any of you!"

His followers stopped when they heard his declaration. Michael and Toga looked in the Rogue's direction. Darren rose in spite of his pain and stepped between the Rogue and Carol.

"No one can stop me now," the Rogue growled, raising his other hand toward Darren.

Darren screamed. Toga ran toward the Rogue and shoved him away from Carol and Darren. Squatting into a defensive stance, Toga waited for him to attack. Michael took his stance behind Toga, waiting to see what the three followers would do. Darren fell unconscious to the floor.

Carol's mind blazed with conflicting ideas, her own and those the Rogue had imposed. The image of a hand broke through the fevered haze. She saw the lone figure of a woman, her body glowed from within. Carol raised her arms and silently pleaded for help. A golden light caressed her. The Rogue's control slipped away. She rushed to Darren's side. He still lived, but at what cost?

The Rogue bellowed at his defeat. Whirling, he spoke to his followers. "Come to me. I am strong. We will win. I promise you."

The three followers spread out ready to fight. One launched an attack on Michael, the other two headed towards Toga. Michael was ready. He whirled and struck his opponent with his foot sending the hooded man unconscious to the floor.

Carol held Darren in her arms. His eyes opened and he looked at her with such tenderness, she found it hard to bear.

Toga kept his eyes on the Rogue as the two followers circled him. One attacked only to meet Toga's iron fist. Toga hadn't even looked in his direction. The Rogue raised his hand towards Toga. Michael turned to help his friend but Toga faltered, dropping to one knee as pain threatened to render him unconscious.

Sarah flew from the circle to his side. Seeing Sarah, the Rogue sneered. "The mortal wants to help a Guardian." He aimed at Sarah and laughed when she crumpled at Toga's side.

Michael hurried to Carol. "You all right?"

"Hurry, we must get to the grotto!" Carol stood.

The Rogue heard her. "Show me this grotto!" he demanded as he attempted to see into Carol's mind again.

Michael was quick to aid her in shielding her thoughts.

Toga stood, released from the mind control when the Rogue became obsessed with the grotto. Painfully he raised his arms and hit the Rogue with all the strength he had.

The Rogue fell forward, realizing he could not control all of them at the same time, the Rogue ran. Michael charged after him.

Carol hurried to Toga and Sarah. "She can't be dead."

Toga's eyes fluttered as his senses returned. When he saw Sarah, he quickly felt her neck. "She's alive."

"How are you?"

"Ready for more," he said as he stood, flexing his shoulder to regain its use. "Where is he?"

Together they ran after Michael and the Rogue toward the grotto. They reached the garden in time to see Michael disappear into the tunnel. Carol guessed the Rogue had learned where it was from her. Could he force the Canyon Powers to do as he willed? Carol and Toga plunged into the tunnel. Sounds of struggle came from ahead. Entering they saw Michael fall, struck by the Rogue.

Carol pleaded, "Help me!"

Silence fell so deep it seemed to thicken the air. Her hands began to hum with a pulsing beat.

She felt the power of the Canyon Spirits meld with her, becoming part of her. Their power raised her arms into the air. She felt a burning furnace churn in her chest.

Her heart beat faster as the fiery heat flooded into her arms. Carol screamed. It felt like her skin began to blister from the incredible inferno that shot through her body.

Pain claimed her. They're going to kill me! She didn't dare look at what her body was doing. She couldn't stop. Her hands began to glow red hot as she stepped towards the Rogue.

He stood transfixed, fear widening the pupils of his colorless eyes. Carol knew he didn't understand what was happening. She laughed.

Shadows oozed from the cavern's walls and ghostly figures rose from the pond. They flew at him, their terrifying faces grotesque with rage.

"Wait! No! You can't..." The Rogue backed away begging to be free of the apparitions. Horror possessed his face as he threw his arms over his head in a feeble attempt to protect himself from such incredible forces.

More power poured through Carol as her soul become one with the Spirits. A beam of white fury blasted from her hands hitting the Rogue where he stood. His cries of mercy went unheard, unfelt by the Spirits whose only desire was to be rid of this abomination forever.

The Rogue's face twisted in anger and defiance. He threw his arms wide and a white glow emitted from his body. He roared, "You will not stop me!" He struggled and managed to turn. He grabbed Michael.

Carol lowered her arms and sank to her knees exhausted. She could only watch unable to risk Michael's life.

Toga started towards the Rogue and Michael.

The white light that engulfed them became so intense Carol had to look away.

Toga stopped.

She squinted, hoping to see a way to stop this madness. The Rogue's body became indistinct. Rushing wind filled the cavern and the Rogue disappeared into the light.

THIRTY-EIGHT

DEAD UNYIELDING silence commanded the grotto. Carol couldn't move, stunned by the physical toll the exorcism had cost her. Toga stood in the pool staring at where the Rogue had been. Michael looked over to her, his face blank, his eyes hollow. She felt a presence and turned to see Darren standing at the entrance, leaning against the wall, his face haggard and pale.

"Carol!" Darren staggered to her. "Are you all right?" He grabbed her and held her tight.

She allowed Darren to hold her. She couldn't feel anything. She couldn't believe anything. She was barely aware that she was standing there.

"What just happened?" he asked. "Where's the Rogue?"

"Gone!" She pulled out of his arms.

She turned to Michael. He still stood in the pond, his breathing hard and fast. Carol went to him.

Toga joined them. He motioned towards the far wall. Standing there, one last Spirit remained. She was beautiful and shone with an inner light. Smiling she floated towards them, reaching out to Carol.

"Be at peace." Her voice was kind, soothing.

Carol felt the comfort of those words in every fiber of her being. Relief hit her like a tidal wave. Tears flowed freely. Carol could hardly speak. "What happened?"

"We are responsible. We sent the Rogue away."

"How? Where?" Michael demanded.

"We sent him to another dimension."

"What dimension?"

"I do not know. Another Earth."

236

Toga stepped forward. "Will he be able to return?"

"We will never allow it. Search your feelings. You know I speak the truth."

Carol felt something familiar as the Spirit opened up to them. "I know you," Carol said with awe.

The Spirit brightened. "You call me George."

"But you're a ghost. What—"

"We of the Canyon have watched over you since you came here. We were foretold of your arrival by the Master Spirits."

Carol reached out her hand and George touched her. "I was sent to watch over you until you found your way to Michael. It was I who persuaded the Powers to help in the fight." She stepped back and held her hand up. "But if the foretelling of the Master Spirits is to be complete, you must ascend beyond what it is to be a Guardian, you must be braver still to keep the balance you have fought so hard to bring today."

Carol's knees were weak and Michael put his arm around her. He addressed the Spirit. "She'll not go alone. I'll help her."

Toga and Darren started toward Carol.

George's calm eyes approved. "Your friends are true although it is you, Carol, who must bring peace. Hope is high and your friends can help you."

Carol's mind flooded with emotion. How could she do more? She looked at Michael and knew in her heart they could do this, but her tears would not stop.

Struggling through her emotion, Carol asked, "What's your name? I can't keep calling you George."

"I have many names. George is who I am to you. It is a good name." The Spirit nodded her farewell and faded back into the wall of the grotto.

Carol stood frozen starring at the wall George had just disappeared through. She did not move until Michael touched her arm. Carol grabbed and embraced him.

Darren cleared his throat. "Let's go back to the library. Sarah needs help."

THIRTY-NINE

AS THEY ENTERED the library, Carol saw Sarah sitting in the protection circle. She was conscious but looked the worse for wear. She smiled weakly at them as they stopped at the door. Shrugging her shoulders, she looked to her left. Five men in white hooded robes stood in front of Michael's desk. Carol knew the device remained inside the circle, she could see it on the floor. But the circle was the only protection it had. Carol closed her eyes. She was exhausted.

Pulling upon the last ounce of energy, she walked towards the Guardian Council. As George said, she was the bringer of peace. Unsure how she could manage, she took a deep breath.

Her head pounded with the now familiar assimilation. She held her head attempting to keep herself in the here and now. She failed.

She stood alone beside a campfire whose smoke rose lazily. Occasional embers flitted into the air with the smoke. A huge yellow moon rose before her and bright stars filled the skies behind her. The calm air felt cool, soothing her face. Her gray hair fell down past her breast. Her supple deerskin dress was beaded with the symbols of her rank as wise woman of her tribe. Deep sadness filled her. Sitting down by the fire, she cupped her hand and pulled smoke towards her to purify and cleanse her spirit. Raising her arms to the moon, she spoke. "Sky Father, we need your counsel." Lowering her arms, she said. "Earth Mother, we need your wisdom. Long have we fought to keep our lands; our way of life. We can fight no longer. How do we go on? How do we keep our sacred path?"

A slight breeze caused the campfire to flare. She threw leaves of sage upon the flames and took comfort from their earthy perfume. Faint music floated down to her from the stars and the earth under her cradled and soothed her.

Unspoken words filled her spirit. Be true to your beliefs. Even when the cycle of life seems at its most desperate, hope remains. The eternal wheel still turns. The spirit of your people has enriched the world. Nothing ever truly dies. Remain true to the core beliefs of the Guardians. This evil shall pass and enlightenment will come again.

Carol felt an arm around her waist. Opening her eyes she realized Michael held her, keeping her from falling.

One of the hooded figures turned to the trio in the doorway. It was the Lord Councilor. "What has happened? Carol, are you hurt!"

Carol steeled herself.

Michael held her by the arm, leading her to a chair. "Councilmen, you are too late."

"And why is that." The Councilman's voice grated with irritation.

Toga answered, "Your rogue Councilman will not cause any more harm."

The Lord Councilor's eyebrow lifted. "You need to tell us what has happened. Is there somewhere we can go to talk?" he said, looking around with disapproval at the devastated library.

Toga answered stiffly, "Yes. Please follow us." His dark eyes glared at them.

Sarah remained seated in the protection circle, a look of resignation on her face. Carol knew she wanted to join them. She motioned for Sarah to come. The Lord Councilor frowned but remained silent.

Sarah bounded from the circle then slowed down, still shaken by the Rogue's attack. Darren helped her. Smiling she regained her composure and walked proudly to Toga taking his arm as everyone walked towards the living room.

When they entered the kitchen on the way, Toga said, "Sarah and I will prepare tea for our guests."

Once the Council was seated, Carol and Michael stood together in front of the huge fireplace. Darren stood off to one side. Carol could read Michael's mind. His irritation with the Council was raging. She felt him compose himself.

"Councilmen, your Rogue came here for the device. He did not succeed and is now imprisoned on another dimension," Michael said coldly.

"I think I can speak for the entire Council, we owe you a great debt of gratitude for taking care of the rogue Councilman. However, there are still followers out there that could be potential trouble. They will..."

Michael remained cold. "We had nothing to do with the disappearance of the Rogue."

"I don't understand!"

Carol entwined her arm around Michael's. "These canyons hold wisdom and power much older than the Guardians. You owe your thanks to these Spirits, Councilman."

The Lord Councilor looked annoyed. "I do not understand. I have never encountered such spirits as you describe. This makes matters even more urgent in my mind. Quickly. Give us the device. We will hide it between dimensions until it is needed or we are evolved enough to use it properly."

Carol sensed Michael's hesitation to discuss any details about the Spirits with the Council. She knew they should be careful. He looked at Carol. She heard his thoughts. "Do not let them have the Device. I'm here for you."

She could barely contain her hostility towards the Council. "Your plan will not work. You already tried to make the device useless to anyone. You failed. We will not, cannot trust you again."

The Lord Councilor blustered. "It must not fall into the wrong hands!"

"No, it cannot. Michael and I are responsible for creating the device. It has become a curse. The repercussions lie squarely with its creators. We will decide its fate."

All the Council members began speaking at once. The Lord Councilor silenced them. He rose from his chair. "We can force you to do the Council's bidding if necessary!"

Toga and Sarah came into the room with trays of tea and sandwiches. Carol knew their arrival had been deliberately timed.

The Lord Councilor fumed, "You must listen to reason."

Sarah began serving tea.

Toga stood next to Carol and Michael, his eyes glared at the Council as he spoke. "Most of the Guardians in this world do not truly understand the seriousness of the events set in motion by the Rogue. Not yet. Therefore, Guardians cannot trust each other until common ground can be found. The Rogue may be gone but he has created doubt and distrust. Chaos is the result of those two demons – they destroy wisdom and logic. I have a great concern about the future of the Guardians and, I now add, the future of the Earth itself. We risk war that no one will win."

Carol looked at Toga, realizing she was seeing the Toga she remembered and respected over many centuries. She knew he could make them see reason. Thankful the meeting was in the best of hands, she relaxed, feeling proud and privileged to be Toga's friend.

Toga continued speaking to the stunned Council. "The device is a major key in the chaos the Rogue has created. Even if it is hidden or destroyed, Carol and Michael still have the knowledge to build another one."

The Lord Councilor interrupted, "Brilliant idea, all we have to do is hide the device and keep Carol and Michael apart."

Carol stared in horror at the Lord Councilor. Would they keep her from Michael so they couldn't make any more devices? Michael put his hand on her shoulder. She turned and saw his calm face. He nodded to Toga.

Toga smiled and shook his head. "You are not listening. Hiding the device is not an option." He paused but a moment. "Think of the possible repercussions. The Guardians have never warred against each other on this scale. Think of the kind of power we possess. Using it against each other is unsupportable. Too many Guardians would be lost forever. We could devastate the entire planet. And the Spirits of the Canyon have demanded there be peace." Toga held out his hand to

Carol. "I will help Carol and Michael. I will help us all find truth and balance to avoid chaos and possible war."

The Lord Councilor stood, visibly shaken. "If hiding or destroying the device is not the answer, do you have any suggestion on what we should do?"

Carol could tell he did not like being out of control, but she also saw how much he respected Toga. She stepped toward the Councilman. "We have to work together. First I believe that spreading the truth to all the other Councils throughout the world would be a good place to start. That is a major task that would be best served by this Council."

The Lord Councilor nodded curtly. "We will alert you to our progress. But, you must keep us aware of what you find or plan."

Carol nodded. "Agreed."

The Lord Councilor frowned.

Sarah showed them the way out.

Carol looked into Michael's eyes. In all of their lives together he had never aspired to lofty desires. He preferred to act in small ways through research and scientific method to benefit humankind. She was proud of how Toga handled the Council and she knew Michael was too.

Darren plopped onto the couch. "The Rogue's followers are not done with us yet."

Sarah had a wry smile. "Grandma always said, 'From the frying pan into the fire.' Here we go again."

Darren laughed in spite of his exhaustion. "And she's right. The device that was created to help has only caused pain. We're now facing the fire of those consequences."

Turning from the fireplace, Carol said, "There'll be more fighting. The followers will be anxious to either find a way to return him to power or grab the power for themselves. It will take time for the Council to spread the truth. The Rogue's faction will be spreading their lies just as fast."

Toga brought them all back to the present. "We need to decide our next moves both offensive and defensive."

FORTY

SARAH FELL into a chair in the library, exhausted. "Okay. Now what?"

Carol looked at Darren. "I've been on this roller coaster since we met you. I've not had time to think of anything beyond a minute from now."

Darren reached for Carol's hand. "Please let me stay and help you. I can't go back to work for the Council. I don't trust them any more than Michael does."

Michael spoke softly, "I know I could use the help and Toga can't do this alone."

Toga laughed. "No Toga can't. I welcome your help."

"Do you think we can trust the Counsel to do what they say they will?" Carol asked.

"No," came Michael's simple answer.

Carol felt exhaustion flood through her. "There's still a lot to think about and I for one am too tired right now. We all need to rest. Make decisions with a clear mind. We can't trust anything here to keep us safe. I'll ask George if she can protect us while we figure out our next move."

"George?" Sarah asked, "You don't mean your ghost? What the hell does he have to do with all this?"

"Turns out George has been my Guardian Angel all this time, since I moved to Briar Cliff Canyon in fact. He, well actually she, gave me the power to get rid of the Rogue."

Sarah only shook her head. "Will I ever hear a normal explanation again?" When Carol started to speak, Sarah stopped her. "Don't answer that. I already know I'm in for a lot more 'weird' with a capital W."

Toga nodded. "I can prepare an energy drink and there are spells to keep us going but most of all we need time to think, to plan things before it all starts again."

Sarah came towards Toga. "Show me what to do."

Toga grabbed Sarah and gave her a passionate kiss. She melted into his arms. Carol looked away feeling she intruded on their privacy. She looked at Michael. He had a big smile on his face.

Toga released Sarah. He caressed her cheek, undaunted by his public display of affection. "Your spirit is the most beautiful I have ever known."

"I love you so much." There were tears in Sarah's eyes.

Toga and Sarah left together to start the energy drinks.

Carol held out her hand to Darren. "I am so glad to have you here. Thank you for staying."

Darren stepped closer. He looked at Michael and swallowed hard. He turned back to Carol. "I still love you. I've not met my life mate yet. If it feels half as strong as what I feel for you, your love for Michael is to be honored above all else."

Carol lowered her head. "Thank you."

Darren stepped away. "There's so much to do, what should be first?"

"I need to see if George will protect the circle for us while we work out a plan. Check with Toga. I bet he has all kinds of projects up his sleeve." Carol smiled. She turned to Michael and held out her hand. "Come with me."

They entered the grotto as the sun was setting. "George, are you here?"

A light shone through the wall next to the flowing spring. As George emerged her light filled the grotto.

"I am here."

"We need your help if you can provide it." Carol spoke.

"Ask."

"Will you protect us while we work on planning our next step?"

"Of course."

Carol turned to Michael. "I know what I want to do next."

Michael smiled. He knew as well. He held her tight in his arms. Their troubles melted away. They were still together. Lying down together on the silver altar, they closed their eyes. Their spirits soared to the astral dimension.

The lake seemed more beautiful now than ever before; peaceful beyond anything earthbound. Night was falling, and stars began to sparkle in the heavens. She turned to Michael. Her heart filled with her love for him. He did not speak as he embraced her. Terrible happiness wrapped them in its ecstatic beauty.

"Tell me we can survive this," she whispered.

"I'll be here. We can never be apart." He caressed her cheek. "Together we can survive anything."

He became a being of light, his pure soul surrounding her with his essence. His love laid bare for her to feel. She too became a being of light and they floated into the night together, entwining their raw energy, embracing their pure emotion, their perfect love, unfettered spirits swirling in a dance that heightened their passions beyond anything they could feel in their earthly bodies. The Universe held no limits for their unbound love and devotion to each other. Hope remained. They would find a way.

THE END